Life is a journey,

Watch for the blessings

Linda Kennedy

As one who reads and listens to Christian fiction for enjoyment and relaxation on a regular basis, I feel privileged to preview Linda Kennedy's winning first novel, Brooke's Miracle.

Linda skillfully draws you into the life of Brooke Erickson whose young choices wreak havoc on her walk with God. Dealing with the difficult subject of abortion, Linda gives us an in-depth view of the mother's trauma, as well as demonstrates the painful ripple effects upon those who love her. You will laugh and cry, rejoice and suffer with Brooke as she struggles toward greater maturity in her walk of faith. Her characters quickly become members of your family and leave you wanting more.

Louise M. Henry, M.A., LMHC, NCC, Counselor
Lakeland, Florida

Brooke's Miracle is a thought provoking story. It is the fictional life of a young woman who could be easily identified with so many girls today. The struggles of an unwanted, surprise pregnancy and the wrong choice of abortion leads Brook to a place of learning and a piece of God's grace that we all need to ponder. This story gripped my heart to stand even more firm on what I know is truth.

Carol Beresford
Founder of Hannah's House, Mentor, Ohio and Tequesta, Florida

BROOKE'S MIRACLE

Linda Kennedy

Salt Life Press

Printed in United States of America
First Printing 2014

ISBN 978-0-9899439-0-1

Salt Life Press
1505 SE Royal Green Cir. Ste U102
Port Saint Lucie, Florida 34952

Edited By: Mary Lou Stark info@infoproductgal.com
Cover Design: Daliborka Mijailovic/99 designs dmijailovic73@gmail.com

DEDICATION

In loving memory of my very special brother, Tom. He was a brilliant writer, a talented actor, and a wonderful man who was generous to a fault. He left us far too soon and now spends his eternity with our Heavenly Father and his beloved wife.

This one's for you, Tom.

ACKNOWLEDGEMENTS

My thanks go to my longtime friends. To Sue, who introduced me to Christian fiction and kept me supplied with all the reading I could consume.

To Louise and Susie who encouraged me and made me believe that God had given me a talent for writing and a story to tell. You gave me confidence when I stood on the edge.

To my friend Laura, always my cheerleader when I was discouraged in my attempts to find my way to publication. You made me believe it was possible.

To my daughter, Sheri, who helped me wade through all the techie stuff and saved me hours and hours of time.

To all my future women friends who need encouragement, confidence, self-esteem and the knowledge that we are all God's daughters. And that he gave us girlfriends to love and be loved.

Chapter One

August, 1974

Numbness worked through Brooke Erickson's body at the young doctor's words. The lights in the exam room seemed to intensify, and her surroundings took on a surrealistic appearance. She struggled to focus. He was asking about a family doctor, advising that an appointment with a gynecologist would be necessary to ensure the health of her pregnancy. Through the fog, his words barely registered. She swallowed to alleviate the dryness in her mouth, but words didn't come. He wrote a temporary prescription for her nausea and left her to gather her things.

As she lifted her purse from beside the chair, the room swam, and she reached for a table to avoid falling. She rested her forehead against her arm, and dizziness threatened to overcome her as she fought being swallowed up in an envelope of blackness. Gradually she regained some degree of control and stood. Walking on wooden legs down the cold and sterile corridor, she narrowly missed a gurney headed in her direction.

Pushing through the glass doors, she squinted against the bright afternoon sun as she strained to see where she had left her 1972 Thunderbird. It was a graduation gift from her parents. After fumbling through her purse, she struggled to get the key in the lock.

Safe inside, she leaned her head against the steering wheel and tried to make sense of the news. *Pregnant. No, can't be.* She never thought. This had to be a mistake. Couldn't there be errors in these tests? Maybe she could try another clinic for a second opinion. *Yeah, right. What good would* that *do?* The slight increase in weight, the nausea, and nearly five months into a pregnancy was too far along to be wrong. Let's be truthful here. Yes, her periods had always been sporadic…yes her mother stopped for a whole year. That made it easier to ignore the waves of nausea she been having all these months. The fact that it had gotten better just gave her an excuse to be convinced there was nothing wrong. She'd managed to keep a flat stomach all this time but her pants were beginning to feel tight around the waist. And really now, why go to this clinic instead of her family doctor?

Got to get out of here. She started her car, pulled out of the parking lot and into the afternoon traffic. Focused on what was in front of her, she mechanically maneuvered toward the beach, with tears now flowing down her cheeks. She needed a safe place. With her car parked in the garage under the Holiday Inn, she stumbled down Clearwater beach and dropped down on a sand dune.

She pulled her legs up, rested her chin on her knees, and watched the rhythmic movement of the translucent green waves that swelled to a curve before they flipped into churning whitecaps. She had grown up on this beach. There were great memories of family and friends, picnics and holiday gatherings, but not today. She dug her toes into the soft wet sand and wiped tears from her face with the back of her arm. A breeze blew her golden hair across her face. Cooler temperatures blowing in from the Gulf brought some relief, but the disturbing thoughts continued to tumble through her mind. She licked her dry lips, salty from the mingling of mist and tears. How could this be happening? Not to her. *Got to clear my head, think this through, and find a solution.*

Mama and Papa—not an option. Brooke graduated valedictorian and won a full scholarship to the University of Florida in Gainesville. In two weeks they would be taking her to get settled in the apartment she was going to share with her best friend, Lisa. The week after that, she would start her new job at the university library for expenses not covered by her scholarship. Her parents were so proud of her accomplishments and encouraged her when she displayed an artistic talent. Good grades had come easy for Brooke, but, she had been driven to achieve the highest standards. No way could she give them this kind of news. Papa was a deacon of their church. How embarrassing for them to face all their friends and church members with a pregnant daughter. She couldn't do that to them.

What about Mark? Brooke had avoided any serious relationship. Group socializing was more her style, and there were plenty of friends and activities to keep her schedule full. That was, until Mark came into the picture. If only she hadn't broken it off with him after that night. He was the only one who knew what happened between them. He was her only option.

She pulled herself up and headed toward the hotel with floundering resolve. First she would have to call her mother with an excuse for being late. As she entered the hotel, she looked for a secluded phone booth. Usually, this was a time of day when there was little activity. A quick glance toward the public phones told her there were none available. A young woman was sitting close by on a couch with two small children. Brooke gave her a forced smile as she settled on the opposite chair to wait.

What can I tell my mom? Who am I kidding? Compared to what I have to hide from her, an excuse for not being home is the least of it.

The woman left with a man who had been using one of the phones. The phone next to her was still being used but, no matter, he was busy and her phone calls would seem innocent enough. She slung her purse to the shelf, dialed her number, and waited for an answer.

"Hello?" The sound of her mother's beautiful French accent hit like a strong punch in the stomach.

"Hi, Mom." She took a deep breath. "Listen, Molly stopped by the office and asked me to meet a group of our friends after work for pizza at Tony's Italian. I'll be home in a couple of hours."

"All right, you will not be too late? Papa and I will be going to dinner at the Franks."

"No Mom, I won't be too late."

"Emma will be here with Benji."

Emma, her older sister by two years, was still living at home and attending a community college while her fiancé was in Viet Nam. Her baby brother, Benji, had just finished sixth grade.

"Great, you and Papa have a good time."

"Of course, it is always a good time with the Franks. We will see you later tonight."

Brooke leaned against the phone and released the breath she had been holding. That was too easy. The real challenge would come when she had to act normal at home. Now for her next call. Her hands trembled as she dialed the familiar number. Her legs stiffened, and the muscles above her knees jerked. The knot in her stomach felt like a large rock. The phone rang…once…twice…three times.

4

Oh please, please be home.

After four rings a soft female voice answered, "Good afternoon."

Why did his mother have to answer the phone? "Uh...hello. Um...is Mark there?"

"I'm not sure."

Brooke didn't want to identify herself, but the hesitation in his mother's voice signaled it was not an option.

"This is Brooke, Mrs. Huxley."

"Oh, Brooke, Mark was just going out. I'll check to see if he's still here."

She heard Mrs. Huxley walk away, and silence filled the receiver that she fiercely gripped in her hand.

"Oh, please God, let him still be there."

After what seemed like days, she heard his familiar voice.

"Brooke?"

"Mark, I need to talk to you."

"Okay—"

"I need to see you—"

"You want me to come over tonight?"

"No. I need to talk to you right now."

"I was going to shoot baskets with Roger. I guess I can swing by your place on the—"

"I'm not at home." She pushed her hair away from her face and turned toward the large glass windows. "Can you meet me at the beach?"

"Well...sure...where—?"

"I'll wait for you in the Holiday Inn lobby, close to the phones." She leaned against the phone booth and took a deep breath. "Thank you."

5

"Are you okay? I mean—it will take me at least half an hour."

"Yes, I'm okay…well sort of—"

"I'll be there as soon as I can."

Brooke collapsed on the soft leather couch, laid her head back and closed her eyes. She had to pull herself together before Mark got there. She needed this time to decide how she would tell him. Bone weary from the day's events, she slipped into a shallow sleep. She awoke with a start and looked at her watch, afraid she might have missed Mark. Only fifteen minutes since their conversation; she had time to wash her face with some cold water. Too bad, she didn't use makeup. She could use something to cover her swollen eyes.

Somewhat refreshed, she went back to the lobby. Minutes later she saw him stroll in the door, his eyes moving around the room in search of her. Dressed in light blue Bermuda shorts and a white tee shirt, Brook noted his tanned muscular frame.

Why couldn't they have waited? They might still be dating. She waved to catch his attention, as he walked in her direction. Guilt washed over Brooke as she saw the tentative hope in those soft brown eyes. This was going to be so hard.

"Hello, Mark. Thanks for coming."

"What is it—?

"Not here." She touched his arm. "Let's walk."

She headed toward the doors leading to the beach with Mark following close beside, their arms brushing against each other until he took her hand. They walked for some time without speaking as he gave her time to gather her thoughts. She liked that about him. Gentle and considerate, he always put her at ease. It helped calm her down. If it hadn't been for the pregnancy, she would have enjoyed this time with him.

"I don't know how to tell you this, except to come right out with it."

He waited, still holding her hand as they stood close.

"I'm pregnant. Almost five months pregnant." She was afraid to look at him. Scanning the horizon over the swells of the ocean, she allowed him time to digest the news.

"You're kidding, aren't you?"

"How could I joke about something so serious? I didn't bring you down here for some kind of sick prank."

He pulled his hand away and took a few steps back. "Well…what are you saying…that I'm the father?" He pointed to his chest. "Or are you asking me for help with some other guy's kid?"

She began to tremble. This attitude was so uncharacteristic.

"What are you talking about? I told you I was five months pregnant. You can count. Have you forgotten our night on the beach? That was five months ago. There hasn't been anyone but you, and you know you were the first."

"How do I know you didn't have some other guy after me? You cut me off right after that. I don't know who you were seeing, but you sure made it clear that you didn't want to see me anymore."

"I guess I deserve that. If I would give in to you, why not someone else?" She shook her head. "I'm sorry for the way it ended. It wasn't fair to you. I was as much to blame for that night as you." She swiped at the tears that trailed down her face. "I felt so guilty for what we did. I couldn't face you anymore, and I couldn't trust us to keep it from happening again. I realize now, I was more concerned about my feelings and I didn't think about what I was doing to you."

"I…I just don't know what to think. I was hoping you wanted to see me again. I never imagined something like this."

He shoved his hands in his pockets. "Why did you wait so long? You had to know way before this that you were pregnant."

Brooke's heart tore as his eyes filled with tears. She hated this. All she'd ever done was bring him hurt. "I'm never regular. My mother wasn't either. She even stopped for a whole year. There were signs but I didn't want to face it; it was easier to think I was doing the same as my mom. I've had some nausea but that's been getting better. I finally couldn't ignore that I was gaining weight." She watched for a show of understanding. "I went to the clinic this afternoon…I…"

He stared past her. "I don't know. Give me some time to think about this. I'm just not sure…"

He turned abruptly and walked deliberately down the beach, leaving her stranded and even more alone.

Chapter Two

It was dark as the little red sports car found its way into the familiar spot. The Erickson's two-story Florida home had a spacious wrap-around porch with a drive to the back of the house. Brooke's father had poured cement parking spaces for her and Emma. A large garage, built separate from the house, was used for storage and as an escape for her father's woodworking hobby. It was an older home when Brooke's parents first purchased it and there had been many remodels and updates. It was the only home she had ever known.

Brooke's step was heavy as she pushed out of her car and contemplated how she could act her normal, bubbly self. *Maybe I can slip in the back door and up the stairs to my room. Nope, that would look even more like something was wrong.* It would be more like her to bounce in, plop down, and chatter away. She couldn't avoid it, time to put on the performance of her life. Her swollen eyes had improved in the time it took to drive home, but Emma knew her too well to overlook a sullen mood. As she opened the back door, she was greeted with the familiar warmth and smells of cinnamon and other rich spices in her mother's kitchen.

Sounds of their favorite program, *Laugh In,* and the aroma of popcorn found their way into the dimly lit room. Brooke leaned against the counter and listened to the laughter coming from the next room. An ache filled her chest at the sounds of normalcy. *How could I be so stupid…nothing will ever be the same.* No point in prolonging it. She took a deep breath and pushed through the kitchen door into the family room. Both Emma and

Benji were engrossed in the show and she dropped into her father's overstuffed chair.

"Hey, great show tonight," Emma said.

"It's always good." Brooke attempted a laugh

"Yeah, it is." Emma glanced her way. "Man, Brooke, you look terrible. What's wrong?"

"Nothing, just a little tired I guess. It's been crazy getting ready for college, and I have to admit I'm feeling a little sad about being away from family."

"Know what you mean. With Robert gone, I can't imagine being away from home. Mom and Dad think I'm still their little girl, but it's better than being alone."

"Yeah, still, I don't know how you deal with Robert in Viet Nam. I would be going crazy." She laid her head back on the chair and tried to concentrate on the TV antics, but her thoughts wouldn't stop. *What a joke, believing Mark would solve her problem on the spot. What could anyone do?*

Emma gave her a serious study. "You really look beat. Have you had dinner?

"Yeah, pizza with the gang, but I do feel tired. I think I'll go up and take a long shower, maybe read for a while in my room."

Emma frowned. "Mom left tuna casserole, and there's plenty in the fridge."

"Thanks, I'll be okay with a little rest." Brooke ruffled her brother's hair as she walked past him and headed upstairs.

She loved her room. A huge oak tree stood guard outside her window, still leaving a view of the backyard and her mother's flower garden. It was like having a little tree house. It was her place to steal away for private thoughts or lose herself in her painting. She kicked off her shoes and felt the cool, smooth wood floor under her feet. She flopped down on her bed under the comfort of a white, ruffled canopy. Eyelet curtains hung softly against pale yellow walls. The easel, holding her current project, was one of her most treasured possessions. Her father made it as a Christmas gift in her freshman year of high school. A few of her paintings hung on the walls, and many more were tucked into folders at the back of her closet.

This should be her safe place, but her mind wouldn't give her any rest. *What am I going to do? This pregnancy is not going away and I can't keep it a secret much longer.* Even if she starved to keep her weight down, her belly was going to swell, and that was going to start soon. She could go on to school as planned but, within a month it would be noticeable. How could she continue in her classes and work at the college library? How will they feel about her having a job at school and pregnant?

What would Lisa think? Lisa had been her best friend forever, and she would understand. If only Lisa still lived next door. Why did her father have to be transferred and move them all to Orlando? A long distance call would show up on their bill. Besides, it was not something she wanted to talk about over the phone. There was too much risk of being overheard, and she wanted to be able to see Lisa's reaction. She closed her eyes, rubbed her forehead, and wished she could stop thinking.

There was a tap on the door. "Brooke?"

*Not now…*she waited quietly hoping Emma would think she was asleep

"Brooke, are you awake? Lisa's on the phone."

Brooke jumped up and grabbed the door. "I'm awake." She rushed past Emma and bounded down the stairs to the phone.

"Lisa!"

"Hey, what are you up to?"

"Oh, nothing, I was just up in my room." She peeked in the family room to see if Emma was within hearing distance.

"You want to meet tomorrow and make plans for the trip up to Gainesville."

"Great." Brooke sank into the wall. "I'll come over there. Maybe we can go to the mall and have lunch." She had to make this sound like their normal chatter with Emma in the next room.

"Cool. What time?"

"Let's get an early start. I'll leave here around eight. That should put me at your place no later than ten."

"Oooo—how can you be up so early?"

"You need to get in practice for school. Classes usually start before noon."

Lisa gave her an exaggerated sigh. "Okay, I'll be ready."

What a relief—some time to pull herself together. At least time to re-group before she spent any time with her mother. Annie would quickly pick up on the tension in her younger daughter.

With a plan in place, at least for the next day, Brooke decided the hot shower she had mentioned to Emma would be a good idea. With clean pajamas in hand, she went down the hall to the bathroom she shared with her siblings. The hot water beat down on her head and shoulders, easing some of the tension in her tight muscles. Hopefully it would help her go to sleep. Pajama-clad, she headed for her room, climbed into bed and dropped into a restless sleep.

Sunlight streamed in the bedroom window as Brooke slowly woke. She snuggled deep into the covers relishing that luxurious time between sleep and fully awake. That peace was soon interrupted, as a blanket of dread washed over her. She pulled the covers over her head. *No! This can't be happening. Why can't it be a bad dream?*

Lisa—her escape for the day—no time to waste. She needed a little time with her Mom, before she left. Mama was having a difficult time sending her away to school.

She winced from sore muscles as she moved across the room. The tension from yesterday left her stiff and sore. Searching through her closet, she found pants that were a little bit large. Thank goodness for shirts from India that fell loosely around her hips. She'd always been grateful for her slender figure, but now she wished she were a little plump. She slipped on sandals, ran a brush through her hair and went down stairs to the kitchen.

Antoinette Erickson, nicknamed Annie by her beloved husband, was humming as she worked in her kitchen kneading bread, while she started breakfast for her family. Brooke leaned against the door frame watching the familiar scene when her mother glanced over her shoulder to see her youngest daughter up and fully dressed.

"Ah, you are awake early, my princess, for a Saturday." She kissed Brooke's cheek.

Brooke smiled and gave her mother a hug and kiss. Her mother knew very little English when her father brought her to America as his bride. Her thick accent remained after all these years.

"It's only because I have things to do today, Mama. I'm going over to Orlando to spend the day with Lisa and make plans for our trip up to Gainesville."

"You are going too much. Emma told me last night how tired you were, and when will you have time to spend with your family?" She brushed a strand of hair from Brooke's forehead. "You will be gone so soon, and then I will not see you except for holidays."

She shrugged. "I just needed a good night's sleep. There's so much to take care of before we go. I won't be late, I promise. Let's do something special tonight, and I'll save all of next weekend just for you."

"Ah, such a naughty child, I cannot deny you. I will make a special dinner." She reached inside the refrigerator to bring out a tray of eggs. "What time will you be home?"

"Probably by four."

"So, you will have a nice breakfast before you go running." Her mother waved a threatening, wooden spoon.

Brooke laughed. "Okay," she said in spite of the lurch in her stomach. "I'll go for one of your wonderful bagels and some hot tea. Some of the tea Grandmere sent from France. Lisa and I are going to have an early lunch, so I don't want to eat too much."

"You never eat too much. You eat like a little bird but you will have a bagel.

Tonight, I will make your favorite beef-tips and vegetables in a nice pastry, hmmm?"

"Cool. I'm sure going to miss your cooking. I'll be home more often than holidays to get a good meal."

14

"That's all you will miss—my cooking?" She attempted some humor but tears filled Annie's eyes and she quickly turned to wipe them away with her apron.

Brooke came up behind, wrapped her arms around her, pressed her cheek against her mother's and hugged her hard.

"Ah, Mama, you know how special you are to me. It's not easy for me to leave my family. Spending time with my friends helps keep my mind off leaving. I've been so lucky to have such a great life, and I'll never forget what you and Papa have done for me."

Chapter Three

One explanation after another scrambled through Brooke's head as she drove the two hours to Orlando. The bond with her friend had been kept intact in spite of the distance between them, but nothing they had shared would have such an impact on their lives. Struggling with the sting of Mark's reaction, she questioned the wisdom of telling Lisa. No choice there. They planned to room together for the next four years. Lisa was her last hope. What answers she might have, Brooke didn't have a clue, but it was enough to know she had a friend to confide in and share this unbelievable situation.

Brooke pulled into the circular drive of the grand, grey-stone estate. A stone wall around the perimeter of the two-acre property opened at black iron gates where lush, green grounds sloped down to the lake. Their lives had gone in such different directions. Lisa was living in one of the most prestigious neighborhoods of Orlando and she in her modest childhood home. This was a friendship that had overcome the distance between them. She had to wonder, given a reversal of their circumstances, if she would have been as faithful.

Brooke grabbed her purse and keys, eager to get to inside. She was half-way up the steps when the door opened and Suzanne, Lisa's mother, ran to greet her.

"Brooke, honey, it's been so long since we've seen you." Suzanne hugged her into her ample bosom before leading her into the house. "And where is your mama? You should have brought her with you so we could visit while you girls go shopping. I miss her so much. Brooke," she held her by the shoulders at arm's length, "you're as beautiful as ever. Child, I can't believe you don't have a dozen boyfriends."

"I'm too busy to be tied down to a boyfriend, Mama Suzanne." Brooked laughed and hugged her second mother. "Mom was busy in the kitchen when I left. Sorry, I didn't think to ask her to come. This college business has left me scatter brained."

"Honey, you're not the only one."

"Is Lisa upstairs?" Brooke loved this woman and would have spent another hour with her under normal circumstances. But the anxiety building inside was ready to explode.

"I'm sure you'll find her in front of her mirror. Go on up, honey, she's expecting you. You are planning to spend the night, aren't you?"

"No, I promised Mom I would be home tonight for some family time. With everything that's been going on, I've kind of neglected her."

"What is it with you girls?" Suzanne shook her head. "Lisa has been crazy; making sure she has everything. As if she can't go shopping after she gets there. You must plan on coming home with Lisa for a weekend. Go on up now. I won't keep you any longer."

Yes! Finally...Brooke's sandals clicked on the marble foyer as she crossed to the circular stairway leading to her friend's room. She tapped softly on the door, pushed it open and stuck her head inside.

"Lisa? Hey, let's get moving."

Lisa called from her bathroom. "In here, Brooke. I'm almost ready, I swear."

"That will be the day."

"Not fair," Lisa called back. "You know I'm not an early riser."

Lisa strolled out of the bathroom, looking the picture of Mama Suzanne in her youth. Dark soft curls fell around her shoulders. Brooke never ceased to be startled by her lavender eyes. Lisa could hold her own in any beauty contest.

"So, can you stand it? We're almost off to college. It's going to be so much fun. Having our own place, making our own decisions, come and go as you please..." Lisa, a talker like her mother, stopped short. "What is it, honey? You don't look so good. Is something wrong?"

The game was up. "No fooling you, is there?" Brooke dropped down on the end of Lisa's bed. "I don't think I'll be going with you to college."

"What do you mean? Is it money? My folks can help. They would be glad to help you—"

"No, it's not money." She shook her head and looked down at the floor.

"What is it, Brooke? Tell me."

Brooke sucked in a breath. Now that she was here, she didn't know how she was going to do this.

"I'm not sure where to begin. I've been trying to figure out how to tell you all the way here."

"Well, just come out with it. You know you can trust me."

"Do you remember last spring when I started dating Mark?"

"Yes...I could never understand what happened with you two. You were so excited when you first started dating."

"There was a big reason." She ran her fingers through her hair and tossed back her head. "One night, Mark took me to a party with some of his friends. They lived in a big mansion on

18

the beach and I felt totally out of place." Brooke shrugged before continuing. "They were pretty uppity and I felt like the maid or something."

"I can't believe Mark let them get away with that. I wish I had known. I would have put those kids in their place."

Brooke smiled at Lisa coming to her defense...*always my protector.*

"It's okay. The worst part was when they brought out pizza; they also brought out the beer. Like an idiot, I drank a can right along with them. I was so in love with Mark that I didn't want to embarrass him in front of his friends. I thought I could just sip on one can and I would be fine."

"So...you got drunk?"

"No...well, I was little woozy. When Mark asked me to take a walk down the beach, I thought it would be a good way to clear my head." Brooke took a deep breath and licked her lips. "We sat on the beach and talked, and it felt so right. Lisa, he told me that he loved me, and that I was the first person to ever make him feel special...you know, really loved." She shook her head. "It broke my heart."

"So what's so bad about that?"

Brooke kept her eyes on her hands clutched in her lap. "The problem is that we let things get out of hand and before I knew it...Lisa, I didn't wait for marriage like I said I would." Tears threatened at the edge of her eyelids.

"Honey, you're not the first one." She sat next to Brooke on the bed and put her arm around her shoulder. "God understands that we mess up sometimes. He knows you're sorry and he'll forgive—"

"That's not the whole story." Lisa's comforting words were like a balm around her soul, but how would she handle the rest of it? "Afterwards, I just couldn't face Mark. I didn't blame him. I knew it was wrong, probably more than he did. But every time we saw each other, it reminded me of what I had done. That's why we stopped dating."

"So why would that keep you from going to college? I don't understand."

"You remember how I was never regular...and would miss a month or two?"

"Yeah—" Lisa began to frown.

"Well, when I missed several months, I didn't think anything about it." She sneaked a quick peek at Lisa to see if she was getting the gist of where this was going. "I just thought it was what I usually do. That is, until I started getting sick in the mornings. I convinced myself there was nothing to it until I started putting on weight. I went to the clinic yesterday." Brooke looked up with a pool of tears spilling down her cheeks. "Oh, Lisa...I'm nearly five months pregnant."

"Oh, honey...no!" She pulled Brooke into her arms and let her weep against her shoulder. "How could...? It was only one time."

"That's all it takes." Brooke sobbed in relief of having the truth out without condemnation.

"Brooke, this is so awful." By now Lisa had joined her with tears trickling down her face. "It's just not fair. You of all people, hardly dating anyone and always been so good. Why did this have to happen to you?"

"I guess...I'm paying...for...not sticking to...my convictions." Brooke struggled between sobs. "I knew it was wrong...whether anything...came of it...or not."

Lisa grabbed a tissue and carefully wiped the running mascara from under her eyes. "Well, we've just got to figure something out." Lisa took hold of Brooke's shoulders and looked into her eyes. "We're not going to let this ruin your life. What does Mark say about this? Have you told him?"

Brooke wiped the tears from her eyes and slowly nodded. "I called him yesterday evening. He met me at the beach."

"And...?"

The feeling the desperation swept over her again. "He was pretty shocked and didn't think it was his at first."

"He's a first class jerk! What did he say...that you were sleeping around?"

"I'm not mad at him. I can see why he would think that since I'm the one that ended our relationship."

"So what's he going to do?"

"He said he would have to think about it and left."

"I can't believe it." Lisa stood and stomped her foot. "Men are worthless! They take what they want and then leave us to live with the consequences. Well, I'm not standing by to let you throw your life away." Brooke watched Lisa as she paced back and forth. "Maybe if we talked to Mama," she suggested. "She's pretty good at figuring out what to do in impossible situations."

Panic shot through Brooke. "No! You know how close she is to my mom. She would be on the phone as soon as we got through telling her."

Lisa gave a knowing sigh. "You're right. She could never keep something like this from Ms. Annie." Lisa sat down again next to Brooke.

"Honey, I know this is going to be hard for you to think about." She hesitated and gave Brooke a side glance. "But, I can't think of any other way." She looked down at the floor to avoid Brooke's questioning look.

"There is a girl...she was a friend at school. Well...she was in the same situation and her parents took her to a doctor. It only took a couple of hours and her problem was solved."

The blood drained from Brooke's face and a new panic washed through her body. "Lisa, are you saying what I think—?"

"Brooke, I know it sounds awful." Lisa hugged her shoulders. "But it's not really a baby yet. What good will it do to go through this pregnancy and embarrass your parents? It will even blow your scholarship for college." She pulled Brooke around to face her. "Oh, honey, you have so much talent and you'll waste all of that, for what? Think girl! Think of all the people this will affect!"

"I don't know, Lisa. We've always been taught that it's...killing...." Brooke's throat constricted. How could she be drawn into such a thing? As ugly as it sounded, she felt herself being convinced it was a viable solution.

"I know, I know, and I could see that if you were further along." Lisa continued to press her view. "But, Brooke, it's not a baby yet."

"How do you know that?"

"Honey, everybody knows that. That's why they allow abortions because at this stage. It's just tissue."

"Oh, I wish I could believe that." Her eyes searched Lisa's for assurance that it was true. "The last thing I want to do is hurt my parents. They are such good people, this would devastate them."

"At least let me see if I can get you an appointment to talk to a doctor. Please, Brooke."

"Well, I guess I could just talk to him. It doesn't hurt to talk." Brooke felt her resolve giving way to the possibility of ending this nightmare with no one in her family finding out what she had done.

Lisa went to the phone by her bedside and dialed. "Hello, is Carol there? Yes, this is Lisa." The wait seemed endless. "Carol, thank goodness I caught you. My best friend is here from Tampa and she is…well, she's in the same fix that you were last year. Yes, it is, but can you give me the number of the doctor that helped you? Sure, I'll wait."

Brooke listened to the conversation. Could she possibly be thinking of doing this? But didn't she come to Lisa for help? Did she have any better ideas? It was time to grow up and face reality. Lisa was right. How could she do this to her mother?

"Yes, Carol, I've got it. Thanks a million." Lisa turned around to Brooke and waved the piece of paper. "Okay, I've got the number. I'm going to see if I can get you in today." She glanced back to assure Brooke. "We were planning to go out shopping today anyway, so Mama won't know any different."

"Yes, Dr. Lewis's office?" Lisa sounded so professional, and Brooke sagged in relief with someone to take over. The exhaustion from the day before seeped into her body and left her ready to be led in whatever direction she needed to go. She would do anything to end this nightmare. "I need to make an appointment for today. No, no, it has to be today. She needs to go back to Tampa tonight and it's urgent!" Lisa was not going to relent. "Eleven-thirty is fine. Her name...her name is...Jennifer...Jennifer Rogers. Okay, we'll be there."

"All set." She turned to Brooke with an encouraging smile. "We need to leave soon, but first we need to do some damage control so Mama won't see we've been crying. Come on." She pulled Brooke toward the bathroom. "Let's get you looking fresh."

An open magazine lay across Brooke's lap as she watched the young couple across from her. Could they be here for the same reason? The girl seemed to be Brooke's age, and him a little older. Certainly not the lady next to her, who appeared to be near the end of her pregnancy, and way beyond having— Brooke stretched her legs to release the tension creeping into every muscle in her body. Her chest had tightened when they first walked in with the familiar smell of the clinic where she had been—could it be only yesterday? She flipped through the rest of the magazine and tossed it to an empty chair. *Why can't doctors be on time?*

"Miss Rogers?"

Lisa bumped her in the ribs with her elbow.

"Oh...yes." Brooke jumped to her feet and turned back to Lisa. "Are you coming with me?"

"Sure, if you want me to."

"Please!" *I can't do this by myself.*

They followed the nurse to a room where she was instructed to sit on the examining table while her temperature and blood pressure was checked.

"The doctor will be with you shortly." The nurse smiled at Brooke as she put her file in the receptacle and closed the door.

The room was cold and sterile in spite of soft pink walls and decorative border. Brooke hugged herself to ward off the chill. It was quiet except for the muffled conversation from the next room. Brooke looked at Lisa. Both of them at a loss for words sat for another long wait before the doctor came through the door. He was a kind-looking man. He seemed more like a grandfather, Brooke thought, than a doctor.

"Good morning, ladies." He perched on a stool at the end of the examining table. "What seems to be the problem today?"

"I've just found out I'm almost five months pregnant." Brooke, unable to look at him, spoke barely over a whisper.

"And you would like for me to be your doctor during your pregnancy and delivery?"

Brooke hesitated and Lisa jumped in. "She's getting ready to leave for college and this is going to ruin everything. She doesn't sleep around. It only happened one time."

Dr. Lewis chuckled. "You have quite a champion in your corner. We could all do with a friend like her." He glanced at Lisa and then turned back to Brooke. "So what you're asking for is to terminate your pregnancy?"

Brooke looked up at him with tears filling her eyes. She had to do this. "It's just that I can't tell my parents. They would be devastated...I...don't know what else to do..."

"There, there." Dr. Lewis patted her arm. "It's a simple procedure. Let me explain exactly what we would do. We'll insert a saline solution that will start the process. There be will something similar to cramps that will lead to the expulsion of the tissue, and you'll be on your way."

25

When Brooke did not respond, he continued. "Does that make sense to you?"

Can it be that simple? She nodded in the affirmative.

"It's much like a miscarriage. We'll insert the saline right here in the office. We have a comfortable room where you and your friend can wait until you feel the cramping."

"Well…I don't know. How much will this cost?" A panic suddenly hit. How could she get this far without thinking of the cost? "I'm going to school on a scholarship."

"We can make arrangements and work with you on that—"

"Don't worry about it," Lisa spoke up. "I've got it covered. Daddy has been generous with my school expense account, but it needs to be soon. We'll be leaving for college in two weeks."

Dr. Lewis turned to Brooke. "Is that all right with you, young lady?"

Brooke nodded. This had to be the answer with everything falling into place.

"You'll be just fine, and before long you'll have all this behind you." Dr. Lewis gave her a kind and reassuring smile. "We'll do a quick exam today to make sure we are on target, and I'll have Tammy see how soon we can get you scheduled."

Brooke closed her eyes to hold back the tears that threatened. How quickly things had been decided.

Lisa hugged Brooke. "It will be okay. You heard him. It's an easy procedure and it will all be over. We can leave for Gainesville as if nothing happened.

"Well, it's not as if nothing happened." Brooke was uncomfortable with how quickly Lisa could dismiss the whole thing. "But at least my parents won't know."

"Brooke, this is the only option you have."

Following the embarrassing exam, Dr. Lewis confirmed what she already knew. "We have you scheduled for Wednesday. You'll need to be here by nine in the morning—only a light breakfast. Tammy will give you some printed instructions before you leave. Do you have any questions?"

"No, I don't think so."

"Then we'll see you Wednesday morning."

As they walked outside, Brooke filled her lungs with the fresh air. "I'm going to have to lie again. I'm supposed to work on Wednesday."

"It might be better if you didn't go back on Wednesday. Why don't you stay overnight?"

"How am I going to explain?" This was getting more and more complicated.

"Well, a group of my friends are getting together for a farewell party before we all go our separate ways. You could say you're coming over for that."

"I hate this. It's one lie on top of another."

Lisa put her arm around her shoulder as they walked to the car. "I know, but sometimes we just have to do things we don't like to protect the people we love. Once this is over, you won't have to make up stories."

"Maybe not, but I still don't like it. I've always been able to talk to Mama about everything. I'll always know I've let her down. For the rest of my life I'll have to keep this from her."

Chapter Four

"Mom, I'm leaving," Brooke called upstairs.

"You have a good day at work." Her mother's cheerful voice came from her parents' bedroom. "Call me when you get to Lisa's tonight."

She was meeting Lisa at the doctor's office rather than risk Mama Suzanne asking questions. Or, even worse, mentioning it to her mother. She'd told the story about going to Lisa's after work. Thankfully, her mother was being more lenient before Brooke left for school. Nancy, her office manager, allowed the two days off. With Brooke leaving for school in a couple of weeks, her contribution involved little more than helping out. A replacement was in-house and ready to take over.

Lisa's VW Bug sat in the parking lot. As she stepped out of the car, her legs began to shake and threatened to give way. *I've got to do this!* Keys dropping to the ground as she missed the front pocket of her purse, she was reduced to reaching under the car to grab them. *Get a grip, it's only tissue...it's not a baby yet.* That argument fell short of conviction, but there was no backing out now. She pushed through the door of the office building and walked down the hall to Dr. Lewis's office. Lisa was waiting at the door and reached out to hug Brooke. "You okay?"

"Scared to death," she managed through a clenched jaw.

"Oh, don't be. My friend said there is nothing to it, and I'll be right here for you."

"I know you will." Brooke hung onto Lisa with a trembling hand. "Let's get this over before I lose my nerve."

Brooke walked into a room that was stark and cold. Everything glared white. A table, covered with stiff paper, stood in the center. What wasn't white was cold stainless steel. She had been instructed to remove her clothing and put on a gown that gaped in the back. She shivered from more than the temperature of the room.

"How are we doing, young lady?" Dr. Lewis smiled as he entered the room. "All ready to go?"

Brooke failed in her attempt to return his smile and simply nodded.

"Okay, here's what you can expect. We'll give you a little something to help you relax, and then insert a needle in your uterus to inject the fluid. There will be a little pain, but with the medication, you should not feel much. Once we are through, we'll call in your friend to wait with you. Tammy will check on your progress, and you can call her at any time. You'll have a menstrual period afterwards." He smiled and patted her knee. "That will provide an explanation for the bit of tenderness you will have. Anything you don't understand?"

"No."

"Good enough. We'll get started as soon as your meds have taken effect."

Brooke lay flat on the table wondering how quickly she could get into her clothes and out of here. Too late. The nurse was there with a capsule for her to swallow. Within half an hour the sedative had done its job. She jumped as Dr. Lewis and his nurse returned, caught her breath, and turned her head away after seeing the size of the needle. Tammy, at her side, instructed Brooke to hang on to her arm. As the needle was injected, Brooke dug her fingernails into the nurse's arm and bit her lip to

29

keep from screaming. The room swam as intense pain consumed her body.

"We're all done, young lady. Give yourself some time before you get up. When you're ready, Tammy will give you a robe and make you comfortable."

Alone, she lay on the stiff table weeping. What was she doing? This was not easy. A wave of nausea hit. *This is barbaric...*and then she felt the small soft kick in her belly. "Oh, God," she cried. "What have I done?"

Lisa waited in a softly lit room with a couch and big comfortable chairs, as *The Price Is Right* played on a television in the corner. Brooke glanced at her and sank into one of the chairs. Lisa jumped up and sat next to her.

"What is it, honey? Was it bad?"

"It was horrible. I thought I was going to pass out from the pain. I wish I'd never agreed to this. What am I doing?"

"You're getting your life back."

"At what cost? After they finished, I felt a kick. Lisa, tissue doesn't kick!"

"It was probably just a muscle jerking. You said it was painful." She reached out to squeeze her hand. Brooke remained silent.

"They left water in this fridge." Lisa indicated the small refrigerator on the opposite wall. "They said it would be good for you to drink a lot of water. Do you want me to get you some?"

Brooke shrugged. There was nothing left but to see it through. She couldn't change what had already been done.

Not more than an hour had passed while the two girls sat waiting, with little conversation between them.

"Do you want to walk around a little?"

"No, I just need to get to the bathroom after all that water."

"I'll go ask where it is." Lisa started for the door.

Panic washed through Brooke. "Lisa, wait!"

"Honey...what is it?" Lisa ran to her side as Brooke doubled over.

"It's...beginning," she managed between gasps.

"I'll get the nurse." Lisa scrambled to the door.

The five minutes it took Lisa and Tammy to return seemed like hours.

"How are we doing?" Tammy chirped as she walked over to Brooke.

Another pain hit and Brooke screamed out, "It feels like a knife through my belly."

"Looks like you're moving a lot faster than usual." Concern crossed Tammy's face as she took Brooke's hand. "I'll get Doctor."

Brooke's head swam and she could barely make sense of the rush of people in and out of the room. Her consciousness was in and out as she felt herself being lifted onto a gurney and wheeled out to a waiting ambulance.

"Dr. Lewis's patient...I'll get her set up...he's on his way here."

She could hear bits and pieces but she was losing the battle. "Lisa...with...me..."

"She'll be waiting for you...try to relax..."

31

She was vaguely aware of being pushed somewhere, and she knew she was lying down. But her focus centered on the searing pain that kept coming in waves.

"I'll be right here." She felt Lisa squeeze her hand.

Her next sensation was one of bright lights somewhere in a cold room…was that Dr. Lewis? She forced her eyes open and looked into the eyes of a nurse beside her. They looked kind and, at the same time, sad.

"Help…me…"

"It's going very fast, dear. It's almost over."

"So stupid…never…should…"

Lisa sat bedside Brooke's bed, rubbed her friend's arm, and prayed for her to wake up. This wasn't anything like she'd been told. She thought Brooke was going to die. Maybe it was because Brooke was so much further along. What was it Carol said, a couple of hours, and she'd walk out of here?

"I wish I'd never talked you into this. If anything happens to you…"

Brooke began to stir. "Can't do…no…don't want…"

"I'm here, Brooke. It's Lisa. Wake up, honey."

Brooke's eyes fluttered. "Where…?"

"You're in the hospital, Brooke."

"Hospital…?"

"Remember…pregnancy?" She whispered and glanced around the room to make sure no one heard.

"It was awful…not true…"

"What's not true?"

"Nothing to it…was a nightmare."

"I'm so sorry, Brooke, but it's over now."

"It will never be over. I'll never forget what I've done."
Brooke cried quietly while Lisa sat helpless to make it right.

"Lisa…"

"Yes, honey."

"I want…to get out of here."

"In a little bit, as soon as you're feeling stronger."

"No!" Brooke rolled her head back and forth in protest. "I want out now!"

"But I don't think they'll let you go. They need to check you first before you're released."

"I don't care what they need to do, get me out of here…get my clothes." She struggled to sit up.

"Brooke, you're going to hurt yourself. Just wait until they check you and make sure you're all right."

"I'm not waiting. Get my clothes…help me get out of here." She jerked at the sheet covering her. "They've…done…enough. This whole thing was a lie." Brooke held her face in her hands trying to clear her head. "That wasn't tissue that came out of my body. That was a baby." She finally managed to stand, clinging to Lisa. "I could feel it…I know it was a baby."

Lisa stood frozen in indecision, "You just thought it was. You were drugged up, and it just seemed that way."

"No! I was not drugged up until afterwards. I gave birth to a baby."

She leaned her head against her friend's shoulder. "I can't stay here another minute. Please, Lisa, help me get out of here."

"Alright, I'll help you, but not because I think you're doing the right thing." Lisa took hold of her by the shoulders. "I'm afraid this is going to hurt you."

33

Brooke looked at her friend, her eyes dull with grief. "Nothing…absolutely nothing…could hurt me more than what I've just gone through."

Chapter Five

Maggie pushed through the doors of the delivery room. Sure had been a lot of commotion. She noticed her friend, Beth, coming out of surgery earlier, giving a resigned look that said they'd done another abortion. Dr. Lewis was a good man, but his stand on abortion went against everything they believed. It didn't help that Beth had been trying for years to have a baby, and all attempts had ended in miscarriage. It was Maggie's job to clean up the mess afterwards, and it never got easier. They called it a D & C...*must make them feel better.*

The work was methodical, pulling off soiled linens, and putting instruments in pans for sterilization, before another procedure. Only a few minutes into the task, a rustling noise caught her attention. She listened, not moving a muscle. It sounded like a mouse scrambling through paper. *How could that be? How would a mouse get in here?* Her eyes scoured the room, looking for the noisemaker. Maybe something was blowing from the air conditioning vent. Nothing. *Nonsense, get back to work.* There it was again. This time it sounded like a...cry...a little cry? It was common knowledge these babies were just tossed into a bin. Could it...no...how *could it live through*--she stood frozen to the spot, waiting. Again, there was a soft cry, coming from that bin. She edged her way toward the sound as though something would fly from the container.

"Be sensible. You've watched too many science fiction movies."

Slowly, she pulled back the cover, and stretched her neck to peek in without getting too close. Maggie gasped and jumped back. There was movement. It was alive! Another ventured look…the baby was breathing rapidly. He'd survived this monstrous attempt to take his life.

With tight throat, she stood immobile and stared down at the baby torn from the safety of his mother's womb.

"What should I do? I can't just leave him here."

The first reaction was to reach for him, but she reconsidered. She knew nothing about these things, and could possibly do him more harm. Beth would know what to do.

"Oh, dear Lord, watch over this little one while I go for help."

Now, where to look for Beth? The nurse's station should know. With trembling body and leaden legs, never had this hallway seemed so long.

Elise, the new graduate, was on the phone. The alarm on Maggie's face reflected in hers as she paused her conversation.

"Can you hold for just a moment?" A hand placed over the receiver. "What is it? What's happened?"

"Where's Beth? I've got to find Beth."

"Has something happened? What's wrong?"

"If you don't know where she is, just tell me,"

"Please, you'll have everyone in earshot in a panic. Try the nursery. I'm not sure if—"

Maggie took off, holding back from a dead run.

"Please Jesus, let Beth be there. Oh Lord, we've got to get back to the baby before someone empties that receptacle." That possibility had just hit. *Why didn't I grab him from that grave?* A quick turn around the corner brought a near collision with the new interns and their instructor, Dr. Melrose. The senior staff member gave a disapproving look as she apologized and adjusted her course.

Just ahead, the nursery buzzed with staff members attending the new babies…but no Beth. Maybe one of them would know. As she flung open the door, she saw Beth sat in a rocker cuddling one of the newborns. Everyone in the room turned to see the cause of the sudden intrusion, but Maggie was on a mission.

"You've got to come!"

Beth stood at her friend's sudden entrance and put the baby in his crib. "Maggie…what is it? Come out here and tell me."

"The baby…the baby…he's alive."

"Calm down. What are you talking about? What baby is alive?"

"The baby, who was just aborted, didn't die. He's alive."

The young nurse stood transfixed while Maggie tugged at her arm to get back to the delivery room. Beth was almost running to keep up with the taller woman's stride.

"Tell me everything." She gave Maggie side-glances as they hurried along.

"The baby…I was cleaning the room when I heard a rustling sound…I…I thought it was some kind of animal, and then I heard him. His tiny little voice called out for help." She was breathing heavy. "I was so afraid to look. But there he was, panting away and determined to live. I didn't know what to do. So I came looking for you."

"I'm glad you did."

"But what if he gave up before—what if someone has carried him out as garbage!"

They were approaching the delivery room when an orderly came out, pulling bins on a cart.

"Wait!" Both women shouted. The startled man whirled around and almost toppled the contents of his cart. With a look of dismay, he watched as the two women started pulling the lids off of the containers…nothing.

"Have you taken anything else from this room?" Maggie asked.

"Has anyone else been in here?" Beth added.

"Nothing…no one else—" He shook his head and pushed his cart down the hall as they rushed into the room.

"Please, let him be breathing," Maggie was the first to get back to where she'd left the struggling life, and lifted the lid. No movement.

"Oh no! We're too late. I should have taken him out."

Beth reached down to touch the fragile little body. He moved against her hand and immediately started breathing rapidly again.

"Get me a clean towel. We've got to get him some help—and fast." She scooped him up to the safety of her arms while Maggie grabbed a towel from her cart. Beth gently wrapped the tiny life, and held him to her breast. "Dr. Lewis will be back in his office by now. Karen is the best neonatal nurse." She checked her watch. "She'll be at lunch." A quick page to Karen for an emergency at the nursery was the first step. "Finish up in here. We'll keep this quiet for now, and I'll let you know how he does." She hugged Maggie. "Thank you for saving him."

Beth rounded the corner by the nursery just as Karen came out of the elevator.

"What's up? What is—?"

"Let's go inside."

38

Karen held the door open for Beth and followed into the nursery.

"It's the aborted baby. Maggie found him alive when she went in to clean up."

"Holy—"

"Yeah, could get sticky. The three of us are the only ones that know."

"First priority is to take care of him. I'll take over from here. You better get Dr. Lewis on the phone, and let the mother know."

"I'm on it." She handed the fragile bundle to Karen and brushed the top of his head. "You're in the best hands now little buddy. Just hang on and let us take care of you."

Beth headed back to the nurses station. "Elise, what's Jennifer Rogers's room number?"

"Gone...took off before they had time to do a final check-up and release. Room 18 had blood pressure going sky high and had everyone flying. Then two of them in a row—came in at the last minute. There was so much going on, we didn't even see her leave."

"This gets worse by the minute. Okay, I'll check with admissions."

Several visitors got off the elevator leaving Beth by herself. She leaned back against wall and closed her eyes. "You didn't want to do this sweet little girl. I saw it in your eyes. I saw your pain."

The doors opened to a quick walk across the lobby and down the hall to admissions.

"Hi Marilee, I need to see the records of a patient admitted this morning—a Jennifer Rogers."

"Sure, I'll be right back." The older woman hefted herself from the chair, and went to the file with the day's admissions. She called over her shoulder. "You sure she came in today?"

"Yes, I was the assisting nurse."

"Nothin' here honey, she didn't come through this office."

"Hmm...I know she was close. We had to rush to get her into delivery. Maybe she came through emergency. I'll check there. Thanks Marilee."

"You bet. Good luck."

Beth walked down the hall toward the emergency ward. Good, things looked quiet, and they would be more apt to look up a file for her. They could be testy. No wonder, with some of the weird things that came through the doors. She walked inside the office to avoid any listening ears.

"Hi. I'm Beth Ramsey, fourth floor. We've got kind-of a difficult situation with a patient. Seems she walked out without being discharged, and I can't find her file."

"She come through here?"

"I think she must have. It was an emergency situation, and they don't have anything in admitting."

"Ooo—what's the name?"

"Rogers...Jennifer Rogers."

She checked through the files behind her, in the basket on the desk, and looked up. "Nothing here, we might have a problem."

"It's looking that way. Have you been here all morning?"

"They just called me in to cover so Sandi could take a break. She was pretty beat. Bus accident—hit a van full of kids."

"Guess I'd better get in touch with Dr. Lewis. Can I use your phone?"

"Use that one in the back office. You won't be heard from there."

"Good idea."

Beth collapsed into the chair behind the desk, and rubbed her neck and shoulders to release tense muscles. The directory for doctors on staff gave the number to dial Dr. Lewis's office.

"Tammy, this is Beth Ramsey. I assisted Dr. Lewis this morning with your patient, Jennifer Rogers."

There was pause. "The hospital called earlier. Seems she left without being discharged."

"Yes, well, there has been a development. I need to get in touch with her."

"I'm afraid that's going to be a little difficult."

"Why?"

"After we heard from the hospital, I called the phone number she gave us. No Jennifer Rogers. It was a pizza parlor."

Beth's heart sank to the pit of her stomach. "So, she gave you fictitious information."

"I'm afraid so. We're only here half a day on Saturdays. They called and insisted on getting in to see Doctor. I worked her in between patients. Our student nurse was at the front desk, and I didn't have time to follow up. At least her friend paid cash before they left."

"Tammy, we have more to worry about than money. I need to speak to Dr. Lewis right away, even if he's with a patient."

Piped music played in her ear. *Should the hospital administration be the first to be notified? No, this was Dr. Lewis's patient. Better to let him know what was going on before he was questioned.*

41

Dr. Lewis came on the phone. "Beth, what's the emergency?"

"Sorry to bother you, but I thought you'd want to know right away."

"Sounds serious."

"Did Tammy tell you that your patient, Jennifer Rogers, used fictitious information?"

"Yes, she did mention that to me. These young girls are so frightened of being found out. They don't realize it's all confidential."

"This one is going to be a real problem. Her baby lived through the abortion. Maggie was cleaning up afterwards, and heard him crying."

There was a long silence. "That's the problem using saline. I've heard of this happening. I just never experienced it. A slim chance he'll make it."

"Karen is working with him now. If he pulls through, we have no mother."

"Right, could be messy if the press gets wind. I'll be finished here in another half-hour, and head over. Let's keep this between us until I can get over and talk to administration."

"Yes sir. Maggie, Karen in neo-natal and I are the only ones aware at this point. We'll take care of our end of it and let you handle the rest. I just wish we could find the mother. This is going to cause quite a mess when the press gets involved."

Chapter Six

Brooke poked at the noodles in her half-eaten bowl of soup. The thought of food had been a stomach-turning proposition, but Lisa was right. With renewed strength and a clear head, the trip home seemed more possible, and the sooner the better.

"I wish I could change your mind. It worries me to think about you driving all the way back home. This didn't turn out to be the minor thing we were told."

"No kidding, but I'm not in a party mood."

"It will help you get your mind off today."

She shook her head. "I just want to go home and be in my own bed. Kinda get my head together, you know?"

"I guess."

"If it's any consolation, you were right."

"About?"

"Eating. I feel a lot better."

"If you call that eating. There's still soup in your bowl."

"Mom will have dinner ready. Besides, my stomach is still a little queasy from the stuff they gave me."

Lisa reached over and squeezed her arm. "I'm so sorry."

She choked back the emotion that tightened her throat. "You didn't know. You did your best to look out for me." She tore at her paper napkin. "I could have said no. I was looking for a way out."

"Do you think we can ever get past this?"

"I don't think you ever get past taking a life." She looked up at Lisa and gave her a weak smile. "But don't think this affects our friendship. You'll always be my friend, and I know you had my best interest at heart. I don't want you to carry any guilt or think I blame you."

"But—"

"I'm the one who got pregnant in the first place. You didn't create this mess. It rests on my shoulders. Don't ever question that."

A single tear rolled down Lisa's cheek. She dabbed it away with her napkin. Brooke watched out the window at the crowds crossing the intersection. People finishing up their shopping or leaving work to head for home. *Amazing how life goes on.*

"I guess I'd better get on the road. Mom won't be expecting me, but I need to show up at my regular time from work."

"Call me. I want to know you got home safely."

Brooke slid out of the booth and grabbed her purse. "I'll call as soon as I get there."

She walked with Lisa to her car. There was nothing left to say, so they hugged each other fiercely. "Don't worry. I'll be fine."

Brooke's car slid into the parking spot like a small ship pulling into a safe harbor. She leaned her head against the steering wheel before climbing out of the car. *This is why I did this…for them.* She had to admit, to have it over was a relief.

She stepped into the warm kitchen filled with delectable smells of pot roast. A hint of cinnamon was evidence of fresh baked goods. Her mom looked up as she came through the back door.

"You didn't go to Orlando, Princess?"

"No, I've got cramps really bad. I wasn't up to a party."

44

"Just as well. Your schedule has been too full." She lifted the pot from the oven and set it on the counter. "Was the traffic bad?"

"Not terribly, not as bad as winter. I'm looking forward to living in Gainesville where the commute will be practically nothing."

"Your father would agree with you. He can't wait to retire so he can sit in my kitchen and get in my way."

Brooke laughed. "You know you'll love it. You and dad should take some vacations to get out and see the country."

"And why would I need a vacation when I already live in paradise? Besides, I'm content right here in my kitchen."

"The world would be a better place if everyone appreciated their blessings the way you do."

Annie waved her away and pulled dishes from the cabinet above her. "Go wash up and tell the others that dinner is ready."

Brooke started toward the door.

"Ah, I nearly forgot. Did Mark get in touch with you?" Annie asked.

"No—why?"

"He called here, and I gave him your work number. You must have been at lunch."

"Yeah, maybe."

"Are you seeing Mark again?"

"No, I'm sure he wants to say goodbye before we head off to school."

"I like Mark. He's such a nice—"

"Mom, we're just friends." She leaned against the door frame and rolled her eyes.

"All right, I will not be prodding. Go call the others so we can eat while it's still hot."

Brooke sat back in her chair and gave a satisfied sigh. "That was the best, Mom."

"You ate like you haven't eaten in a week." Emma laughed.

"I dunno. Everything just tasted so good."

"It's time you ate a good meal. You're going to waste away to nothing." Annie glanced at her husband for reinforcement.

Brooke raised her hands and got up from her chair. "Enough. You, Mom, are going to take your coffee, and watch TV while we clean up the kitchen."

"But, I don't need—" Annie stood to clear the table.

"No arguments. Out." She took the dishes from her mother's hands and shoved her with her hip. Brooke cleared the table while Emma was up to her elbows in soapy water. The phone rang.

"Hello."

"Brooke—"

"Hi Lisa, what's up?" *Ahhhh...forgot to call.*

"Well, I guess you made it okay."

"Sorry, I had really bad cramps. I went straight home from work, and Mom sat me down to dinner."

"Honestly, Brooke, I've been picturing you off in a ditch somewhere."

"That sounds like fun. Did you find some good sales at the mall?"

"What—? Oh, I guess you can't talk."

"You could probably say that."

"Okay, I get it. Do you know what time we're going to leave for Gainesville?"

"I imagine our moms will work that out, but I'd like to get an early start."

"Me too—there's the doorbell. Must be the group arriving. Call me soon."

"Right. Catch you later."

Emma gave her a side-glance. "That was the shortest conversation I've ever heard between you two."

"I was supposed to spend the night at her house for a big farewell party. I forgot to call her."

Emma emptied the dish water, reached for a towel and dried her hands. "How do you think you guys will manage living together?" She hung the towel on its hook and leaned back against the sink. "A lot of good friendships have gone down the tubes with too much togetherness."

"I'm not worried about us." Brooke sat in a chair and pulled her feet up on the edge of the seat. "It's not like we don't have other friends. We're both pretty independent. I think we're a good match."

"I hope so. It would be pretty awkward for Mom and Suzanne if you had a falling—"

The phone rang again. "She probably forgot to tell me something." She laughed as she reached for the phone. "Okay, what did we forget?"

"Brooke?" She eased herself back into the chair, recognizing Mark's voice.

"Hi, Mark."

"Listen, I'm sorry I haven't called, but can we get together tomorrow night?"

47

"Well—"

"Please, we can go out to the pier for dinner. It'll be quiet there and we can talk."

She leaned her elbow on the chair back and rested her head in her hand "Well...I guess."

"I'll pick you up around six."

"Better make it six-thirty."

"Sure, I'll see you then. It's going to be okay, Brooke."

She held the receiver for a minute before replacing it on the wall.

Emma's eyebrows rose. "Are you and Mark getting back together?"

She swatted her sister on the arm. "No, we're not getting back together. We're just friends going out for dinner before we leave for school."

"I think he wants to let you know he's still around before you go off to a college loaded with a bunch of cool guys."

"Yeah right. He's had a dozen girlfriends since me."

"C'mon, anybody can see he's still nuts about you." Emma wrung out the dishcloth and spread it over the edge of the sink to dry. "I feel sorry for him. Why did you break up?"

She pulled her hair back from her face into a ponytail and then let it fall loose again. "We never argued or anything, just drifted apart."

"You mean you drifted. He was hanging on like his life depended on it." She leaned against the cabinet and folded her arms. "I don't know what you're looking for in a guy. You couldn't get much better than Mark Huxley."

"I'm not ready for a serious relationship, Em. I've got enough to worry about making good grades while I keep a part-time job."

"Don't get so busy you can't have any fun. You're still young. You need to enjoy life a little. The world isn't going to end if you don't have straight A's. You don't want to end up being an old maid, and—"

Brooke reached her bare foot over to give Emma a little kick. "Don't give that a second thought. They don't call it the party school for nuthin'."

"Well, you don't have to go too far," She laughed as she jumped out of the way. "C'mon, let's see what's on the boob tube." She wrapped her arm around Brooke's shoulder. "I'm going to miss you. Don't make yourself too scarce around here."

Chapter Seven

Brooke watched the familiar sports car pull into the front drive. She'd barely had time to take a quick shower, pull on a simple blue sundress, and slip on white sandals. Her pulse quickened as she watched him walk toward the front door.

"Mark's here, Mama. I'll see you later."

"Not too late, Brooke," Annie called from the kitchen.

"I'll be home early." She opened the door to the tantalizing smell of his cologne.

"Hi." He grinned at her. "You look great." Brooke's heart twisted in her chest. Emma was so right.

She indicated her outfit. "I hope this is—."

"Perfect." He took her hand, helped her down the steps, and into his car with great care. *Of course, he still thinks I'm pregnant.*

The drive to the restaurant was filled with trivial conversation and a few awkward silences. They now sat across from each other in a quiet corner of the restaurant overlooking the gulf. It had been one of their favorite places when they were dating. It was an upscale establishment, with a rustic, nautical decor. Outside, seagulls marched up and down the shore while sandpipers scurried back and forth pecking at the sand.

"I thought we'd go for lobster tonight. Is that okay with you?"

"Lobster sounds fine."

He placed their order and they sipped sodas as they waited. Unless she was mistaken, he was intent on making this a special night. Maybe it was just nervousness. She was curious at his last comment the night before, about it being okay.

"I've been working with my dad this summer," he said.

"In the law office?"

"I know, it sounds crazy doesn't it?"

"You still have your sights set on the NBA, right?"

"Yeah, that's my dream." He wiped the moisture from the outside of his glass with his finger. "Only thing is, I have to be realistic. If I don't make it in the pros, I've still got to make a living."

"So, you're thinking about becoming a lawyer?"

"No way. It's been good though, spending time with my dad this summer. We've actually gotten closer."

"I'm glad. You needed to do that." Brooke shook her hair back from her face and took a sip of her soda. "So, if you're not going to be a lawyer, what will you do?"

"I dunno. I'll probably major in business. You can do a lot with that. I've got plenty of time to decide, if basketball doesn't pan out."

Brooke sensed Mark was trying to tell her something, but she didn't have a clue where this was headed. They made light conversation, talking about family and mutual friends while they ate their meal. Their server cleared the table, brought them coffee and left them undisturbed.

Mark shifted in his chair and cleared his throat. "Brooke, I need to apologize for the way I reacted last week. I…uh…it was such a shock…I had to come to grips with what you told me."

"Mark, I—"

"No, please, let me finish. I couldn't even think about what to do. I was just plain scared."

Brooke smiled at him. "I know its scary stuff."

"I wandered around until I finally figured out I needed to talk to my dad."

"You told your father—"

"Don't worry. He was angry at first but got over it, after a while. Said it was understandable. You made quite an impression when we were dating. It might've been different if it'd been someone else." He took her hands in his and rubbed the back of them with his thumbs.

"My dad insisted I shouldn't miss out on college, but he's concerned about you, too." Mark reached out to touch her face. "My parents will help us out financially until we're out of college and get on our feet."

Brooke's heart began to pound in her chest. "What do you mean they'll help us out financially?"

He frowned, and shook his head. "I'm not explaining this well—after we get married. You can have your records transferred and go to school with me. You have excellent grades and with a word from my dad, you'll easily be accepted."

Brooke sat stunned and speechless.

"Of course, you might not be able to take many classes until after the baby is born. But this way, you won't have to drop out completely."

She pulled away from his hold and lowered her face into her hands.

"I know that having a baby is not the best reason to get married, but you've got to know I never stopped loving you. I want you to be my wife."

"Please, don't say anymore." She looked up and flinched at the disappointed look in his eyes. "I had no idea this was coming." Tears threatened but she choked them back. "When I called and told you about the pregnancy...I...I was confused. I

52

didn't mean to push for marriage. I…I'm not sure what I wanted."

She took a deep breath. "I was desperate for someone to tell. I was scared and I was embarrassed. I knew I couldn't talk to my parents. That night, Lisa called. I went to Orlando the next day and, after I told her about my problem, she arranged for me to see a doctor…and well…there is no more pregnancy, it's over. We don't need to get married." She reached for his hand and squeezed it. "You can go on to school just like you planned."

Mark stared at her, shaking his head. "What do you mean, there's no more pregnancy?"

"The pregnancy was terminated. It was done yesterday and no one has any idea."

"You mean…you killed our baby?" Mark's knuckles turned white as he clenched his fists on the table.

She avoided his look and stared out the window. "It wasn't a baby yet. It has to be further along before it's a baby. Besides, what was I going to do?" She turned back to him. "You walked away from me. I couldn't tell my parents. It was the only solution to keep us from ruining our lives any more than we already had." Her heart was not into the lie she was telling him. Now she was double scum. She'd gone for the easy way out while he intended to do the honorable thing.

"I can't believe you made that kind of decision without even telling me." Mark's voice was husky and broken as tears ran down his cheeks. "That was my baby, too. No matter what you call it—it was my baby."

She stared at her hands on the table. They sat quiet for what seemed like hours. He finally wiped his face with his napkin and touched her arm.

"Let's go."

The drive home was awkward and silent. No hope of keeping him as a friend now. *Will this nightmare ever end?* She watched absently out the window to avoid his look. Any other guy, she supposed, would be driving recklessly to vent his anger. She could see his fierce grip on the shift but his driving was calm and deliberate.

Brooke was surprised when he took her hand as they walked up the steps to the front door. Without a word, he pulled her into his arms and held her close for a long time.

His cheek on top of her head, he spoke softly. "I'm sorry I failed you. First in taking your virginity and then running away when you needed me. If I'd just had better control, you never would've been faced with this decision." She felt a sob run through his chest as he held her tightly against him. "I don't want to lose touch. Please don't cut me off because of what's happened."

He lifted her chin and cradled her face in his hands. She looked into soft brown eyes and waited. He slowly bent his face to brush her lips with a soft kiss, turned and walked to his car. Brooke watched him drive away before opening the door. What a mess she'd made of things and, in spite of her good intentions, she'd hurt them both even more.

Brooke spent a restless night having nightmares of her dead baby. He appeared fully developed and staring at her, as if to ask why she didn't want him. Mark burst into the room, grabbed the baby and held it to his chest while he cried, "Why? Why? Why?"

She awoke with a start, soaked with perspiration, and sobbing.

"Oh Lord. Is this what I'm going to live with the rest of my life? I didn't realize. God, can you ever forgive me? Can I ever have peace?"

She lay back on her pillow, quietly crying and waiting for dawn.

Chapter Eight

Brooke, Lisa, Annie, and Suzanne surveyed the new apartment. Stark would be the best description. A picture of nothing but white walls and the usual beige carpet. A small galley kitchen was separated from the living room by a bar and two stools, giving definition to the two rooms. A bathroom at the end of a short hall had bedrooms on either side.

Goose bumps rose on Brooke's arms. All the plans she and Lisa had made, talked about for months, were actually happening. Could it be only two weeks since her life had come apart? When it seemed none of this was going to happen? She was so ready for a fresh start. To put it all behind her. This was a chance for a new beginning, and she welcomed the challenges ahead.

Suzanne slung her arm around Annie's shoulders. "It looks like we have a little work to do." She turned to her husband. "Ronnie, if you and Carl unload the van, you can get to your golf game while we tackle this place."

"You ready, Carl?" Ronnie slapped Carl's shoulder. "What she's really saying is get the van emptied so they can take it to the mall and fill it up again."

Carl chuckled. "Sounds like we need to get it done and get out of here."

Brooke exchanged a grin with Lisa. A little thrill ran through her. This sounded like fun and more than she'd expected.

"What if we use the lime green, orange and yellow in these cushions on the bamboo couches for our colors?" Annie said.

"I like it." Suzanne turned to the girls. "How does that sound to you, Orange, lime green and yellow throughout?"

"How about something a little different in the bedrooms? I don't think I can sleep in all that noise," Lisa suggested.

Brooke laughed. "You could sleep with a train running through your room. I love it out here, but I think I'd like a calmer color in my bedroom."

"That's what malls are for. Help your dad get the rest of your stuff in here and we can get started."

The apartment was a blur of four women armed with curtains, rugs, lamps, bedspreads, pictures and plants while the rooms were transformed.

"Neither one of us will need a bridal shower when the time comes," Lisa said as they set up their new kitchen.

Brooke lined up the bright-colored canister set. "I guess they actually think we're going to cook."

"But this will come in handy." Lisa held up their new coffeepot. "How about here?" She set it on the bar next to a coffee-mug tree.

"Perfect. It'll be handy for first thing in the morning."

By late afternoon, the apartment bore no resemblance to its original state.

"How about some coffee?" Lisa said.

"I'm ready." Suzanne collapsed into the chair.

"I brought some fresh pastries."

"You're a doll, Ms. Annie. In here?" Lisa searched through a box from Brooke's car.

"In those red and blue tins. There's enough to last you for several weeks."

The girls sat cross-legged on the floor in front of the coffee table as they tore into the goodies.

"It's very comfortable and cozy. Maybe we should move in with them, Annie."

"Not a chance. We're ready to be on our own, right, Brooke?"

"You got it."

"What's this?" Ronnie and Carl stepped in the front door.

"And we were just about to ask them if they wanted to go to dinner." Ronnie winked at Carl. "Guess we'll have to go by ourselves since they've already eaten."

"Not so fast. That was just an appetizer." Suzanne scooted out of her chair. "Ladies, get your purses; we're ready to celebrate a job well done."

The shouts and laughter of children carried from the distance as the two co-eds relaxed by the pool. Brooke loved their location. There were several apartment complexes in the area but the oak-lined street led to a single family home development. A hint of neighborhood and family helped to hold down insecurities about college life and how she would fit in. Mixed emotions surged when their parents left the night before. She was ready for the new freedom ahead, but her heart gripped watching Annie's struggle to leave them behind. Papa had practically dragged her out the door. Lisa rode with her yesterday on the drive from Orlando. Given the time alone she told Lisa about the evening with Mark.

"He was going to marry you?"

"Yeah, I felt like a slug. Emma told me he was still in love with me. I knew she was right as soon as he walked up to my house. He confirmed what I saw and told me he still loved me at the restaurant. I don't know when I've been so ashamed. He

58

poured his heart out to me and I had to hit him with the cold hard fact that I'd killed our baby."

"Sad. Too bad he didn't speak up when he met you on the beach."

"I wasn't exactly thinking straight myself. I can't blame him for needing time. Truthfully, I'd been sitting on this for months. I just didn't want to face it. As if it would just go away. When he walked into the hotel that day at the beach, I was thinking about how I wished we were still dating. I don't know, too much has happened between us. I suppose I might have considered his offer if I'd still been pregnant, but what a way to start a marriage."

"I guess you're right. He didn't have much of an opportunity to help. And he did try to do the right thing."

Someone jumped into the pool and brought Brooke back from her thoughts. She rolled over in her lounge chair to her stomach. All this remembering and rehashing had to stop. What was done was done. She had her whole life ahead. The warmth of the sun soaked into her back and lulled her into a drowsy state. *Maybe I can check out my job at the library*, she thought and drifted off to sleep.

Brooke organized her room, went through school instructions and several cups of coffee while waiting for Lisa to stir. She checked her watch and decided to head over to the library. With their apartment only blocks from the campus, walking seemed like a good idea. Even with humidity, the air smelled fresh and there was a magnificent display of voluminous white clouds against a clear blue sky. She breathed deeply as she walked through the campus. A quiver of excitement ran through her as she walked up the steps to the library.

Cool air enveloped her at the door. She shivered at the size compared to their high school library and walked toward a long marble check-out area.

"Umm…I wonder if you could help me?" A young woman was busy stacking books on a cart.

"Sure." She pulled back long hair that reached her waist and adjusted the strands of beads around her neck. "What are you looking for?"

"I'm not sure. I'm going to be working here starting next week. I thought I'd check things out."

"Cool, you're a freshman, huh?"

"That obvious?"

"We all have a glazed look our first semester. Everything seems so big and unfamiliar."

"Yeah."

"Don't let it get to you. It's cool." She pushed the cart to the side. "You'll have to fill out some forms before you start. You can do that if you like."

"Great."

"Down that hall, third door on the right…says *Elizabeth Schoope*. Her secretary, Kathy, can give you the forms."

"Thanks."

Her heels clicked on the terrazzo floor and echoed down the hall while she read the names on each door. "Elizabeth Schoope; that's it." She pushed through a heavy wooden door. A woman seated at a large desk looked up and smiled.

"Can I help you?"

"The girl at the front…umm…she said I could get the forms to fill out for employment."

"I'm sorry. All our positions are filled for the semester."

"I have a job here this semester. My name is Brooke Erickson"

"Oh, I know what you're looking for." She got up from her desk and went to the file cabinets. "Those are usually filled out the day you report for work, but it won't hurt to do it ahead of time." She handed her several pages.

"Thanks."

"It'll save me some time later." The door opened again. "Good morning, Mrs. Schoope."

"Good morning, Kathy. Who do we have here?"

"This is one of our new freshmen. She'll be working with us this year...was it Brooke?"

"Yes, Brooke."

"I'm pleased to meet you, Brooke." She turned back to her secretary. "Is there anything pressing, Kathy?"

"Nothing more than usual."

"Good. Do you have a minute, Brooke? We can get acquainted before you begin."

"Sure."

She followed the older woman to another office with a generous group of butterflies juggling for position in her stomach. She stepped tentatively into the room. Getting ahead of the game was one thing, but the director's office felt a bit like being sent to the principal's office. Well, no turning back now.

A cherry wood desk filled the center of the room. At one end was a small library table and chairs. Floor to ceiling shelves filled with books, photographs and an eclectic selection of art pieces hugged the wall.

"Have a seat over there," she said as she dropped her things on the desk and indicated a small seating area at the other side of the room.

"So, where is home?" She took the chair opposite Brooke.

"I'm from Clearwater." In spite of her original awkwardness, the woman's warmth put her at ease. Maybe this wasn't such a bad idea after all.

"Ahh...so you're a beach girl."

"Yes, ma'am."

"Have you lived there long?"

Brooke grinned. "I've never lived anywhere else."

"You're first time away from home?"

"Yes, that is, on my own. Well, not really alone since I'm with my best friend."

"Do you have a major yet?

Brooke leaned forward in her chair. "Oh yes! I'm majoring in art."

"Do I detect a bit of passion?"

"I guess. It's all I've thought about since Junior High. It's the only thing I ever wanted to do." She held back the urge to say more. A babbling teenager wouldn't be very impressive. Besides, she had a feeling this wouldn't be the last time she'd spend with Mrs. Schoope.

"If you'll notice, I have quite a selection over there. I'm not artistically talented, but I'm an avid collector."

She ducked her head and grinned. "Yes ma'am, I noticed those when I came in."

"So are you all settled in a dorm?"

"Well, I'm settled, thanks to my mom and my roommate's mother. In an apartment that is."

62

"So you and your mother are close?" The warmth in her eyes told Brooke she understood how hard it was to leave her mother.

"Yes, I'll miss her the most. She's French. All of my friends loved her accent, and her French pastries."

"Really? Charles and I have been to France several times. Once, when we were much younger, we took a whole summer to tour the French countryside on bicycles. It's one of my fondest memories. Do you go often?"

Brooke shook her head. "My mother has been back several times but it wasn't possible for all of us to go."

"I would enjoy talking to your mother sometime. Please bring her in when she comes to visit." Mrs. Schoope stood. "Now, perhaps we can have Kathy take you to meet your supervisor. Would you like that?"

"If it's not too much trouble, it'd be super."

Brooke followed Kathy down the hall. College was going to be everything she anticipated and she already had a new friend.

Chapter Nine

Brooke sat at a back table in the library and absently stared at her paper. Three weeks and she would be on her way home for Christmas vacation. *What a way to spend a Friday night, writing a term paper. Oh well, better than spending the evening with Lisa and her new boyfriend, Jack. If only they would quit trying to set her up. Why didn't they leave well enough alone? A heavy load of classes and work at the library was enough. Lisa, of all people, should understand she wasn't ready for another relationship.* The wounds from the last one were too deep. How many times had Lisa jumped out of bed to her screams from that horrible nightmare?

"What have we here? Studying on a Friday evening?"

Brooke looked up at Mrs. Schoope. She'd only seen her to say good morning or briefly during the workday since they'd begun school. "I've got a term paper due next Wednesday."

Mrs. Schoope smiled. "I thought those were saved for Sunday afternoons."

Brooke laughed. "My roommate and her boyfriend are cooking dinner at our place. Figured I could give them some space, and get this knocked out at the same time."

"Have you had dinner?"

"I'll grab a burger after a while."

"That doesn't sound very appetizing. If you don't mind spending time with an old woman, I find myself at loose ends this evening. Charles is having dinner with his department. Why don't you come home with me and we'll see what we can put together? Or better yet, we can pick up something on the way."

Brooke fiddled with her pen. "I wouldn't want to impose—"

"Nonsense, I would love the company, and it will give us a chance to get better acquainted. What kind of food do you like? There's an Italian place a couple blocks from here."

Now what. She'd walked into this one and there were no more excuses. "It does sound better than a hamburger." Brooke closed her notebook. "I'll follow you in my car."

"Perfect, I'll meet you out front."

The two women snuggled deep in oversized chairs and sipped hot coffee. Brooke watched the fire burning in the fireplace, reflecting soft shadows on the walls in the dimly lit room. It had turned out to be an okay night and their conversation now came easy.

"Our daughter, Diane, is living in Africa. She went there with the Peace Corps. I miss her terribly but she loves her work. Todd is a junior at West Point."

Brooke couldn't imagine living in a place so remote and without modern conveniences. "I'm afraid I'm not so noble. You must be very proud. I've never been out of Florida. Didn't you say you went to France?"

"We did. Charles and I were juniors in college. We spent almost an entire summer there. Now that Charles is head of the science department, we can't always get away, but we've been back for a few short visits.

"My mother lived just outside of Paris and worked in a restaurant downtown. It's—"

The doorbell rang. "Now who could that be? Hold that thought, I'll be right back."

Brooke leaned forward to catch the conversation. Sounded like some college guy. *Time to get out of here.*

65

"Mitch, I'm afraid Charles is out for the evening, but please come in out of the cold. I have coffee made."

Brooke was out of her chair. Rats, her purse and books were out in the kitchen.

"Come in here. I have someone I'd like you to meet."

She looked up into startling deep, blue-green eyes. "This is our friend, Mitch. Brooke is one of our girls from the library."

Trapped. She couldn't leave as soon as he walked in the door without seeming rude. "It's...um...nice to meet you."

A grin spread across his face. "Likewise."

Their hostess headed toward the kitchen. "Do you want anything in it?"

"A little cream," he called in her direction. He tossed his leather jacket across the back of his chair, ran his fingers through sandy red hair, and sat down.

Brooke sat down. She'd have to wait for Mrs. Schoope to come back and then make her exit. "So, you're friends of the Schoope's?"

"Ms. Liz and my mom were college roommates."

"Oh." What was wrong with her? She'd never felt so awkward.

"You work at the library?"

She shifted in her chair and then crossed her legs. "Uh...yes...cover expenses. Scholarships don't do it all."

"Right."

"Mrs. Schoope is wonderful." *That was dumb. As if he didn't know.*

"Mr. Charles is great, too. He's helping me get through chemistry. I wish I could get by with math classes."

66

Brooke wrinkled her nose. "I hate math. I'll take just enough to graduate."

"What's your major?"

"Art, but you couldn't tell it by my schedule."

"Mmm—the required general studies. It goes pretty fast though."

"Here we are." Mrs. Schoope handed Mitch the steaming mug. "Brooke, I should have asked. Would you care for a warm up?"

"No, I'm fine. I need to be going soon—"

"I guess our boy has been filling you in on our family history. His mother is my dear friend." She settled on the arm of his chair and asked Mitch. "When will you be finished for Christmas break?"

"Not until the last day. I have a big exam on Friday before vacation. When will Todd be home?"

"We expect him the Wednesday before. I do hope the two of you will have time to spend together. Of course, Diane won't be able to come home from Africa. It will be difficult."

Brooke looked at her watch and shifted to the edge of her chair.

Mitch shook his head. "I still can't imagine Diane in the jungle. Have you heard from her lately?"

"Just last week. She's so excited about her work. We mailed her Christmas package months ago so she would have it in time." Mrs. Schoope laid her hand on Mitch's arm. "By the way, would you be able to help Charles set up some tables for our Christmas party?"

"When?"

"Our party is next Saturday evening, but I'd need the tables set up in the afternoon. We're having a little gathering for everyone at the library."

"Sure, but you'd better call and remind me on Friday."

"Of course, and while I'm thinking about it, Brooke, could you help me set up?"

This was turning into more than a break from a term paper. *Maybe I should have stuck it out with Lisa and Jack.* "Well, I'm not sure I know how to get here—"

"Mitch, why don't you pick up Brooke and save her the drive?"

He grinned. "Not a problem."

How did that happen? "Really, it's okay, I can—"

"I've got to come here anyway. You may as well ride along."

Brooke sank back in her chair, just as a door opened, and all eyes turned to a stately Charles as he walked into the room.

He gave Mrs. Schoope a kiss on the forehead. "I see you found some company to occupy your evening." He reached to shake Mitch's hand. "I didn't forget a meeting, did I?"

"No." Mitch shook his head. "I was just struggling with some homework and took a chance you might be home. It can wait."

"I would appreciate that. It has been a rather challenging day. How's Sunday after church? Perhaps you could join us for lunch." He checked himself. "Did you have any other plans, Liz?"

Mrs. Schoope smiled up at her husband. "No, that's fine, Charles.

"And where are my manners?" He turned to Brooke. "Who is your lovely guest, Liz?"

68

"This is Brooke Erickson, she works at the library. She's also an art major."

"Ah, hang on to your work. This wife of mine is always on the hunt for good art."

Brooke laughed. "I owe her. I was headed for a burger."

Mrs. Schoope hugged her husband's waist. "Would you like some coffee, dear?"

He rubbed the back of his neck. "No, I've had more than enough coffee this evening."

Brooke noted the look between husband and wife and scooted out of her chair. "I've enjoyed this evening so much, but I need to get home."

Mitch followed her lead. "Me too, I have swim practice early tomorrow morning."

Mitch put on his coat while Mrs. Schoope retrieved Brooke's things from the kitchen.

"We'll see you Sunday, my boy," Dr. Schoope said as they both followed their guests and waved their good-byes at the door.

Brooke pulled her coat around her against the cold as they walked toward their cars. "They are lovely people."

"Yeah, like a second set of parents to me. I grew up with Todd and Diane. We even took vacations together. They'll be spending Christmas with us."

"So you live close?"

"My parents live in Ocala but I live here on campus. You know how it is. Independence has its benefits. Where are you from?"

"Clearwater."

"Cool—right on the beach."

"I love it." She reached into her purse for her keys. "I guess I'd better get going. My roommate will be worried."

"Yeah, I should head out." He started to go and then turned back again. "Wait, I need directions to your place for Saturday."

"Oh, I'm afraid I don't know all the street names. Can you stop by the library on Friday? I'm there after one."

"That works. If you follow me, I'll get you back to campus."

"Thanks, I'd be lost getting out of here."

"See you Wednesday." Mitch gave her a wave and climbed into his Jeep.

Brooke started her car and waited for Mitch to move from behind her while she battled the butterflies in her stomach. *Come on, Brooke, you don't need a distraction. He's just a guy, even if he is good-looking.*

Chapter Ten

Brooke watched out the window for Mitch. He'd stopped by the library for directions on Wednesday, but she hadn't heard from him since. All week, she'd fought the anticipation of their next meeting. The sight of his Jeep gave her heart a little start. She grabbed her things, hurried out of her apartment and met him halfway.

"What's all this?"

"Mrs. Schoope told me to bring my clothes to change for the party, so I wouldn't have to come back again."

"She's always one step ahead," he said as he took them from her.

Securing her dress and bag in the back, he helped her into the passenger side and walked around to climb in beside her. "Not exactly a limousine."

"It fits you." She laughed.

He gave her a lop-sided grin. "Meaning?"

"Nothing. I mean, you just look like someone who would drive a Jeep."

"You mean a country boy?" Looking her way, his blue-green eyes took her breath away.

"Well, I guess."

"Are you saying that's a good thing?"

"Of course." She gave him a light punch in the arm.

He was smooth. She would give him that. There was something about him but she couldn't quite put her finger on it. Maybe that he was so comfortable in his skin. She could imagine this guy fitting in wherever he went, and at ease with leaving when it pleased him.

"I don't imagine you see much country in Clearwater."

"Palmettos are about it."

"Maybe we can remedy that." He reached over and gave her hand a squeeze. Her heart swelled. Already they were pulling up to the Schoope's drive…way too soon, as far as she was concerned.

"I saw you drive up. Welcome, welcome." Mrs. Schoope greeted them with a hug at the door. "Charles is in the kitchen, Mitch. You know your way. Come with me, Brooke, and we'll hang up your things."

She led her upstairs. The banister was decorated with a heavy garland of pine, burgundy and silver ornaments, red berries, pine cones, and yards of white ribbon. Brooke breathed in the scent. Memories of family holidays flooded in and she could almost smell the gingerbread in her mother's kitchen.

"How beautiful." A ten-foot tree stood next to the stairway. Christmas lights flickered between pearl rope, glass balls and Victorian style ornaments of delicate satin purses, umbrellas and tassels.

"You like it?"

"It's so different."

"I know the trend is silver trees with colored spotlights, but most of these belonged to my grandmother and I'm rather sentimental."

"I can see why."

"This is Diane's room." She hung Brooke's dress in the closet. "In here is a bathroom for you to freshen up when we're through working."

Brooke dropped her bag next to the bed and took in every inch of the beautifully decorated room. *What would it have been like to grow up with a room like this? Imagine having my own bathroom.*

"Ready?"

"Ah—yes, ready."

They found the men in the kitchen, coffee in hand, helping themselves to the trays of cookies and candies.

Mrs. Schoope waved them away. "Out of there, you bad boys, or we'll have nothing left for the guests."

"We're just making sure it's adequate fare." Charles winked at Mitch.

"We can do without that kind of help." She laughed and slapped Charles on the shoulder. "Now off with you to the sunroom and get finished before we run out of time."

Mitch and Dr. Schoope grabbed a couple more cookies on their way, and Mrs. Schoope followed them out.

"Just put all this lounge furniture in the garage. I had the party rental people leave the tables and chairs out there." With the men busy moving furniture, she turned to Brooke. "If you'll come with me, we can bring out the linens and centerpieces to decorate the tables, as soon as they have them set up."

Two hours later, the four stood back and admired their work. Tiny white lights winked out of green garland that hung around the perimeter of the room. Candles glowed softly on each table covered with pale pink linens.

"I think this will do nicely." Mrs. Schoope rested her arm around her husband's waist. "We couldn't have done it without your help. I promise we'll save you both a plate for later."

"Now that sounds like a deal. In the meantime, I'm getting out of here before all the women arrive. How about you, Mitch? Could you go for a plate of ribs?"

"Just lead the way." He grinned at Brooke. "You have everything you need for the party?"

"Yes…thanks." Wow all this attention and concern was more than she was prepared for.

He hesitated for a moment. She could swear he was reluctant to leave but out of excuses to stay.

"Okay." He gave her a wink that was just between the two of them. "I'll be back to take you home."

Brooke's heart skipped. She was losing this battle, and fast. She may not be ready for another relationship but this guy was tossing those fears out the window.

Charles gave his wife a kiss on the cheek. "We're on our way. What time will it be safe to return?"

"I should think we'll be finished by nine or nine-thirty."

"We'll make it nine-thirty to be safe."

"Looks like all we have left to do is make ourselves presentable." Mrs. Schoope led the way upstairs. "Let me know if you need anything."

Brooke took her time getting ready, pampering herself in the luxury for as long as possible. She slipped her long, dark blue velvet skirt over a pale blue blouse before fastening on small diamond earrings. She did a quick survey in the mirror. *Just a bunch of women who won't be impressed.* But she knew she was dressing carefully, not for the women, but a certain young man who would be taking her home.

"In here, Charles." Mrs. Schoope called out. The party was a big success and they'd been relaxing amid the clutter of empty plates, discarded napkins and cups holding left-over punch. They sipped cups of fresh coffee as they shared stories of the evening.

Brooke noted the look of approval from Mitch, and gave him a quick smile.

"So, where are those promised plates, Liz?" Charles rested his hands on his wife's shoulders.

"After ribs, you're still ready for more?"

"That was several hours ago, right, Mitch?"

Mitch grinned and gave Brooke another glance. "You know me, Ms. Liz. I can always find more room."

"You're both impossible." She stood and headed for the kitchen. "Come with me, Charles, and carry the coffee. Would you like another cup, Brooke?"

"I'll take a warm up, thanks."

Mitch turned a chair around and straddled the seat, resting his arms on the back. "So, how was the party?"

"It was lots of fun. Mrs. Schoope is quite the hostess." Brooke cringed at the pink she knew was creeping up her neck and would soon cover her face.

"Yeah, she's a southern belle just like my mom. You'd like my mom, too."

"I'm sure I would," Brooke said, wondering if that might be in her future.

"Here we are." Mrs. Schoope brought in a plate of cookies and candies while Dr. Schoope followed with a tray of coffee mugs. They shared stories for another hour before Mitch and Brooke left the Schoope's with assurances they didn't need to stay for the clean-up.

Mitch helped her manage her long skirt as she climbed into his Jeep, before jumping into the other side. "Like I said, it's no limousine."

"I'm sure it's a lot of fun."

"Well, it's economical, especially while I'm in school."

They drove in silence for a while.

"So when do you finish up for Christmas?" he asked.

"My last exam is on Thursday, but my roommate has her last one on Friday morning."

"You're traveling together?"

"Yeah, I'll drop her off in Winter Park and head for Clearwater."

"That's kind of out of the way, isn't it?"

"Lisa and I go way back. We've been friends since we were little. I don't mind the drive."

"Here you are." He pulled into a parking space. "Hold on, I'll help you out."

She thought about asking him in but, wasn't it a bit soon for that? She didn't want him to think she was too forward. And wasn't she trying to avoid another serious relationship. This was moving too fast. *Got to get a grip here.* Her heart was getting way ahead of her common sense.

"I appreciate the ride."

"Glad to be of service." He gave her a mock bow as they reached the stairs.

She gave him a soft shove. "Mrs. Schoope volunteered your services. You didn't have much choice."

They walked up to the landing of her second-story apartment. After setting down her bag, he stood watching her for a moment. Brooke couldn't breathe.

He pulled her gently into his arms and spoke softly against her ear. "I'm glad she did." Releasing her from his embrace, he lifted her chin and brushed a gentle kiss against her lips.

"I'll see you again soon, okay?"

"Okay," she whispered…and he was gone.

Chapter Eleven

Brooke finished the dishes, dried her hands, and walked over to the window to watch for Lisa. She checked her watch...nearly ten. She dropped onto the couch and leafed through a magazine, tossed it aside, and got up to check their bedrooms for anything they might have forgotten. Lisa's bags were on the bed, so she carried them out to the car and stuck them in the back with hers. Another check on the time...ten thirty. What was taking her so long? She went to the kitchen for a drink of water and then back to the living room window, staring out at nothing.

I should have known better than to get my hopes up. I didn't want to get involved with another guy anyway. Don't see why he had to lead me on and make me think he was going to call me. Men, I don't need 'em. Or...maybe this is God's way of making me pay. How could I expect him to forgive what I've done? Stupid...stupid...Brooke. You've ruined your life. No guy's gonna want someone like you. Just forget it. Just need to go home and have a good time with my family. Lisa...where are you?

Lisa burst through the door. "Let's go. Do we have everything? Where's my bags?"

Brooke grabbed her purse. "Put a lid on it. I've got everything in the car."

Lisa stopped short, the smile fading from her face. "Hey, what gives? Did I say something wrong? I just aced my test and I can't wait to get home. Is there something wrong with that?"

"Nothing, let's just go."

Lisa put her arm across the door. "No way, José. I'm not spending three hours in a car with you in this rotten mood."

Brooke dropped down on the couch, propped her feet on the coffee table and crossed her arms.

"I mean it, Brooke. What's your problem?"

"I'm just stupid. Okay?"

"Well, you're a lot of things, but stupid isn't one of them."

"When it comes to guys it is."

"Ah, is this about that library guy?"

"He doesn't work in the library; he's a friend of Mrs. Schoope's."

"Whatever! Is that what this is all about?"

She got up from the couch and went to the window. "How dumb could I be, thinking he was interested in me?"

"Maybe he's been cramming for exams and finished early." Brooke heard the exasperation in Lisa's voice.

"He had his last exam today," she shot back.

"You see, he's been bogged down clear to the last minute. I'm sure he'll call you after break."

Brooke grabbed her purse. "Maybe, but I'm not banking on it. I'm ready to get out of here."

Lisa took hold of her friend's shoulders. "Brooke, it's not like you have a big red letter on your chest. Get a grip and give yourself a chance. Just because the guy didn't call you the next day doesn't mean he's not interested. You make up people's minds and decide what they're thinking before you know the facts."

Brooke's shoulders sagged. "I—all right. I'll wait and see. In the meantime, can we just go? I'm ready to be home."

Brooke rolled down her window as she pulled out of Lisa's driveway and breathed in the crisp air. The sky was such a bright blue it almost hurt her eyes. This winter held the promise of temperatures cold enough to hail a Christmas spirit in the worst

79

of scrooges. The pressures of homework, term papers, and work at the library melted away as Brooke sped toward home. Familiar landmarks plunged her into excitement. She shook her hair back and laughed out loud as she drove into her parking spot next to her father's truck and Emma's car. The whole family was home.

Brooke reached for her purse and hurried up the steps. As she pushed open the door, the smells of her mother's cooking wafted through the air to greet her. She watched for a moment, taking in the familiar sight of her mother expertly putting together a meal.

"Hi, Mama."

"Look at you, princess." Annie reached out to pull her daughter into a warm embrace. Unshed tears filled her eyes. "You look wonderful and I've missed you so much."

The rest of the family came through the kitchen door to welcome her home. Her father pulled her into a warm hug while Emma asked a hundred questions. It was so good to be home.

They lingered long around the dinner table as they caught up on the events of the past few months.

"I can't believe how much Benji has changed." She grinned at her little brother who was showing signs of losing his little boy look. "You'll be a grown man before I know it."

Her mother smiled and rubbed his arm. "Yes, he will be a big Swede like your papa."

"Lucky the girl who wins his heart."

Benji's face turned bright red. "C'mon, Brooke, lay off."

"Okay, but anyone interested in you will have to meet my approval."

"Oh! She's gone for three months and comes home the authority of the household," Emma mocked.

Brooke stood and slapped her sister's arm. "What, I can't look out for my little brother? C'mon, Em, let's run these people into the family room and get the dishes done."

Her mother stood and reached for a couple of plates. "You've just come home, Brooke, you needn't trouble yourself."

Brooke took the plates from her mother. "Out of here. You fixed dinner and we'll clean up."

Benji frowned. "Do I have to?"

"No, Benji, we'll let you off the hook as long as you get the suitcases out of my car and put them up in my room." He was out the back door before she could finish. Brooke and Emma broke into laughter and started clearing the table.

"What do you hear from Robert?"

"Things seem to be going okay for him, considering he's in Viet Nam. He puts the military newspaper together so that keeps him out of the battles, and off the front line."

"How much longer does he have?"

"Another year." Emma rinsed a bowl and handed it to Brooke to put in the dishwasher. "I'm praying he can be home for Christmas next year."

"He's not planning to make it a career is he?"

"No, once he's served his two years, he will be eligible for veteran's benefits to help finance the rest of his college."

"Do you think you'll get married as soon as he gets back?"

Emma grinned. "I guess that's up to Robert and the Lord. I'll just be glad to have him home safe. It's so hard waiting for his letters. Even when I get a letter, I know its old news and I can't help but imagine what might be happening to him. It keeps me on my knees."

81

A tinge of guilt poked at Brooke. She and Lisa hadn't been in church since they left. It was Brooke that held them back, and Lisa didn't want to make her any more uncomfortable than she already was. After what she'd done, God certainly didn't want her there. Brooke reached for the dish cloth and started wiping the table.

"I wish you could meet Mrs. Schoope." Better to change the subject. "She's the head of the library."

"Really, you know her personally?"

"Actually, it came about because of Lisa and her boyfriend."

"They knew her?"

"No, Jack and Lisa were fixing dinner at our apartment." Brooke tossed the cloth into the sink. "They invited me but I didn't want to be in the way. So I went to the library to finish up a paper."

"Yeah, kinda like being a single at an all couples party."

"Exactly."

"So what did that have to do with you meeting this lady, what was her name?"

"Mrs. Schoope. I actually met her when I went to fill out the forms for work, the week before school started."

"That sounds like you. Got to get the jump on everything and have all your ducks in a row."

"Shut up. Do you want to hear this or not?" Brooke grabbed the towel from Emma's hands and threw it back in her face.

"All right, all right, I'm listening."

Brooke sat down and pulled her feet up on the chair. "So, Lisa and Jack were cooking things up at our place, and I was doing a paper at the library. Mrs. Schoope happened by and wanted to know what I was doing there on a Friday night. Her husband had a dinner meeting, so she invited me to go over to her place. We picked up some to go food on the way. Emma, you should see their place. It's even more spectacular than Lisa's house."

Emma emptied the water in the sink, dried her hands and turned to lean her back against the counter. "I can't imagine."

"I was a bit nervous about going home with the head of the library, but they are such sweet people. She made me feel so comfortable and, before I knew it, we'd spent two hours talking about our families. Then a friend of theirs, Mitch, showed up. Well, we talked for another hour before Dr. Schoope came home. What a handsome dude he is, Em. Mrs. Schoope asked me to help with the annual Christmas party. Mitch was helping Dr. Schoope move furniture. So he picked me up on his way and—"

"Whoa, whoa, hold on a minute. I keep hearing the name Mitch. Did my little sister find a new love at college?"

Brooke's cheeks flamed red. "No."

"I'm not buying that. Out with it."

"Nothing to tell. I thought he was interested, but I guess not. I didn't hear from him after that night."

"But that was just before Christmas, right? Maybe he finished up early and headed home for a long vacation."

"Hardly, he told Mrs. Schoope he had an exam on Friday."

"Didn't you guys leave this morning? He probably finished his exam and tried to call after you and Lisa left."

Brooke got up from her chair. "I'd like to believe that's the case, Em, but—we'll see when I get back. I'm not holding my breath."

Emma squeezed Brooke's shoulders. "Just give it to the Lord, Brooke. If it's meant to be, then things will work out. God has the perfect man for you and if it's not this Mitch person, well, you're better off finding out now."

Chapter Twelve

Their junior year! Returning early for Lisa's benefit was an easy decision. Jack was back for football practice. How could she tell Lisa no after all she'd put up with last year. When there was no sign of Mitch after the Christmas party, Brooke lost her enthusiasm for everything. Down on herself, she started hanging with a new crowd. In spite of Lisa's warnings, she continued in a downward spiral. It took a near escape from being arrested for the drugs they were using to bring her back to her senses.

Now back at their apartment, an afternoon by the pool was a nice wind-down, and Jack was on his way to pick them up for the first campus group meeting. Brooke smiled to herself, thinking how much her life had changed. Telling her parents about her drug experiment was hard and they'd kept a close watch on her. It was okay. She'd had enough of that scene and a quiet summer had been good for her soul. Now she was ready for the Christian band playing this evening. It would be a good way to get back into the swing of things.

"You girls ready?" Jack hollered from the front door.

Brooke pulled her purse out of the closet and headed for the living room. "Be right there."

Lisa called from her room. "In a minute."

Jack rolled his eyes at Brooke.

Brooke laughed. "Better come on in."

Another five minutes passed. "Lisa," Jack called out. "We need to get there early unless you plan to sit in the back row."

"Okay, okay." Lisa hurried down the hall, swinging her purse to her shoulder and slipping on shoes.

Brooke breathed in the familiar smell as they walked into the old southern style church. She was flooded with sweet memories and her body tingled with excitement as they started downstairs. They were met with shouts and hugs from friends. Scott, the campus group minister, caught her eye and walked toward them.

"Hello there. Welcome back." He shook Jack's hand and hugged both girls.

He looked directly at Brooke. "How was your summer?"

"Great. My sister got married. I was her maid of honor, and the place was a zoo for a couple of weeks. Then I just hung out and did a lot of painting."

"And church I hope."

"And church, yes. It was a good summer." Scott had counseled with Brooke after her psychedelic experience. He felt like family now, and she was not going to let him down. She'd talked to him about everything, except the abortion. That was still guarded information to anyone other than Lisa.

"Glad to hear it. We've got a great schedule for this semester. Tonight is just the beginning. Wait till you hear this band. The disc jockeys are already playing some of their tunes."

Jack slapped Scott's shoulder. "We've been looking forward to it."

"You'd better get your seats now. This place should be packed. I'll catch you after."

"Later," Jack said as Scott went back to setting up lights. They walked toward the front rows. The room was buzzing with laughter and happy chatter as returning friends found each other.

"Okay—" Scott whistled through his fingers. "Okay, guys, let's get started."

The hum settled.

"We are honored to have a new and upcoming band to kick off our first meeting. *The Apostles* are a name you're going to be hearing a lot of in the future, and after tonight, you'll understand why." He scanned the audience. "We're thrilled to see so many familiar faces and new faces, too. It's going to be a great year in the house of the Lord, isn't it?"

There was loud clapping and hoots from the guys.

"Before we begin, let's stand and ask the Lord to be with us this evening."

The room echoed with the sounds of the crowd standing, their chairs scraping on the floor.

"Father God, how we love you and thank you for what's ahead of everyone here. We thank you for opportunities to reach the lost on campus, and for decisions that will affect the rest of our lives. We glorify you, Lord, with our service. Let your hand rest on *The Apostles* as they minister to us. Lead and guide them as they strive to serve you in this ministry. And we ask your Spirit to come upon us as we worship you tonight. In Jesus' holy name we ask it. Amen and amen."

"Okay—without further delay—I give you—*The Apostles.*"

A wild cheer and clapping filled the room as the band began. Brooke was vaguely aware of a late-comer moving into their row. Scott was right. This band was headed for success. She was on her feet with everyone else, soaking up the words in her soul.

The concert ended way before the crowd was ready to let them go. After two more encores, Scott turned up the house lights and raised his arms to signal for quiet. Brooke glanced to her left and caught her breath. Two seats down stood Mitch Harris. Scott ended the evening with a short message, but it was all lost on Brooke. She stared ahead, trying to decide whether to speak or let him make the first move. Why was she acting like this? If he was interested, he would've called way before now. Blast it all, there was no denying the stirring in her heart, whether he was interested or not. Scott finished with a prayer.

"Brooke?" She felt him touch her arm.

"Oh. Hi, Mitch." She looked over at him, praying her face would not betray the turbulence going on inside.

He shoved his hands in his pockets. "I didn't know you went to church here."

Great, how do I explain this? "I, well, I didn't until the end of last year, that is, go to this church."

He grinned and gave her an appreciative once-over. "It's good to see you."

"Yeah, it's nice to see you again, too." *Wait a minute. He was a senior last year.* "I thought you graduated last spring."

He shrugged. "Well, I should've, but I took some time off."

"Oh, you weren't here last year?" Brooke's heart lifted. *Maybe he wasn't ignoring her.*

"No. Miss Liz didn't tell you?"

"Actually, I haven't seen that much of Mrs. Schoope. I've...ah... had a busy schedule. You know. The dreaded requirements."

Mitch laughed. "Yeah, I know, like math."

Lisa's elbowed her in the ribs.

Brooke gave her a look and turned back to Mitch. "This is my friend, Lisa."

"Mitch Harris. It's nice to meet you. Brooke and I worked on a Christmas project once."

"Yes, I believe she mentioned something about that." Brooke kicked Lisa's leg.

"I was telling Brooke I took off for a special project. I'll be finishing up this year."

"Oh, so you've been away?" Lisa raised her eyebrows and Brooke gave her a frown. Lisa pulled Jack to her side. "This is my boyfriend, Jack."

The two men shook hands. "Mitch Harris."

"Hey, man. So how do you know Brooke?"

He grinned at Brooke. "We helped the Schoope's get their Christmas party together."

Jack dropped his arm around Lisa's shoulders. "We're going out for burgers. How about joining us?"

"Thanks, but I'm driving back to Ocala tonight. I'm commuting this week."

"Too bad, Butch's makes some mean burgers."

"I know all about Butch's. How about a rain check for next week?" he asked as he directed his gaze at Brooke.

She felt goose bumps rise on her arms.

"You got it. Next week it is," Jack said.

"I'll see you all then," he said to the group. He winked at Brooke before turning to leave.

"So, that's the infamous Mitch Harris. No wonder you were in such a wad when he didn't call." Lisa bumped Brooke with her hip. "What a hunk!"

"Hey, hey, remember? Boyfriend?" Jack protested.

"That's right, honey, but a girl doesn't go blind." She gave Jack a kiss on the cheek.

Brooke laughed at their easy way with each other. "Don't read anything into this, Lisa. He just happened to find a seat in our row after the lights were out."

"But he asked for a rain check next week."

"What else was he going to say? I'm not getting my hopes up." Now, if she could just convince her heart.

Brooke easily slid back into her work at the library. It was like an old friend and, as a junior, she had more privileges. She smiled as she watched a freshman fumbling her way around, remembering that lost and inadequate feeling. She loved her job and was quickly absorbed in her work. Several hours passed before she checked her watch. Good, she would finish in time. If she hurried, she could get to the art supply store to pick up paints for her new class.

"Hello, Brooke." She looked up to see Mrs. Schoope. "How was your summer?"

"Perfect. My sister was married in June, and I spent the rest of the summer working on several paintings."

"Sounds lovely. Are you looking forward to this year?"

"I am. Last year was tough but the Lord got me through it."

Mrs. Schoope's eyes reflected an understanding of a year gone awry. "Sounds like you are back on track."

"Yes, ma'am."

"Good to see you, Brooke." She started to walk away and then turned back. "By the way, we're having a few friends over for lunch after church on Sunday. Diane is home from Africa. I'd love for you to meet her."

"I'd like that."

"We'll look forward to it."

Warmth and contentment, like hot chocolate on a brisk day, washed over her. *How did I ever get away from this life? This feels so normal.* It still amazed her that she could sink so low.

Lost in her memories, Brooke hurried down the library steps and headed across campus.

"Brooke!" She turned to see Mitch jogging in her direction.

A foolish grin took over her face. "Hi, where are you headed?"

"Well, I intended to catch you before you left work," he said as he caught his breath. "I thought you were there until five."

"Yeah, I did leave a little early. I'm trying to make it to the art supply store before they close. I need to pick up some things for my class in the morning."

"How about a ride? My Jeep is right over there."

"That would be super but we need to hurry. I'm not sure what time they close."

Mitch helped her in and hoisted himself into the driver's seat. "You'll have to give me directions. I don't shop very often for art supplies." He laughed as he started up and pulled out into the street.

She feigned a shocked look. "Why, Mr. Harris, I can't imagine."

He gave her a mock frown.

"Turn right at the stop sign, three stop lights and then take a left. It's about half-way down the block on the right. It's a big store. You can't miss it."

Following her directions, they pulled into the parking lot and saw neon lights still blazing. They'd made it in time. Moving down the aisles, Brooke followed the signage and found the section she needed. She was a bit overwhelmed at the paint selection. She wanted to take one of each but her budget was limited. She picked up one, then returned it and chose another.

With ten in hand, she began the elimination process to fit her available cash. "What are you doing?"

"I'm trying to decide which ones I need the most. I won't get paid for another two weeks."

He took the paints she had in her hands and retrieved the ones she'd replaced. "I'll get these. You don't need to worry about next payday."

"I can't let you do that."

"Why not?"

"Because that's a lot of money and you have your own expenses."

"I will survive, trust me." He caught her hand in his and headed toward the checkout. "C'mon, let's pay for these and get something to eat. I'm starving."

Brooke stood, dumb-founded for a moment, before he tugged her into motion to follow him. She couldn't wait to see what else developed this evening.

Chapter Thirteen

They sat across from each other in a cozy diner at the edge of town. The green-checkered table cloth and pine-covered walls gave it a woodsy atmosphere. Their booth, tucked away in the corner of the room, gave them a nice seclusion. It was perfect for private conversation and time to get to know one another better. Things had moved so fast since seeing him again at church. She was torn between a hesitation to trust another man and excitement at the way he made her feel when they were together.

"I like to get away from the college crowd," Mitch said. "This is one of my favorite places. Just good home cookin'."

Brooke dove into her chicken fried steak, mashed potatoes and gravy. "Umm. I'll have to bring Lisa here. This is definitely her style."

"Not yours?"

Brooke noted a twinge of disappointment and mentally kicked herself.

"Of course." She felt her cheeks flush pink at her blunder. "I'm just saying...Lisa would love this and we share almost everything...I mean—." She scrambled for a change of subject. "So what's the special project? The one that kept you out of school all year."

"I've been learning to fly."

This man seemed to be full of surprises. "And it took you all year? Couldn't you do that on weekends and after classes?"

He grinned at her. "It's not that simple. I've been learning to fly for aviation missions and it took me to Colombia.

Brooke's fork stopped midway between her plate and her mouth. "You're kidding."

"Actually, I'm dead serious. Why is that so surprising?"

Brooke set her fork down and leaned against folded arms on the table. "Think about it. How many people in this school are going to Colombia on a mission? Besides, isn't that dangerous?"

Mitch shrugged. "Some, but you take your life in your hands getting out on our highways. It's all relative."

"There's a lot more people on the road. I'm not up on missionary work but I imagine the proportionate risk is a lot greater."

He leaned toward her. "But they need God. Until now, the missionaries have had to depend on translators to teach the gospel and interpreters were getting the message confused. Now we have it written in their language. There's no telling how many can be saved."

Brooke was surprised at the compassion she read in his eyes. She took a sip of coffee and contemplated her answer. Could she be setting herself up for another let down? He left her before, without explanation. Here she was getting involved with him again and he was talking about leaving for a foreign country. She could feel her defenses rising.

"So, you're going to be a missionary and live in the jungle?"

"No," He smiled easily. "Not quite so noble. I'll be flying into South America with supplies for missionaries on the front lines."

She felt the knot in her stomach ease a bit. "So how long does it take for a trip?"

"Depends on how quickly we're able to make contact with those in charge of the pick-up. Trips are not usually more than a week, sometimes less. Third-world countries don't work on the same time schedule, and we don't like to leave our cargo unattended. Too much stuff gets into the wrong hands. That's why I couldn't carry a regular schedule at school. We had to go when we were needed and we're never certain how long it will take."

Brooke pushed away her plate and pulled her coffee closer. That didn't seem quite so bad. "It does sound interesting. What kind of supplies do you take?"

"For the most part, we take medical supplies, some food, clothing, the new translations of course, mail and personal items for the missionaries. Once in a while, we carry passengers and short-term mission groups."

The waitress cleared the table and refilled their cups.

"I hope you don't hold it against me but I know nothing about missionary work. I mean, we've had missionaries come to our church, but I'm afraid I have to plead guilty to passing notes to my friends during the slide shows. Where do you stay while you're waiting for the pick-up? Do you stay in a hotel?"

He laughed. "Hardly. When we go to Colombia, we stay with a missionary couple who run an orphanage."

She must sound like a selfish clod. "It all sounds amazing. How did you get involved in aviation missions?"

"A friend of my dad is the one who's been teaching me to fly and taking me to Colombia."

"Weren't you afraid? I mean, I've heard about missionaries being killed. Speared right through by the natives." She gave an involuntary shudder.

He paused for some time before looking up at her. "If you tell anyone else, I'll deny it. Yes, I was a bit afraid my first time.

After I met some of the Americans working there, I saw how they've won the confidence and love of the locals. It was as clear as anything that God was speaking to me and telling me this is what He wants me to do."

Brooke felt as though that native spear had gone right through her. She'd never known a man who was as close to God and willing to follow His lead. Sure, her dad was a strong Christian, and she knew that he and her mom prayed about big decisions. But he owned a hardware store for crying out loud. She was shamed by Mitch's dedication, especially in light of her past. "Your parents must be very proud."

"I wish that were true. I guess my mom is, in her own way."

"Not your dad?"

Mitch played with the handle of his coffee cup and stared into its contents for a time before answering. "He had big plans for me to work with him and eventually take over the farm so he could retire."

"The farm?"

"Not the plowing up field's kinda farm. My dad owns a horse farm just on the outside of Ocala. It's a beautiful place and my dad's raised some champion horses."

"Not your bag?"

"I love the farm, don't get me wrong. It was the one thing that I struggled with in this decision. It's just that, when God calls you to do His work you gotta go."

Brooke thought of the way her parents had encouraged her in her painting since Junior High. "Your dad doesn't understand that?"

Mitch shook his head and took another drink of his coffee. "To hear my dad talk, you'd think he was a preacher. I'm just

96

not sure about his relationship with God." He reached out to take Brooke's hands. "I've never told anyone else this but, I'm not totally sure that my dad is saved."

"That's scary."

"I don't want to give you a bad impression of my dad." He gave her hands a quick squeeze. "He's a great guy and I know you'll love him."

A little thrill passed through her. Did that mean she'd be meeting his father or was she reading things into his conversation? Noticing the clock on the wall, she was surprised to see how much time had passed. She wouldn't mind an all-nighter, talking right here in this booth. But her sense of responsibility, and a concern for him, took precedent. He still had a drive after he took her home.

"Hey," She gave his hands a little squeeze back. "Do you know what time it is? You still have to drive back to Ocala."

He caressed the back of her hands with his thumbs and looked straight into her eyes. "Time flies when you're in good company." How was she supposed to control her heart when he looked at her like that?

They made the short drive and pulled into a parking spot in front of her apartment. Mitch turned off the car and made no effort to get out. He turned to face her with his arm stretched across the back of the seat.

"I appreciate your listening ear tonight." He reached for a strand of her hair and placed it behind her ear. "There aren't many people who know what I'm planning to do and I kinda needed to talk to someone about it."

"I'm glad you felt comfortable...I mean with me." Brooke felt the warmth of his gentle touch all the way to her toes.

"Hey, I have an idea," he said. "Miss Liz invited me over for lunch on Sunday. Her daughter is back from Africa and I know she wouldn't mind if you come with me. I can call and have her set an extra place if you'd like."

"She beat you to it." Brooke laughed. "She invited me this afternoon."

"There, you see, it was meant to be." He took her hand and played with her fingers. "I could pick you up for church and we could go from there."

"I'd like that, a lot." So much for guarding her feelings and not jumping into things. "But for now, you need to get on the road."

"All right, I can take a hint." He gave her chin a mock punch and got out on his side. At the apartment door he waited for her to find the key, and then turned her around to face him.

"Do me a favor," she said as she looked up at him, memorizing every detail of his handsome face. "Give me a call when you get home."

"Okay, if it will make you feel better," he whispered as his eyes held hers.

"Yes," she managed with held breath. "It will make me feel better. Then I can go to sleep without worrying about you being in a ditch somewhere."

"Deal," he said. "I'll talk to you in a little bit." He drew her to him, placed a soft kiss on her lips and was headed down the stairs before Brooke could grasp what had just happened.

Chapter Fourteen

Brooke grabbed the phone on the first ring to keep from waking Lisa.

"Hey, I'm home. No ditches for me tonight." He chuckled.

"Super," she said as she snuggled under a blanket on the couch. "What time do you have to be up?"

"Not till eight. I don't have a class until nine."

"But it's eleven-thirty. We'd better call it a night."

"I'd rather talk to you."

He was sure making it hard for her to be cautious.

"You probably say that to all the girls you date."

"Nope, I'm not usually comfortable talking to girls. I guess you just bring out the chatty in me."

A satisfied smile spread across her face. "Is that a good thing?"

"I'd say it's a good thing." His voice was warm.

Maybe she could trust in the relationship that seemed to be developing. She couldn't quite put her finger on it, but something about him made her feel safe.

They spent the next hour talking. She told him about her older sister, and her little brother. How she and her friends spent all their free time at the beach and how important her painting had been. He shared about an older brother, now married and living in New York. The time spent caring for horses, bringing colts into the world, and the pleasure of realizing they had a champion in the making. She could have spent the whole night talking, but practicality reared its ugly head

"I hate to be sensible, but I've got an acrylics lab at eight."

Mitch exaggerated a sigh. "If you insist. I'll think of you when I crawl out of bed."

"Thanks a lot." She giggled. "Good night."

"Good night...and sweet dreams."

Brooke climbed into bed, but her thoughts were on anything but sleep. Where was this going? She'd been disappointed before, thinking he was interested in her. Yes, he'd been busy learning to fly, but Ocala was not that far. He could have called and kept in touch. Now he was coming on like gangbusters. And what about his mission career? Could she be on board if this developed into more than someone to date? She tried that on for size...*a missionary wife*. Could she be the support he needed? It was a decision she needed to make soon because her heart wasn't paying any attention to reason.

Wrapped in her bathrobe and a towel around her wet hair, Brooke sipped fresh coffee and watched out the window. This was her favorite time of day, while the neighborhood still slept. She pulled her feet under her. Mitch would be picking her up in another hour. She thought about Diane and wondered how she could live in a place like Africa in poverty conditions. Now Mitch wanted to be a missionary pilot to South America. It was a world Brooke knew nothing about.

"Lord," she prayed silently, "Is there some significance in this? I mean two people you've brought into my life who are interested in missions. Surely there's no use for an artist in a third world country."

"What time is it?" Lisa staggered into the room and shielded her eyes. "How can you stand all this light so early in the morning?" She dropped into a chair.

Brooke grinned at her friend, hair disheveled and eyes barely open.

"How about some coffee to open your eyes?" She poured a cup and handed it to her.

"You're a life saver." She reached for the hot brew and took a healthy drink. "How do you get up so early?"

"I love it. It gives me time to think and get my day started."

"Ugh! My brain doesn't function before noon." She lifted her long hair away from her face. "So what time is Mitch picking you up?"

"He'll be here at nine so we can make Sunday school. Do you want to ride along with us?"

"Thanks, but I'll wait for Jack." Lisa sipped her coffee. "Mitch seems very nice. I hope this works out for you."

"He does seem like a comfortable fit. His father owns a horse farm in Ocala, you know."

"Really? Is that what he plans to do after graduation?"

"I don't believe so." Brooke was hesitant to tell Lisa what Mitch had told her on Wednesday night. She would leave that up to him. "He doesn't seem to share his father's interest."

"That happens a lot. I guess you have to have the dream."

"I guess you're right. I can't imagine doing anything besides art. God has a plan for each of us."

"Yeah, He hasn't clued me in yet." They both laughed.

"Well, He does have a plan for us today," Brooke said as she took her coffee mug to the sink. "We'd better get ourselves together before we're caught looking like this."

"Come in," Dr. Schoope said opening the door, as they arrived after church. "We're out here getting in Liz's way." He

101

led them into the kitchen. "I didn't realize you attended our church, Brooke."

Brooke's felt her face go hot. "I have to admit, I didn't go until the end of last semester."

He smiled and patted her back. "Easy to get sidetracked when you're away from home the first time. It happens to a lot of our students."

"Oh, good, we're just waiting on the Millers." Mrs. Schoope came around the kitchen island to give both Mitch and Brooke a hug. "Come meet Diane." She led Brooke into the dining room where a tall, slender young woman was giving a final touch to the table settings.

"Sweetheart, I want you to meet Brooke. She's the one I've been telling you about."

Diane's smile was warm and welcoming against her sun-darkened skin. "I'm glad to finally meet you. Mom has been telling me about your work."

"I have a lot to learn," Brooke protested.

"Hey, kiddo," Mitch strolled into the room. Diane moved to his open arms with the ease of a finely tuned athlete. The two embraced.

"Mitch, you're looking fabulous."

"You're looking pretty good yourself."

A twinge of jealousy filtered through Brooke at their warm familiarity.

Mrs. Schoope patted Diane's arm. "Why don't you all go in the den, and I'll get us some tea while we wait for the Millers. Their church goes a bit longer than ours."

Leading them into the other room, Diane turned to Mitch, her eyes dancing with excitement. "Dad tells me you're interested in aviation missions."

"The Lord definitely has my attention, but I don't need to explain that to you."

Mitch sat on the couch next to Brooke while Diane sat in the chair across from them.

"No." She shook her head. "When did this happen? When I left, you were still trying to decide on a major."

"My dad's friend, Guy, came to visit and told us about his trips to Colombia. It had me so intrigued; I had to go see for myself."

"So, he took you on a trip with him?"

"Yeah, after a lot of talking to convince my mom."

She laughed. "I can relate to that."

"My first trip was amazing. The kids are what get to you. I knew God was tugging at my heart when I saw those big hungry eyes, starving for even the basics of life. Now that I'm back at school, my friends seem shallow. Americans don't have a clue how the rest of the world lives."

"Oh, yes!" Unshed tears glistened in Diane's eyes. "I have several, what you might call, adopted children. My favorite was Maya. Well, that was my nickname for her. Her mother died when she was just an infant. An aunt nursed her along with her own baby. She was barely more than a child herself, and she was glad for my help taking care of Maya. Maya was my shadow and it nearly ripped my heart out to leave her."

"Will you go back?"

"Possibly. Mom's awfully glad I'm back."

Brooke sat quietly listening to Diane and Mitch. Wasn't she shallow compared to these two selfless people? Yet, the thought of doing the same brought an inkling of fear that shuddered through her.

"Here we are." Dr. Schoope balanced a tray with glasses of iced tea and passed one to each of the young people. Taking one for himself, he sat down in his leather chair.

"So, has Diane convinced you all to head for Africa?"

"Nope, wrong direction for me." Mitch reached for Brooke's hand and squeezed it. It felt like he was including her in the plan. Could she comfortably fit in his future?

"That's right. You hope to go to South America—Colombia wasn't it?"

"Yes sir."

"How's that going?"

"Just need to finish this year, before I start real training. Since I've already been flying, it will cut down my time. It shouldn't be long before I can make solo flights."

Brooke watched Mitch's excitement as he shared with his mentor. Yes, she was definitely going to have to examine her feelings about all of this.

"I think you'll find that very rewarding, Mitch."

"What's this?" Mrs. Schoope came in the room to catch the end of their conversation. "Mitch, you aren't leaving us are you?"

"Not for a while. I've got to finish school first."

"Thank goodness for that. We've just got Diane back. I'm not ready to send another one of you off for—" The doorbell rang. "That's the Millers," Mrs. Schoope said as she left the room. Brooke watched as Diane and Mitch exchanged a knowing look.

Dinner conversation was lively as they enjoyed a tasty roast, browned new potatoes, parsnips, fresh green beans and a crisp salad. The finishing touch was Mrs. Schoope's famous key lime pie, and coffee. Brooke was in the kitchen helping Mrs. Schoope with the clean-up where they could hear Diane telling the Millers about her experiences while her father listened. Mitch popped his head in the door.

"Brooke, come here. I want you to see this."

Brooke reached for a cup to put in the dishwasher. "We'll be done in just a sec."

"Go ahead," Mrs. Schoope said. "I'll be finished in no time."

As Brooke stepped outside, he motioned her to follow him and cautioned her to be quiet. Leading her out to the far end of the yard where the plants were thick, he pointed through the foliage to a mother cat nursing her kittens, along with a tiny baby rabbit.

"Oh my goodness, why would she do that?"

"Just a mother's instinct, I guess. You'd be surprised what you see in the wild. C'mon, I'll show you around."

He led her to a woodsy area with a small stream flowing through. They walked for a while in silence, enjoying the sounds of nature. Mitch stopped close to the stream, sat down on a log and patted a space beside him.

"So what do you think of Diane?"

"She's beautiful, and such a tender heart." She could only imagine how she looked in comparison. And if he knew what she had done...Brooke shuddered at the thought.

"She is that. Her brother and I will make sure she finds a guy who can measure up."

"You're not interested?"

"Me?" He laughed out loud. "Diane and I have grown up together. She's like a sister. Why would you ask that?"

"You do have a lot in common, and she is beautiful."

"My feelings for Diane are nothing but admiration and affection."

Relief washed through her, and she mentally kicked herself for sounding like the jealous woman. Nothing like exposing yourself when you want to impress a guy. *Nice move, Brooke.*

They sat in silence for a time and watched the stream as it carried leaves and sticks to an unknown destination. The only sound was the water bubbling over the rocks.

Brooke spoke softly, unwilling to disturb the quiet around them. "I feel a bit ashamed listening to you and Diane."

"Why?" He turned to face her with uplifted eyebrows.

"I'm one of those who never gave a thought to how the rest of the world lives."

He reached for her hands. "Brooke, you haven't seen the things that Diane and I have, but you have a tender heart. I knew that from the first time we met." He looked down, rubbing her hands with his thumbs. "I guess you wondered why I never called after the Christmas party."

"I did get the impression—"

"I wanted to, but there were a lot of uncertainties in my future. And I made the decision a long time ago that I would never date a girl who was not a Christian. I sensed a sweetness about you, but you never mentioned going to church." Mitch

106

looked into her eyes and gave her a broad smile. "You can't imagine how happy I was when I saw you at that campus rally."

Brooke lowered her head as tears threatened. How much should she say? She didn't want to chase him away...but she couldn't be completely dishonest. She took a deep breath and plunged in with what she hoped would be enough. "You made a wise decision. I was a Christian but I wasn't acting like it. And after you disappeared...well, I kinda went off the deep end."

He slid his hand into her hair and left it against her cheek. "None of us have led an exemplary life, love. That's what grace is all about." He watched her for a moment. "I can't say for sure where we'll end up. I have some pretty big ambitions." He leaned his forehead against hers. "I just know I've never felt so comfortable confiding in anyone like I do with you." He brushed his lips against hers leaving her wanting more. "For now, I would like to spend as much time with you as our schedules allow. Time will tell what our future holds."

"I would like that. I would like that a lot."

He leaned forward and placed a tender kiss on her lips. She reached her arms around his back and met his kiss with eagerness. He pulled her close and held her there for a long time before breaking the embrace. "For now, we'd better get back to our hosts."

She recognized his caution in holding down the intensity that had been building with their kiss. "Of course, they must be wondering where we got to."

He took her hand to pull her up from the log and swung his arm around her shoulder, holding her close to him as they walked back to the house. From the looks of things, she had a lot of praying to do.

Chapter Fifteen

Brooke rode with Jack and Lisa to Wednesday night church, since Mitch's class finished too late for him to pick her up. She was pleased when, after the program, he begged off the group plans and took her to a quiet place downtown.

"Outside okay?"

"Perfect."

He took her hand and led her to one of the sidewalk tables. Surrounding trees were filled with white lights creating a soft illumination. The cool air hinted that fall would soon be here. Stars glittered against a darkened sky while warm jazz played in the background.

Brooke loved their time together, and how eager he seemed to share his week with her. Could this be a picture of their future? She'd given it a lot of thought and was warming up to the idea of being a missionary wife. But then, how hard could it be with a guy like Mitch. Just a look from him and she couldn't imagine living without him.

"So, do you have any plans for this weekend?" he asked as the waitress left them with their coffee and a large piece of chocolate cake to share.

"Some homework and a painting in progress. Other than that, no."

"How would you like to go to the farm this weekend?"

That caught her off guard. "You mean your parent's place?"

"What other farm is there?"

She giggled. "I don't know."

He took a drink of his coffee and set down his cup. "I'd like you to meet my parents."

"Well, I guess…"

A small frown creased his brow. "You seem a little uncertain."

Tread carefully. "I thought you wanted to take things slow."

"Are you uncomfortable with it?"

She slowly let out the breath she was holding. "No, just surprised."

Mitch grinned. "What time is your last class on Friday?"

"Art History at two. I'll be done at three."

"Perfect, I'm finished at two. I can grab a few things at my apartment and pick you up…say three-thirty?"

"Sure, I can pack the night before." She held back a giggle as she visualized jumping up and down when she told Lisa. "What kind of clothes shall I bring?"

"Jeans are a must. Probably need to bring something for dinner on Saturday and church on Sunday. We'll come back in time for campus group Sunday night, and pick up that rain check with Lisa and Jack."

Brooke managed to keep her cool but bubbles of excitement were churning around like an overflowing soda. "Sounds like you have everything worked out."

"Sorry, I'm an organizer. Does all that work for you?"

She reached over and squeezed his arm. "It sounds great. Besides, I like a man who knows how to take charge."

"Now how did I get so lucky?"

She smiled back at him. *It's me that's lucky.*

"Hey, Mom."

"Mitch, what's wrong?"

"Now what makes you think something is wrong?"

"That's usually when we hear from you."

Mitch could imagine the twinkle in her eye. "Okay, Mom, enough of the guilt trip. I thought I'd make up for it and bring a friend home this weekend."

"Michael?"

"No, her name is Brooke."

"You have a girlfriend?"

"I guess you could call her that. I'd like for you and Dad to meet her."

"This sounds serious. How come you've never mentioned her before?"

"Actually I have. Remember the girl I met at Ms. Liz's place?"

"Hmm...not ringing a bell."

"She's an art major and works part-time at the library. We helped them set up for Ms. Liz's Christmas party."

"I guess I do remember you mentioning her, but I didn't think you were that interested."

"I was. But I was concentrating on Colombia, and I didn't want to get sidetracked."

"I see. So we are to be on our best behavior?"

Mitch loved his mother's sense of humor. "You got it, Mom, make one of your famous pies. And I'd like to go to the club for dinner Saturday."

"Will that be a private affair or will your father and I be invited?"

"We'll bring you along so Dad can pick up the tab and impress my lady."

She laughed. "Well! I won't be passing that on to your father. What time do you think you'll be here?"

"Probably four or four-thirty on Friday."

"Okay, honey. I'll sweep out the dirt and put some fresh straw on the beds."

He laughed. "Thanks, Mom. We'll see you then. You're going to love her."

Mitch dumped his books on the desk and headed for the bedroom. He pulled down a bag from the top of his closet, and began throwing in clothing and toiletries. He stepped back and took a breath. *What's the rush?* He flopped down on the bed, stared up at the ceiling and prayed. "Lord, if this isn't the one for me, you need to close the door. I could sure use your wisdom. I'm not sure if you are opening doors or if my heart is clouding my perspective."

He rubbed his forehead, then laid his arm across his face and closed his eyes.

"I know you have your own timing, but I'd be thankful for a quick answer." He lay there for some time, hoping that God would speak to him at that very moment. Nothing, but he had a peace about seeking God's will.

Brooke struggled to concentrate on the pop quiz in front of her. Her thoughts kept leaping forward to the weekend with Mitch and her stomach churned at the idea of meeting his parents. Maybe they would hate her and think Mitch was crazy for bringing her home. *Okay, deep breath. No more of that kind of thinking.*

She giggled as she remembered how she and Lisa had danced around the room after she told her about the weekend plans.

The shell of protection she had carefully built was beginning to crumble. Mitch was teaching her to trust again.

The test was easy and they were allowed to leave as soon as they finished. Great, an early escape meant time to freshen up. No such luck. Mitch was at her apartment, leaning against the front of his Jeep.

"You're early." He swung his arm around her shoulder and walked along beside her.

She gave him a look and poked him with her elbow. "So are you. I thought I would have time for a shower. I don't want to meet your parents looking like a scrounge."

"That's not possible." He gave her a little squeeze as they headed up the stairs to her apartment. "But I'll give you time to do whatever you think is necessary."

On the way, he filled her in on the weekend itinerary. A turn off the highway took them under a canopy of giant oak trees reaching their leaf-covered limbs across the road. White fences marked off the lush green fields of each farm.

"Looks like you're not the only horse farm in the area."

"No, this is horse country."

"It's beautiful. I never imagined."

He seemed pleased with her appreciation. "I know. I grew up here and I'm impressed every time I come home."

"How much farther?"

"We'll start seeing our property in a couple of minutes but the house is a ways back."

As they pulled into the circular drive, it appeared as if they had stepped back in time to visit Beulah land. Surely Scarlet would greet them at the door. She realized she was not far wrong when Mitch's mother came out to meet them. *So, that's where he got his auburn hair and those startling blue-green eyes.*

"Mitch, honey." She gave him a hug. "Are you going to introduce me to this lovely young lady?"

Mitch put his arm around Brooke's shoulders and beamed. "This is Brooke."

"Well, I'm glad to meet you, darlin'."

"It's nice to meet you, Mrs. Harris."

"None of that Mrs. Harris stuff, honey. You call me Janet or I'll feel like an old lady. Son, grab your bags and drop them in the hall. I was just finishing up a pie to pop in the oven."

They walked toward the kitchen, following the smells of cinnamon and fruit.

She talked as she finished crimping the edges of the crust. "How about some iced tea. I've got it ready in the refrigerator."

"I'll get it, Mom. I don't want to take you away from those pies." Mitch gave Brooke a wink. "What kind did you make?"

She turned to Mitch with her hands on her hips. "What do you think? Your favorite, apple, banana cream for your father, and chocolate meringue, just because everyone loves chocolate."

He filled two glasses with ice and poured tea from the refrigerator. "I can't wait."

"I figured that much." She opened the oven door and slid in the pie. "There's some fresh cinnamon rolls on the counter to go with your tea."

They sat at the kitchen island where Brooke could look through French doors at the pool and screened patio. How her mother would love this kitchen with white cabinets gleaming against marble counter-tops and a pantry as large as their whole kitchen.

113

"You just missed Rose. She made your favorite pot roast and homemade noodles before she left." She explained to Brooke, "Rose helps me keep up this place. Honey, I wouldn't even try to do it all myself."

Brooke laughed. "Oh, I was beginning to think you were Wonder Woman."

"Hardly. I was in this kitchen making pies because a certain young man had someone to impress."

Brooke felt her checks warm with embarrassment. "You shouldn't have."

"Don't let her kid you." He raised his hands in protest. "She's proud of her pies. If I hadn't asked, she would have made them anyway."

After a quick unpack in her upstairs room, she met Mitch in the kitchen to explore the rest of the farm. He took her hand and led her to the backyard. She got a tour of the stables, and a detailed explanation of how they cared for the horses. He reminded her of a little boy showing off his toys. Just outside the stable, he climbed to the top of the fence. Brooke climbed up with him.

"Watch this." He gave a loud whistle. Within a few moments, a beautiful chestnut galloped across the pasture, ran up to Mitch and shoved its nose into his chest.

"Hey, Red. How ya doin', buddy?" He rubbed the horse's nose. "I've got someone for you to meet. Say hello to Brooke." He pushed the horse's head in Brooke's direction and she reached out timidly to pet its neck.

"Red's been my horse since he was a colt."

"He's magnificent!"

"He's getting ready to be a papa again, his third one."

"Really?"

"He's sired a couple of champions for us." He flashed a grin in her direction. "Do you ride?"

"Hardly. This is the closest I've been to a horse."

"Well, it's time you learned. We'll go first thing in the morning. You can ride the bay. She's nice and gentle. Mom named her Silky because she rides so smooth."

Fear ran through her like a small lightning bolt. She definitely wanted to learn everything about Mitch's world but the prospect of sitting on a horse and giving it directions was a scary thought. "Sounds like the one for me."

On Saturday night, they drove to the country club that nestled among giant pine trees on the bank of a lake. Brooke and Mitch sat across from Janet and his father, Roland, with an unobstructed view of the lake and the forest beyond. Birds flew in unafraid and watched for dropped crumbs.

Brooke was beginning to feel more comfortable with Mitch's father as he teased her about her introduction to riding. "You'll be hobbling tomorrow."

"Oh, please, don't say that." Brooke begged.

"Roland, you'll worry her to death." Janet slapped his arm. "Honey, you may be a little sore but that soak in the tub should take care of most of it."

Mitch reached for her hand, pulled it into his lap, and squeezed. She thrilled to his touch that was becoming more frequent. Several friends stopped by the table to say hello and were introduced to Brooke.

Roland chucked. "We'll have a quiz tomorrow morning to see how many names you can remember."

"I've been taking notes."

After dessert and coffee, Roland turned to his wife. "I believe I'm ready for my comfy chair and the sportscast. Let's leave the party to the young folks."

"I'm ready." Janet stood and leaned over to hug Brooke. "You two stay as long as you like."

Roland leaned down and gave her a kiss on the cheek. "Good night, my dear. It's been an enjoyable evening."

As they watched them leave, Mitch put his arm around her shoulder and pulled her close. "You've made quite an impression."

She squeezed his hand and leaned into his shoulder. This was encouragement she could use. "Your parents are lovely people."

"I've never seen my dad give anyone that much attention, much less a kiss on the cheek."

"He seemed very affectionate with your mother."

"Always has been, but she's the only one."

As the band started in the background, he moved his arm from her shoulders and reached for her hand. "Like to dance?"

"Lead the way."

Mitch was a smooth dancer and they glided around the floor to the Big Band music that fit the majority of an older crowd. Brooke loved his arms around her, his face resting against the top of her head. The band played Johnny Mathis' song, "Chances Are" while Mitch sang softly into her ear. Brooke snuggled closer and hoped that the words came from his heart. After several numbers he guided her out to the deck. The still, glistening lake and the birds calling to each other across the water left no need for words between them.

"Beautiful night," she whispered, unwilling to disturb the magic of the moment. "Thank you for asking me to come."

Mitch turned her to face him and looked into her eyes. "I hope this is just the beginning of many weekends like this." His voice was husky with emotion.

Any doubts she might have had were dissolved to complete surrender. "No argument here."

With her face in his hands, he softly kissed her mouth. Then pulling her into an embrace, he cradled her head against his chest.

"Lady, you are really getting to me. I want this to go on forever."

With her arms held tightly around his waist, feeling the rapid beat of his heart, she whispered back. "Me too, Mitch...me too."

Chapter Sixteen

Visits to the farm were soon a regular thing, and Roland let her name the new colt sired by Mitch's horse.

"Lady Esther," she said without hesitation. "She has a regal look about her. She's definitely a queen."

"She's all yours, Princess," he said with a twinkle in his eye. She'd given him a hug with all the warmth of a daughter.

After spending so much time with Mitch's parents, Brooke was thinking it was time to introduce him to her family. They sat on the hood of Mitch's Jeep after an evening of burgers and a movie with Jack and Lisa.

"I was wondering. I haven't asked my parents yet but, if it's alright with them…umm…how about going to Clearwater for Thanksgiving?"

"I would like that." He took her hand and kissed her fingers. "I was beginning to think you didn't want me to meet them."

"I didn't want you to think I was rushing you."

"Honey, I've been rushing you since the first night I saw you at church."

She looked down and said, hesitantly, "I didn't want to make any assumptions."

Mitch drew her into his arms. "Baby, forget assumptions. I'm not going anywhere without you."

Brooke listened with a warm glow inside, as Mitch explained his future plans to her family.

Her father leaned forward, resting his arms on the table. "I must admit, I haven't heard much about the aviation end of missions. We've had missionaries come to raise funds and show pictures of their work, but I never thought about how they get supplies. It sounds like an admirable vocation, son. We'll keep your future in prayer."

She smiled to herself. How silly of her to worry about overwhelming him with such a large group. He'd blended in like an old family member. She watched him go with the men as they moved into the family room for football, while the women cleared the table and stored left-over food for snacking later that evening.

Brooke's eyes sparkled. "What do you think, Mama?"

Annie pinched her cheek. "I think you have a fine young man. How do you feel about him flying to South America?"

"Mom, he won't be gone all the time. It will only be long enough to take the supplies."

"It is a wonderful thing he is doing, just make sure you understand. You will be a part of his ministry if you two are married."

"He hasn't asked me yet Mama."

"Anyone can see he's very much in love with you and it won't be so long."

At Mitch's suggestion, he and Carl went out for a tour of the workshop. After listening politely while Carl showed him around, he took the plunge.

"Sir, I really asked to see your workshop so I could talk to you privately."

"I thought as much."

"I know we've just met but I'm very much in love with Brooke…and…well…I would like to ask permission to marry your daughter."

"I see. Have you spoken to Brooke?"

"No, Sir. I mean, not exactly. I've hinted at my intentions, but I wanted to speak to you before I actually proposed."

Carl leaned his back against the workbench. "I have no doubt her answer will be yes. I have only one concern. Does she fully understand what your work in missions will involve?"

"I'm sure she does. We've talked about it a lot."

"I see. So what time frame did you have in mind for this marriage to take place?"

"Soon, I'll graduate this year and, after some training, I'll start flying in late summer. I know it seems rushed but I've been in love with your daughter since we met in her freshman year."

"Really. I didn't realize the two of you had been involved that long."

"Mr. Erickson." Mitch hesitated a minute. "When I first met Brooke, I didn't realize she was a Christian and I made a promise to God I would not date a girl who didn't share my faith." He gave a nervous laugh. "You have no idea how happy I was when I ran into her at church this fall."

"Yes, Brooke had some lessons to learn." He folded his arms across his chest and nodded. "I admire your principles, but what about Brooke's last year of school?"

"We can live in my apartment and I'll drive back and forth to Orlando until she graduates."

"Sounds like you have things all worked out."

"I've done a lot of praying. I believe the Lord brought Brooke into my life."

Carl extended his hand to Mitch. "Welcome to the family, and you can call me Carl."

Mitch's grin spread across his face as he reached for and clenched his future father-in-laws hand.

"Thank you, Carl. I'll take very good care of her, I promise."

"I'm sure you will. You seem to answer to a higher authority than me."

The kitchen was clean and Brooke snuggled up in a chair with Mitch as they watched the game with the rest of the family. The second game was beginning when Mitch whispered in her ear. "I would sure like to stretch my legs. How about showing me your beach?"

"I'd love to. Let me get a sweater and you'd better take your jacket. It will be cool."

Carl and Mitch exchanged knowing looks as they went out the door.

They rolled up their jeans, left their shoes in the car and walked through the fine white sand. Mitch put his arm around her waist and pulled her close. The sun warmed their faces and the air was filled with the smell of salt water and sea weed.

"Wow! This is beautiful, Brooke. You must miss living here."

"Not as much as I used to. Even though it has that home feeling whenever I come back, I've learned to love the farm just as much." She stretched up to place a kiss on his cheek.

"That's good to hear," he gave her a squeeze.

"Because…?"

"Well, I wasn't sure I could take you away from all of this."

She gave him a curious look.

Mitch stopped, pulled her hands against his chest and looked into the smiling blue eyes that grabbed his heart every time she glanced his way. *This is it buddy.*

"I mean, lady, I want to spend the rest of my life with you. I want you to be my wife." Just the hint of moisture rested in his eyes. "Will you be my wife, Brooke?"

He watched tears well up in her eyes as she broke into a huge smile and giggled. "Yes! I'll be your wife. I'd love to be your wife." She threw her arms around his neck as he pulled her to him and kissed her softly.

"My Brooke, my precious Brooke. How I love you." He pressed his mouth against hers again, a little longer and more intense.

"I love you, too. I can't believe I'm so lucky."

He pressed a finger against her lips. "Not luck, my love, God." He suddenly stepped back. "Wait, I almost forgot." He reached into his jacket pocket and pulled out a large solitaire diamond.

Brooke covered a gasp with her hand. "You had this planned all along."

He slid ring the on her finger and leaned his forehead into hers. "I've just been waiting for your dad's permission."

"Ahhhh…the trip to the workshop."

"A man's got do what he's gotta do." Lifting her off the ground, he declared his love with kisses all over her face. He slowly lowered her back to the sand and looked into her eyes. "I have one more thing to ask you."

"Anything." She grinned.

"I don't want a long engagement."

Brooke hesitated. "How long?"

"How does Christmas sound?"

"Christmas? That doesn't leave a lot of—"

"I know you haven't had much time to think about all this, but I've been thinking a lot."

"What about school?"

"We can live in my apartment, its big enough for the two of us."

"But I'll have another year after you graduate."

"And you can finish your last year while I commute to Orlando for training."

"But that's a long commute."

He held her head in his hands and kissed the end of her nose. "Not when I have you waiting for me at home."

"You are unbelievable." She laughed. "I suppose you have everything else worked out too."

He grinned. "Well, yes, if you agree."

She stepped away from him and put her hands on her hips. "Give it to me. I'll let you know if it meets my approval."

He laughed and grabbed her hand to walk her down the beach. "Call me sentimental but I'd like to get married in our church at school. It's where we fell in love, and all of our campus friends are there…even have Brother Scott marry us."

"Hmm…go on."

For the first time since talking to Carl, he began to relax. She was good with his ideas. "The reception, I was thinking the farm, or talk to Ms. Liz about having it at their house."

"It all sounds wonderful, but I have to think about my mother. She will be crushed if she doesn't play a major part in all of this."

"I thought about that and it's time for our parents to meet. Do you think your folks would come over to the farm next weekend?"

"I don't know, I guess."

"You and our mothers could spend the whole weekend planning food, dresses… all that stuff that goes with a wedding." He put his arm around her neck and kissed her cheek. "Of course, part of that weekend you would have to save for me."

She grinned. "I could maybe work you in."

"We can get married, before everyone leaves for the holidays, and we'll have Christmas break for our honeymoon."

"Okay, you win." She laughed. "But first we need to run this by our parents."

He pulled her into his arms and kissed her long. "Just remember, it's all I can do to keep from dragging you off to my cave right now. I want you as my wife as soon as possible.

She rested her head against his chest. "Hmm…I like the sound of that. Your wife."

The weeks flew by and the anticipated day was here. Mitch pulled Brooke away from Lisa.

"It's time for our first dance," he said, his eyes taking in every inch of her.

Brooke laughed and followed her new husband to the dance floor. Their ceremony had centered on the Christmas theme. The church was already decorated with heavy garlands and Christmas lights. There was little to do besides add the crimson rose arrangements at the front. The church had been packed with family and friends but Mitch could see no-one else but his lovely vision in white. Tears trickled down his cheek as he watched Brooke's father escort her to his side.

The deck and pool, at the farm, was now covered for dancing. Lights sparkled in the pine garland draped around the top of the screen. Heaters were placed around the perimeter to keep away the coolness of the night. Annie, Suzanne, Janet, Liz and Rose had outdone themselves with a wedding feast to rival any celebrity affair. Mitch's brother, Peter and his wife Megan had flown in from New York and would stay for the holidays with his parents. Michael, Mitch's best man had wished them well and God speed. Lisa had complained to the group that she no longer had Brooke to wake her in the mornings and brought the house down. Then, in an emotional finish of how much their friendship had meant to her, she broke down, bringing all the women to tears.

Brooke glided easily across the floor in Mitch's arms. "I love you, Mrs. Harris." He smiled and stared into her eyes.

"Love you more."

"Not possible."

"Well, how about just as much."

"That will do." He pulled her in a little closer. "How long before we can ditch this crowd?"

"Mitch! We can't leave our own reception."

"I can't wait to have you all to myself." He kissed her forehead. "I'm tired of sharing. Can't we go soon?"

"We haven't even cut our cake yet. You need to dance with your mother and I need to dance with Papa."

"All right, but let's hurry up."

"We can't disappoint our parents and we have the rest of our lives."

"But, we still have to drive to Orlando, and we have an early flight to Hawaii tomorrow."

"I promise, not too late, but this is a once in a lifetime." Her eyes pleaded with him. "I want to enjoy every minute."

The music stopped and he leaned down to give her a kiss. "Let's get the parents' dance over with."

"You are impossible." She laughed and headed toward her father.

A couple of hours later they were in their traveling clothes ready for a rice-filled send off in the rented limousine. Speeding down the highway, Mitch held her in his arms, his chin resting on top of her head. They would have two weeks on the beaches of Honolulu before returning to their little nest on campus. He was so full of love for this woman he couldn't speak.

Chapter Seventeen

𝓜itch's apartment walls were decorated with poster-size photographs, of barely-dressed children, staring out with sorrowful eyes. Her heart melted the first time she saw them.

"That's why I want to be a missionary aviator," he whispered, as he came up behind her and encircled her in his arms.

She stared at them now and wondered if she felt quite as strong in her convictions. Mitch was training in Orlando. For all his good intentions, it was too far for him to commute each day, especially with early morning classes. Brooke declined Janet's invitation to stay at the farm. That would mean sharing Mitch with his parents on the weekends.

She kept busy with a couple of classes and a summer job at the library. It made the week go faster, and supplemented his meager salary. No longer under his father's financial umbrella, he was determined to follow through with his goals.

Brooke collapsed into her big, comfortable chair and rubbed her forehead. Why was this so difficult? She knew there would be some sacrifice, and didn't her mother point that out before Mitch even proposed. Maybe she was coming down with something and it was making her impatient with their circumstances. She'd gone without breakfast when her stomach lurched at the smell of coffee.

Hmmm…twelve-thirty. Mitch wouldn't be home until this evening but he had promised to call before noon. She shrugged off her irritation. *This is no way to begin a weekend with my husband.* She decided to start a pot roast and put on a better attitude. Her head spun as she stood. She reached for the chair until her head cleared. Then her stomach gave another lurch and she raced for the bathroom.

"Honey?" Mitch called as he came in the door. "Brooke, where are you?"

After checking the kitchen he headed toward the bedroom and found his wife with her head in the bathroom sink.

"Honey, what's wrong?"

Brooke wiped her face and tried to sound cheerful. "It must be something I ate."

He pulled her into his arms and cuddled her. "Do you want to lie down? Can I get you something?"

"No." She pulled back and gave him a smile. "I'll be okay." She hugged him around the neck. "It's so good to have you home. I miss you when you're gone."

"I miss you too." He squeezed her tight. "It will be better after I've finished training."

She gave him a mischievous grin. "I'm looking forward to that. For now, I need to get the roast in the oven if I'm going to feed you a good meal."

She headed for the kitchen, calling over her shoulder. "How did I get so lucky to have you home early?"

"Our instructor's wife is having a baby so they cancelled this afternoon's classes," he said as he followed her into the kitchen and perched on the counter.

"She gave him a nudge with her arm. "You'll have to move if you want dinner tonight."

He took the vegetables out of her hands, placed them on the counter and pulled her to him. "Maybe I'll just take you out for dinner"

"And what am I going to do with this roast? "

"Can't it wait till tomorrow? You've been home by yourself all week." He softly kissed her mouth. "Besides, I want to show off my beautiful wife."

"I think I can handle that."

"On second thought," he said smoothing her hair back. "What would you think about going over to the gulf?"

"To my parents?"

"No, I had something a little more private in mind." he twisted a strand of her hair around his finger.

"I'm listening."

"What if we get a room on the beach? It's not too expensive this time of year."

"Yes…"

"If we leave now, we could get in a swim before we go out to dinner. I'm thinking, a nice little place on the water. How does that sound?"

"It sounds heavenly. Give me ten minutes to throw a few things in a bag." She was so ready for this.

Brooke's mind whirled as she paced back and forth in the apartment. The weekend had been wonderful, in spite of her recurring nausea. Rather than leave her on Sunday evening, Mitch had opted for an early Monday morning commute. Rolling over in bed, after he left, she felt her stomach roll. What was going on? This was almost like when she was preg—. *No, we're not ready.* I've just got the flu she decided. *I'll go early and stop by the clinic on the way to work.*

Her conversation with the doctor replayed in her mind.

"I would say congratulations are in order, young lady. The test will confirm, but it looks like you're about to be a new mother."

"How...? I've been on the pill—."

"That's usually effective but not a guarantee. Have you taken any antibiotic?"

"Umm...a while back...I had respiratory infection. I took it for about ten days."

"That will do it. An antibiotic can render birth control ineffective."

"But—." How could this be happening? "I have another year of college and my husband is still in training."

"There are other options."

Brooke sucked in a gasp. "No!"

He shrugged and walked toward the door. "Leave your phone number with Peggy and we'll call you with the results."

She stopped by the library and told her supervisor she wasn't feeling well. Maybe she should have stayed at work. But that would risk missing the call. It came with the news she was dreading. They didn't need the expense of a long-distance call, but she was going to explode if she didn't talk to someone. She grabbed the phone and dialed before she changed her mind.

"Mama?"

"Brooke, what a surprise."

"Mama... I... I'm... pregnant."

"Wonderful, you're going to be a mama."

"No, this is not good. I have another year of college, Mitch is still training and we're barely making it financially."

"Princess, God knows all these things. It can be worked out."

"But...I want to finish school."

"Of course you do. There will be a way to work it out. When is your baby due?"

"February second." She sighed. *She just doesn't get it.*

"You have taken extra classes since you started and you're taking summer classes, right?"

"Right—"

"So how many classes do you have left? Can you take them in one semester?"

"I could, but I need to work. I can't carry all those classes and work too."

"Let me speak to your papa, perhaps we can help."

"You've already done so much I hate to—"

"I will hear no more. You've worked too hard to quit now. What does your fine husband say about being a papa?"

"I haven't told him yet."

"He doesn't know?"

"He's in class and I didn't want to upset him."

"Brooke! Why would you say such a thing? Mitch will be happy."

"But what about his plans for missions?"

"I can't see Mitch letting this be a problem. You worry too much, Brooke. He will be a happy papa."

Mitch's shout could be heard throughout the apartment complex, as he lifted Brooke and swung her around. Then, remembering the pregnancy, he gently set her down. "I'm sorry, I didn't think."

Brooke laughed. "I'm not fragile, just pregnant."

He pulled her into his arms. "I can't believe it. We're going to have a baby."

Brooke sighed against his chest and he pulled back to look at her.

"Honey, is there something you're not telling me? You don't seem very happy about this."

She lowered her eyes and a tear trickled down her cheek.

"Is there something wrong with the baby?"

She shook her head.

"Then...what?"

"I wanted to finish school."

"You can still do that." He took her hand, led her over to the couch and pulled her into his lap. "Now what makes you think you can't finish school?"

"Because...our baby is due in February...the only way to...finish...is to take a lot of hours." The tears wouldn't stop.

"So, you've taken extra classes before."

"But, what about the money? We need my income. I can't do a full load and work too."

"Of course you can't and you won't have to." He cradled her in his arms and stroked her hair. "You know I'm a take-charge kinda guy."

"Yes."

"I can handle this. That's why I'm your husband. I'm here to take care of you. I'll be finished with training before you start the fall semester, and my pay increase will make up for what you're earning."

Brooke was silent.

"I won't be gone every week and I can earn a little extra working at the farm."

"But I don't want you to have to work two jobs."

Mitch laid a finger on her lips. "Hush, I don't want you to worry another minute." He leaned in and gave her a kiss. "Okay?"

"Okay."

"Now," he said as he wiped away tears and pulled her to her feet. "Why don't we go get something to eat and cruise by the mall to check out the baby stores?"

"That sounds nice, Papa."

Mitch's grin spread across his face. "Papa! Boy does that sound good. I'm going to be a papa."

Brooke was warming up to the idea of being a mother except for the nagging reminder of her first pregnancy. She was inordinately protective of this new life. Lisa was back at school but, between her involvement with Jack and Brooke's full load of classes, they hadn't spent much time together. Mitch was usually gone a week on each trip. The adjustment hadn't been too difficult with her studies to keep her busy and the reward of having him home for a week. Mitch was scheduled to fly out the next morning and had, again, opted for an early morning commute.

"No...you can't have my baby...leave my baby alone...Noooooooo!" She sat straight up and woke with her scream.

Mitch pulled her into his arms. "It was just a dream, honey, it's okay."

A shudder ran through her. "I dreamed they were trying to take our baby.

He held on tighter, as if to protect her from the fear, and nuzzled his face against her head. "No one is going to take our baby, it was just a dream."

The baby kicked and realization hit. That had triggered the dream. The first one had kicked just after... A sense of foreboding pressed down on her chest. If only she could tell Mitch the truth, and explain these nightmares. But he would hate her and she couldn't stand that. She began to relax as he rubbed her back, but the guilt gnawed at her heart.

Chapter Eighteen

The ringing phone jarred Lisa from her bed.

"Lisa, I guess I woke you."

"Mitch?"

"I know it's early, but I'm flying out in half an hour and I'm worried about Brooke."

"Why, there's no trouble with the—"

"No, I mean…not exactly."

"Spit it out, Mitch. What's going on?"

"She keeps having nightmares, some kind of crazy dream that someone wants to kill our baby."

Lisa closed her eyes and leaned her head against the wall. She knew what this was all about. "Maybe she's just a little apprehensive."

"I don't know where it's coming from but she woke up screaming last night."

"You want me to see if I can get her to stay with me while you're gone?"

"Would you? I'd feel a lot better. I'll be gone for two weeks this time. I'm doing Larry's run and he'll cover for me when the baby comes."

"You got it, Buddy. I'll get her over here tonight. We'll see you in two weeks."

She was on the phone as soon as she hung up with Mitch.

"Hey."

"Lisa? Isn't this a bit early for you?"

"Yeah, well, it's the only time I can reach you. What time do you go to lunch?"

"Let's see…noon. Why?"

"Want to meet somewhere? Now that you're an old married lady, I don't get to see you that much."

Brooke giggled. "Sounds good to me, where?"

"How about Harry's, across from the Science building?"

"Great, I'll see you then."

Brooke sat in a booth close to the front of the restaurant and searched the crowd for her friend. It was almost twelve-twenty. Finally bursting through the door, Lisa spotted Brooke and hurried over.

"Sorry, Alex got carried away in our Oral Interpretation class and we got out late.

"Oral Interpretation?"

"Yeah, I figured it would be an easy grade. I surprised myself and I'm actually good at it."

"Maybe you've found you're calling."

"I don't know if I'd go that far." Lisa reached for a menu. "What time do you have to be back?"

"Next class is at two."

Lisa scanned the menu. "What are you having?"

"I think I'll go for a salad."

"You'd better do more than a salad. You don't want to starve the little guy."

Brooke grinned and shook her head. "Not much chance of that. Mitch stuffs me every chance he gets."

"Good for him. Speaking of your handsome man, what's he up to today?"

"He left this morning for Colombia."

Lisa folded her arms on the table in front of her. "Bummer, how long will he be gone?"

Brooke shifted to stretch her back. "A couple of weeks this time."

"And you'll be all by yourself?"

"I'll be fine. He was only home on weekends during the summer."

"But you weren't pregnant then."

"Not at first, but I do okay."

"I've got a better idea. Your room is just like you left it, and I'm dying for some company."

"Oh, I don't know—"

"Why not?"

"What if Mitch tries to call?"

Lisa leaned back in her seat. "How many times has Mitch called you from South America?"

"I guess...never."

"C'mon. Don't be a party pooper. It'll be like old times." Lisa reached over to squeeze Brooke's arm. "Remember the first night we spent there after our parents left?"

Brooke grinned. "Well maybe, for part of the time."

"Super. What time can I expect you?"

"I have a night class that doesn't finish until nine. Maybe I should wait until tomorrow."

"Are you kidding? Remember, night owl here?" She pointed her finger at her chest. "When do you break for dinner?"

"I'll be done at four. My night class is at seven."

"Perfect, you go by your place and pick up your things. I'll have dinner ready when you get there."

"You're going to cook?"

"I didn't say that. I just said I would have it ready."

Brooke burst out laughing. It felt good to let go and be carefree. Lisa was good medicine.

Brooke's scream brought Lisa straight out of bed. With a groggy head, she groped with the covers to free herself. She could hear Brooke crying.

She sat on Brooke's bed, pulled her into her arms and rocked "I'm here. Want to tell me about it?"

"Anyone who says you can have an abortion and go on with your life is a liar."

"I'm so sorry I ever talked you into that."

"Don't blame yourself. I could have said no."

"But I'm the one that suggested it. I found you the doctor."

"And I'm the one who got pregnant to begin with." She shook her head. "I couldn't face the consequences. I brought this on myself."

They were both silent for a time. "You want to tell me about your dream?"

Brooke shuddered and took a deep breath. "Do you remember me telling you that the baby kicked right after they injected the saline?"

"Yeah…"

"Every time this baby kicks, I remember the first one."

"Oh."

"In the daytime it makes me sad, but at night I start to dream." She looked out the window to the dark, star filled sky. "I dream that I'm back in that room. The doctor is coming toward me with a sinister grin. He has on black gloves, he's carrying a big knife and he starts to cut open my stomach. Then I wake up."

"That's awful."

"What makes it so hard is I can't tell Mitch why I'm having these dreams. I know he's worried about me but he'd think I'm a monster."

Lisa took Brooke's hands in hers and squeezed them. "He could never think that. He loves you more than life."

She shook her head. "Think about it. He wouldn't even date me because he thought I wasn't a Christian."

Lisa contemplated her answer for a moment. "No one is perfect, not even Mitch. Everyone's made mistakes, and done things we wish we hadn't." She searched her memory for scripture. "What's that verse, 'for all have fallen short of the glory of God?' You've prayed and asked God for forgiveness but, you haven't forgiven yourself."

"How can I forget a thing like that?"

"You can't completely forget, but God has. When we repent, it's like it never happened."

She dropped her chin to her chest. "Maybe in God's eyes but it's etched in my memory."

"Don't you think maybe this baby is a second chance?"

Brooke looked up at her friend "I was even upset about this one. I didn't want it to interfere with my life. I was worried about graduating and I wanted more time with Mitch before I started a family." A tear ran down here cheek. "I'm a poor excuse for a Christian. I couldn't even be grateful for a baby with the man I love."

"You're being way too hard on yourself. Maybe some counseling would help. I know our pastor would be glad to do that."

"No." Brooke shook her head. "I don't want anyone else to know what I've done."

"Okay, but I'm here for you, no matter what."

"I know," she said smiling through her tears. "Maybe I shouldn't stay here though. I don't want to wake you up every night."

"Not on your life. You're staying here until Mitch gets back and every time he's gone. At least until the baby is born."

"I can't do that to you—"

"Not another word. I'd be awake all night worrying."

Brooke gave her a crooked smile. "I do feel better having someone with me."

"Then it's settled."

"All right." She hugged Lisa's neck. "Thank you."

Two more days of finals and she would be finished. *I'm finally graduating. What a relief.* A little thrill traveled through her, remembering Mitch would be home in less than a week. Then, they would move to the farm until the baby was born. She rubbed the nagging ache in her back as she headed for the last final of the day. Mr. Owens, one of her favorite instructors, suggested his desk rather than squeeze into the chair made for a flatter stomach. The exam had just started when the ache moved around to her abdomen. The urge to cry out was stifled by biting her lip until it subsided. She'd almost finished the last section of the exam when another wave began. *No, it's not time.* But it was obvious what was happening. She got through the last few questions and signaled to Mr. Owens.

"I've finished my exam and I believe my labor's started."

"My goodness, why didn't you say something?" He reached out to steady her "You could have done this test later," he said in a hushed voice.

"It's all right. It just started."

"Can I call someone for you?" He helped her from the chair.

"No, I'll be fine."

He walked her to the door. "Good luck, and keep in touch."

"Thank you, Sir, I will."

She walked gingerly toward the library and the only person she could think to help.

"Please tell me Ms. Liz is in her office," she said to Kathy.

"Yes, she is. Is there something wrong?"

"I believe I've started my labor, and Mitch won't be home until Saturday."

Kathy punched the intercom. "Mrs. Schoope, we have a little emergency."

Ms. Liz came out immediately. "Brooke?"

"I think it's time."

Ms. Liz helped her to a chair. "Do you have your doctor's number?"

"Here." She pulled out her address book and read the number while Kathy dialed and handed the receiver to Ms. Liz. Brooke leaned back against the chair while Ms. Liz talked to the doctor.

"How close are your pains?"

"I've had two…I think…about 40 minutes apart."

Ms. Liz repeated the information. "Very well," she said and hung up the phone.

Brooke scowled, "I don't want to do this by myself. I was counting on Mitch."

"Of course you don't, and he'll be terribly disappointed. Since this baby seems to be in a hurry, I believe we should give your mother and Janet a call."

"Do you think my mom can get here in time?"

Ms. Liz smiled and squeezed her hand. "I don't think that will be a problem. The first one usually takes longer. Let's go into my office and you can have a cup of tea while I make those phone calls."

Brooke gratefully let Ms. Liz take over but a bit of panic floated through her mind. This wasn't her first and maybe her mother wouldn't have time after all.

At ten-thirty that night, on the twenty-first of January, McKenzie Beth Harris, wrapped in a soft pink blanket, was laid in her mother's arms. Brooke gazed down at her tiny daughter, perfect in every way. Her bright blue eyes peered out in a look of wonder as she examined her mother's face. Brooke brushed the soft auburn fluff on top of her baby's head and prayed. "Oh Lord," she whispered against the silky soft cheek. "Thank you for a second chance."

Stretched out in a chaise lounge with the baby asleep on her chest, Brooke was in a peaceful slumber. Snuggled into comfortable sweats and a throw across her legs, the cold wind outside went unnoticed. A crackling fire added to the warmth of the room. Mother and daughter had been swooped away in a car waiting at the hospital entrance. A message had been left for Mitch that his wife and daughter would be found at the farm. Annie and Carl returned to Clearwater after an over-night, with plans for Brooke to be with them the next time Mitch flew out. Delectable smells drifted through the house from the kitchen.

Janet and Rose, anticipating Mitch's arrival, had been baking since early morning. Several pies and pecan rolls were cooling on racks while chicken and dumplings cooked to perfection. Janet looked up just as Mitch walked through the door.

"Mitch, I didn't hear you drive in." Her eyes glistened as she gazed at her handsome son. She gave him a warm hug. "They're in the living room, both asleep."

"What happened, Mom? She wasn't due for another week."

Janet laughed. "Babies have their own timing. These things happen."

"I wanted to be here for her."

She hugged his shoulder. "There was nothing you could do Mitch, she did fine. Now go on in and meet your beautiful daughter."

Mitch crept quietly into the living room. He stood over the two and gazed down at his daughter nestled against her mother, tiny lips sucking as she slept. He gently lowered himself to place a kiss on the downy soft head. Brooke stirred and opened her eyes in time to see the tender moment of father meeting daughter. She reached out and caressed the back of his head and whispered, "Do you think she's a keeper?"

Mitch looked up at his wife. "Just try sending her back." He leaned over to give Brooke a tender kiss. "You're wonderful. I'm so sorry I wasn't here with you."

"I know you wanted to be. I understand. She decided to come whether we were ready or not."

Mitch knelt down, took her hand and pressed it to his lips. "I promise you. You will never go through this alone again." He pulled her into his arms. "I love you babe, don't ever forget that."

143

Brooke breathed in the familiar scent of her husband. It was so good to have him home, but she wondered. *Was that a promise he could keep, or was this an indication of her future?*

Chapter Nineteen

McKenzie sang a happy tune as she pushed and poked a mound of sand.

"Look Mama, makin' castle for Papa." Her strawberry blond ringlets bounced as she danced around her project.

She was bright and daring. Definitely her daddy's little girl. "That's a nice castle, sweetie. I'm sure Papa will love it."

Brooke stood from her beach chair, stretched her back, and rubbed her swollen belly that held their second child. The baby was due the first week in July and Mitch was on his last run until after the birth. This week with her parents had been a blessing. She could afford late mornings, knowing that McKenzie would be in her mother's care. Benji, now eighteen, adored his little niece. He would come home from his summer job to scoop her up in his arms and throw her into the air. McKenzie would squeal in delight.

Brooke glanced at her watch. "C'mon 'Kenzie, it's time to get back to Grandmere's."

"No." McKenzie shook her curly head and continued to play.

"Yes, sweetie, Grandmere will have dinner ready. Aren't you hungry?"

"Not hungry. Want to play."

"McKenzie, Uncle Ben will be home and you won't be there. He will be so disappointed."

"Unca Ben?" She paused to give her mother a wide-eyed look.

Brooke pictured the wheels turning in her head. "Yes, sweetie, Uncle Ben and Grandpapa are probably on their way home. C'mon, help mommy get your toys in the bag." Brooke started picking up the toys while McKenzie watched, uncertain of her resolve. "Quick, we want to get there before Uncle Ben!"

McKenzie grabbed up a toy and ran to put it in the bag. Brooke laughed at how easily McKenzie could be caught up in the excitement as she ran back and forth, one toy at a time. Mitch was missing out on so much. Why couldn't he see that?

Dinner dishes were done and McKenzie was down for the night. Brooke sat with her mother on the big wrap-around porch. She breathed in the fragrance of jasmine wrapping tendrils around the porch pillars. Bright green ferns swung on their hangers in a soft breeze.

"How are things going for Mitch?"

"Oh fine. Seems he can't wait for the next flight."

"What does this mean?"

"I'm just getting tired of spending half my time alone." Brooke rested her arms against her swollen belly.

"Brooke, I thought you were excited about Mitch's work."

"Well, I'm not very excited about it now."

"But, didn't you understand what his work would involve?

"It just gets old, Mama. He wasn't even here when his daughter was born."

"But McKenzie was early. How could he help that?"

"I know Mama, but that's the nature of the beast. I just wish he had a regular job and could be home every night. Besides, it's not easy living on a missionary income. Sometimes I think I should go get a job so we could have a few things."

"Are you doing without? Do you need some help from me and Papa ?"

146

Brooke sighed heavily. "No, we meet our basic needs. It's just that...well, there's never enough for anything extra."

"You knew when you met Mitch this was his calling, and you should have known it wasn't a profession of wealth. If you didn't intend to stand by him, you never should have married him."

The truth stung and she had nothing to say.

"Have you prayed about this? This is a great concern for me. If you force your husband to go against God's calling, you'll be asking for a miserable life."

Brooke concentrated on a squirrel that ran up and down the oak tree in the front yard. "Then why am I so miserable when my husband is *in* God's will?"

"Maybe because it's your husband who is in God's will...where are you Brooke? There was never great wealth in this home. Did you have an unhappy childhood?"

"No."

"Money does not bring happiness. Having a marriage that is centered on the Lord and being supportive of each other...that's what brings happiness."

"What about Ronnie and Suzanne? They have money."

"And they have a God-centered home. Who knows why God chooses some to have money and some not. Being content with where God puts you is where you will find peace."

Brooke squirmed at the disappointment in her mother's eyes. She should have known the stand she would take. "I suppose you are right, Mama."

She could see her mother was not persuaded, but dropped the subject. She would know better than to complain to her again.

"Papa...Papa." McKenzie jumped up and down as Mitch came in the door.

"How's my girl?" He dropped his bag to the floor, scooped her up into his arms, and swung her around. Brooke heard the commotion and hurried from the kitchen. With his daughter in one arm, he embraced his wife and gave her a warm kiss. "How's our little mama doing?"

"I'm about ready to pop." She rubbed her enlarged stomach. "You're home early. I didn't expect you until Friday."

"We had someone waiting to pick up the supplies. Not disappointed are you?" He snuggled his face into her neck.

"Are you kidding? If I had my way you wouldn't be going at all."

Mitch stopped short. "What do you mean?"

She laughed nervously. "Oh...I mean I just miss you so much. I hate to see you go."

Mitch shrugged. "I know. It's hard for me to leave both of you."

Brooke called over her shoulder as she walked toward the kitchen. "I was just getting some dinner ready but it's not much."

He followed her into the kitchen, holding McKenzie on his hip, then slipped into a chair and swung his daughter onto his lap.

"I wish you could see what I do, babe." He tousled McKenzie's hair and watched his wife as she cut up tomatoes over the sink. "I know you would fall in love with the orphans. Maybe, after this baby is born, we could leave the kids with your folks and I could take you with me."

"Do you think you could?" She turned around to her husband, surprised at her intrigue.

"I'm not sure, it just occurred to me. There might be some regulations, and we'll need to get you a passport. I'll ask Bill and we can get things rolling right now." His eyes sparkled with excitement. "Then you would feel more like a part of the mission instead of just sending me off and waiting for me to come home."

They sat on the porch to share the week over iced tea. Crickets were already in song as the day gave in to dusk. Sitting out here gave her a sense of peace, listening to the shouts of children still at play as they took advantage of the late summer daylight. McKenzie slept in her father's arms, her head resting against his shoulder. Brooke had offered to tuck her into bed but Mitch preferred to steal this moment of contented closeness with his baby girl.

"I made a quick run over to see Roger and Mary Ann before I left today."

Brooke took a sip of her tea. "That's the people who run the orphanage?"

"Yeah, do you remember the little girl I found in the street... too weak from malnutrition to stand?"

"Of course, what was it you named her... Doodles?" Brooke pulled over McKenzie's stool to prop up her feet and rest her legs.

"That's the one. You should see her now. She's running around with all the other kids. She has a slight limp but the doctor is hopeful that will diminish. Every time I go to visit she runs to me...calls me Mr. Mish."

149

Brooke wiped the drips of water from the bottom of her glass. "Any hope of finding her parents?"

"Not really. They're probably dead. I would guess that's the reason she was in the street in that condition." He smoothed McKenzie's curls away from her face with his fingers. "Between poverty and the Communist guerrilla groups, life doesn't have much value there."

"Guerrillas?"

"Yeah, between the National Army and the Revolutionary Armed Forces, it's pretty unstable for the normal Joe just trying to take care of his family. They never know when violence is going to break out."

Brooke leaned forward in her chair. "Mitch, I didn't realize you were in that kind of danger."

Mitch waved the idea off with his hand. "I'm not in any danger, honey. I fly into Bogotá and stay in the residences of the other missionaries."

"But, I thought you said you found this little girl in the street and her parents probably dead. Her parents lived in the city; why wouldn't you be under the same threat?"

"There is some danger I suppose but it's so slim. I could be killed right here, in a car accident. When the Lord is ready for me, it won't matter where I am."

She was not completely convinced. "I suppose."

"Honey, I can't wait for you to meet Roger and Mary Ann."

Brooke recognized the change of subject. She was not buying it but she didn't want to argue when they had so little time together.

"We can stay with them. Mary Ann would love your company."

"Really?"

"Sure, it's hard for women being cut off from family and friends. There's no one to share their frustrations or successes. That's why my part is so important. I bring them mail and connect them with home."

"I can understand that. I don't know what I would do without Lisa." Maybe a trip to Colombia would be a good idea. She'd spent her entire life in Florida. Going to a strange new country could be quite an adventure.

Brooke was preparing a light Sunday lunch of sandwiches; potato salad; cold, sliced, beefsteak tomatoes; and sweet iced tea while Mitch was in the living room entertaining McKenzie. She'd felt the familiar ache in her back during church, but didn't mention it to Mitch. She didn't want to distract him from the message.

"Hey, you guys, lunch is ready. Mitch." She couldn't be heard over the squeals of laughter as Mitch tickled McKenzie's stomach. She'd just walked into the living room when the first birth pain began. She reached for the back of the couch, leaned over and waited for it to subside.

"Brooke...?"

"Just... a... minute"

"Is it time?"

She laughed as the pain released. "Not quite. It's the beginning, but don't panic. You're in for a long night."

"Well...well...shouldn't we be going to the hospital...calling the doctor?"

"We have plenty of time. Let's have lunch and then I'll give my parents a call to come watch McKenzie."

151

"You feel like eating?"

"Yes, Papa. We'll need our strength for later on." She led McKenzie into the kitchen leaving Mitch standing with his jaw dropped.

Mitch sat, with his son in his arms, filled with wonder. Mitchell Conner Harris lay in peaceful slumber with an occasional wiggle or stretch.

"So what do you think, Papa?" Brooke whispered as she watched her husband.

"Brooke, this is more wonderful than I could've imagined."

She could see the moisture in the corners of his eyes. Maybe this is what it would take for him to realize how much he was needed at home. She leaned over and kissed her husband's cheek.

Chapter Twenty

Brooke strained to hear Mitch's phone conversation as she laid her sleeping baby in his crib. She crept softly across the room. With McKenzie down for a nap, she was hoping for some time alone with her husband.

"I just can't believe it, Bill. Well, yes, I know…there's always that possibility. I assume their family has been notified…how are the kids—their grandparents are picking them up…right…right…no, please…I understand. I want to go, Bill. They were my friends…right…give me a couple of hours. I'll meet you there."

Brooke quietly closed the children's door and found Mitch in their room throwing things into his flight bag. "What are you doing?"

He stopped his packing and pulled her into his arms. "Honey, we've had a real tragedy. Ivan and Marie Reed." His voice was hoarse. "They've been killed by the Medellin cartel."

"In Bogotá?"

"No." He sank to the end of the bed and shook his head. "They're in the valley…valle del cordilleras. We don't have the details but someone intervened before the children were killed. They're bringing them to Bogota. I'm flying out this afternoon to pick them up."

"But why you? You promised me this time! Can't someone else take this run?"

Mitch stared at her. "Brooke, Alan and Larry are already out in Ecuador and Brazil." He continued throwing things in his bag wiping tears from his face as he did so.

"Well, if they're already down there why can't they just stop on their way back?"

Zipping up the bag, he glared at her. "We don't know how long it will take to bring them out of the jungle, Brooke. They're on their way out now. Alan and Larry need to get back. Remember? They're covering for me."

"All you care about are your precious missions." She turned and stared out the window.

"So what would you have me do?" He stood with his hands on his hips. "Two little children are finding their way through the jungle. They've just seen their parents murdered. You want me to just leave them down there?"

She continued to stare out the window, her fingernails digging into her arms folded across her chest.

Mitch tried again. "What if those were our kids? Would you want someone to just leave McKenzie down there?"

She whirled to face him in a rage. "That's my point. Half the time your children don't have a father, and one of these days the same thing may happen to you. What about your kids then?"

Mitch's jaw dropped. "What happened to the woman who was excited about my work?"

Her voice raised an octave. "She got sick and tired of being here alone."

Mitch grabbed his bag. "I have two little kids who are frightened and traumatized, counting on me to be there to bring them back to their grandparents. If you have a problem with that—well maybe you should think about that attitude." He turned and left the room.

"Fine!" she yelled at his back.

Mitch sat in his car at the airport, his head down and his hands gripping the steering wheel. He was shaken to the core by his wife's reaction. He had no idea she was so unhappy.

"Lord, what's happening here? I thought I was in the center of your will. I don't understand."

Raising his head, he leaned back against the seat. He had to put this aside for now.

He had a job to do. Hoisting himself out of the jeep, he grabbed his bag and hurried toward the hanger where Bill would be waiting. He would need a clear head to check his plane and file a flight plan. It was a struggle to keep the ugly scene behind him but he had to concentrate on the task ahead.

"Mitch, I didn't expect you for another hour."

"May as well get to it."

"Something wrong, Son?"

He shrugged. "It seems my wife is not happy about my choice of career."

"Hmmm...it can be hard on women sometimes."

"I...I...just had no idea she felt this way."

"Remember Mitch, she just had a baby. Women get a bit emotional at these times. I'll have Betty give her a call."

"That would be great, Bill. I'd appreciate that."

Mitch secured his aircraft in Bogotá, went through customs and jaunted out to the waiting, Ford station wagon where Bill was settled in the back seat. He tossed his bag into the back, slammed the door shut and swung into the front seat. Their driver, Poco, had worked with Roger for the last two years. A young man of eighteen, he adored Mary Ann who had become the mother figure denied him at the age of three. His broad

155

smile flashed a row of white teeth and lit up his dark brown eyes. A tee-shirt, with the sleeves removed, revealed the smooth hard muscular arms developed in the construction of the new orphanage that was near completion.

"Good to see you, Mr. Mitch."

Mitch grinned back at him. "Same here, buddy."

"But not so good the reason."

Mitch squeezed his shoulder. "No, I'm afraid it's not."

"Mr. Roger...Ms. Mary Ann...they very upset."

"We're all upset Poco. Any word yet on how soon they'll be here?'

"No senor, still waiting...maybe tomorrow...maybe tomorrow night." Poco pulled the car out into the street. Traffic was heavy at night and throngs of people were milling about doing their shopping and socializing in the cool of the night. Mitch watched the familiar sights from the car window as Poco expertly maneuvered his way through the crowds and down the narrow streets in disrepair. Within half an hour they pulled onto a dirt road and parked next to an adobe-type structure painted a brilliant blue.

Before they were out of the car, Mary Ann was there to greet them. Her hazel eyes, usually sparkling with joy, were now clouded with sorrow and a deep concern. She greeted them with a warm smile and gave Mitch a strong hug.

"How was your flight?"

Tears threatened at the corner of his eyes. "A sad one, but easy otherwise."

Reaching for Bill, she gave him the same hug. "A sad day, Bill. They are with the Lord."

They all nodded as Mary Ann wiped the tears from her cheeks. "Come on in. I've got fresh coffee and some dinner almost ready."

Mitch and Bill followed her as Poco gathered their bags from the station wagon. He carried them to the room where they would sleep, and quietly left to return to his work at the orphanage. The two men collapsed into chairs while Mary Ann headed for the kitchen. Mitch looked up at the wall covered with pictures of their orphans. It was a simple home full of love and welcoming. A true place of refuge.

Bill called out to Mary Ann. "Did Roger go with the rescue party?"

"No. They're finishing up the last wall of the new orphanage. He should be here anytime now."

Her words were barely spoken when the door opened and Roger walked in. He crossed the room to greet them.

"Glad you were able to come." Roger squeezed Mitch's shoulder. "I know it would mean a lot to Ivan and Marie."

"It's the least I could do. I can't imagine my children—"

Roger shook his head. "That's the hard part."

Mary Ann came in from the kitchen and hugged her husband's neck. "Dinner's almost ready. Wash up and we can eat."

Mitch and Bill joined Roger the next day to work on the new structure. It helped to keep their hands busy while they waited. Mary Ann brought them fruit and pita sandwiches for lunch and then stayed to help with the children in the old orphanage. She was the adopted mother to over forty children and she loved each of them as if they were her own.

That evening, they lingered over their coffee, discussing their progress and plans for the following day.

"Mr. Roger...Mr. Roger." Poco burst in the door. "They here—they here."

The group simultaneously came to their feet and headed for the living room.

"What is it, Poco?"

"The children from the jungle and—at the orphanage. They not sure where to go."

He turned to Bill and Mitch. "Coming? Honey, you'd better stay here and get some things ready for the children. They probably haven't eaten much and I'm sure they are exhausted."

"Of course," she said, realizing that he was protecting her from what they might find.

Mary Ann busied herself making up a bed in Roger's study. She cleaned up their dishes and laid out clean plates, silverware and glasses of milk. There would be plenty left from their meal. She'd dealt with the grief of many children losing their parents in this foreign land. She sat briefly asking the Lord to guide her in comforting the two who would be coming to her now.

"Mary Ann?" She heard Mitch calling from the front door. He held a little girl of about five in one arm. Her long matted hair fell across her face almost covering wide blue eyes, dull from shock and grief. Her jeans and tennis shoes were splattered with mud and one pant leg was torn from possibly a branch as they had trudged through the jungle. She clung to Mitch's neck. Her brother, clinching Mitch's other hand was about seven. His hair was matted like his sister's. The trails of tears still showed down his mud smeared face. His eyes had the same dull appearance from the horrors they had experienced. Mary Ann's heart was pierced as she ran to them.

"Denise...Michael...this is Mary Ann. We're going to be staying with her until we can take you to your grandma tomorrow."

The two children gave her a blank stare. Mary Ann reached for Michael and pulled him into her arms. "I'm so glad you're here with us. I've got a room made up for you. We'll get you a warm bath and how about something to eat?"

The children nodded their heads only slightly.

"Did they bring any clothing?"

"I didn't see anything. I thought I'd better get them here as soon as possible."

"I'm sure we have some things at the orphanage that will fit them. I'll go down first thing in the morning."

Brushing Michael's hair from his face she headed toward the bathroom. "Let's get you a nice bath first and find some clean clothes." Mitch followed with Denise still clinging to his neck. As Mary Ann reached for her she pulled away and clung even tighter to Mitch.

"It's okay honey, I'm not going to leave you. I'll be right here."

"Poor child. Maybe you'd better see if she'll let you put her in the bath. She seems to be secure with you."

Mitch gently rubbed her back and spoke softly. "It's okay, Denise, I'm not going anywhere. Wouldn't you like to take a nice warm bath and get all that mud off of you?" Denise began to relax but kept her eyes on Mitch. He bent down to put her on the floor, careful not to let go of his touch. She released his neck but clung to his arm as he began to remove the torn and dirty clothing. Between the two of them, they managed to bathe and wash her hair. Dressed in two of Rogers soft tee-shirts they took them to the kitchen. Only from Mitch's lap, and with his coaxing, did Denise eat part of her meal. Mary Ann sat close to Michael giving him hugs and attempted bits of conversation. With a little food in their bellies they were rocked to sleep in the safety of loving arms. Having just tucked them into bed, they heard Roger and Bill return.

"We had to get the body bags from the plane," Roger reported. "Mitch, I think it'll be best if you stay here with the kids tomorrow while I take Bill. We'll get the bodies loaded and he'll head out for the States. Then I'll come back for you."

Mitch nodded. "The less they have to see the better. Next people they should see are grandma and grandpa."

Mary Ann brought in mugs of fresh coffee and the four talked long into the night, reaffirming the desperate need for the work they were doing.

Chapter Twenty-One

The clock glowed menacingly in the darkness. Three-thirty. Sleep eluded Brooke as she wrestled angrily through the night. *It's not fair, why should my children do without their father? Why doesn't he understand?* She turned her back to the clock that stared silently like a determined foe. *He just wants to follow his precious calling. Being a father and a husband is a calling too.* She pounded her pillow and threw her head down again. *Maybe he would be better off without us. Then he could go any time he pleased. He could just stay down there with his orphans and not have to worry about coming back to us.* The pain of that thought drew a fresh flood of tears and soaked her pillow. *Maybe that's what he wants—to be free of us. We just tie him down.* She reached for a tissue and blew her nose.

Why can't I get a grip? If I'm going to be left alone, I've got to be stronger than this. She threw the covers back and reached for a robe. Moving quietly, she found her way to the kitchen in the darkness and turned on a light over the stove. She made a cup of tea and moved to the front porch. The floor felt damp from humidity on her bare feet. She pulled them under her in a wicker chair, snuggled deeper into her robe and leaned her head back. *I've got to do some clear thinking. It's time to grow up and be responsible. I have two children to think about, even if their father doesn't.* She closed her eyes, weary from her sleepless night and tried to stop the endless thoughts on replay.

The sky was just beginning to show a light shade of grey as the dawn gave evidence of a new day. The outlines of trees, heavily laden with hanging moss and clinging vines loomed black against the lightening sky. It fit her mood perfectly and did nothing to lift her spirits. *I wish Lisa was here.* She felt a lump in her throat as tears threatened. Lisa had moved to Arizona after she and Jack were married. Jack was just beginning his career as a business executive while Lisa kept her life busy teaching third grade. It would be four in the morning. Too early to call. A thought began the germination of a plan. *What if I took the kids to visit Lisa? She would be thrilled to see us and it would be great to get away for a while.* The idea began to excite her. She missed her friend and it wouldn't hurt Mitch to find out what it's like to be left alone. *Give him a taste of his own medicine.* Spurred on by such a delicious revenge she thought, *yes, Mitch, let's just see how you like being left alone.* Maybe you'll appreciate *what you have once it's gone. I'll just pack us up and leave you a note that says "See Ya." Let you figure it out.* You *can worry about whether we're going to come back, just like I have to worry every time you leave.* She returned to her bedroom and began pulling out clothes to pack.

Brooke sat in the Orlando airport waiting for her flight to be called. The only seats available on such short notice was at five that evening. They would gain time flying west and Brooke was hopeful that her babies would sleep most of the way. She hadn't been completely honest with Lisa, telling her that she couldn't stand being away from her any longer. Lisa's school year wouldn't start for another month and was happy with the idea. They'd kept in touch through letters and an occasional phone call, but it wasn't the same. She smiled at the thought of Jack and Lisa waiting for them at the other end.

Conner lay sleeping in his infant seat while McKenzie sat in her mother's lap, wide-eyed at the activities around her.

"Where's Papa?" She broke into Brooke's thoughts. "Is Papa coming too?"

"No, Papa is in Colombia."

"We're going to see Papa?"

"No. Papa is too busy."

She looked at her mother with a bewildered look at her harsh tone.

"We're going to see mama's friend, Lisa. You'll like her. She's lots of fun."

McKenzie didn't respond.

"Lisa and I were friends when we were little girls just like you. We lived together in college."

"Did Papa live with you too?"

"Well no, I met Papa much later."

"Does Papa like Lisa?"

"Oh yes. We're all good friends."

"Then Papa can come see Lisa too?"

Brooke was relieved to be rescued from this conversation with the announcement to board small children. "Oh—that's us, McKenzie. We need to get on the airplane. Can you help Mama with that bag while I get Conner?"

Lisa and Brooke sat talking in the spacious living room of their rambling ranch-style home. The children had barely wakened at their arrival and were now sleeping soundly.

Jack, after a short visit had excused himself for the evening. "I'm headed for bed, girls. I'm sure you two will be up for hours and I have an early appointment." He bent over to kiss his wife. "Don't worry about getting up in the morning, I'll get myself off."

"So," Lisa got down to business. "Tell me what really brings you here."

163

"What do you mean?"

"I know you better than anyone, Brooke. You don't bring two babies all the way across country on the spur of the moment for a friendly visit."

Tears welled up in Brooke's eyes. "Can't fool you, huh.

"So tell me what's going on."

"I just can't take this anymore. Mitch lives and breathes his work and we take second place."

"That doesn't sound like Mitch. I can't picture him putting anything before you and the kids."

"Well, first of all, he wasn't even there when McKenzie was born."

"Brooke, she was early—"

"I know, but that's the problem. I can never count on him to be there when I need him. Just like this week. I was barely home with Conner when he got an emergency call. What does he do? He goes right off…leaves his brand new baby. We're just not important to him, Lisa. His missions are his priority, not his family."

"What was the emergency?"

"One of the missionary couples was killed by somebody down there. Mitch went to get their bodies and their two children."

Lisa's eyebrows shot up. "Oh my goodness, the children were killed too?"

"No, they're bringing them out of the jungle. Their grandparents will be waiting for them in Orlando"

"How awful for those poor babies."

"It—was a terrible situation." Brooke faltered. "It's just that there's always a reason why he has to go and my children are left.

And what if Mitch gets killed down there, then my children will be in the same situation."

"Hey." Lisa placed her hand on Brooke's arm. "You keep saying my children. They're Mitch's children too."

"Not that you would notice," Brooke snapped back.

"Doesn't Mitch have anything to do with them when he's home?"

"Oh, yes." Brooke shrugged. "McKenzie adores him but that doesn't make up for all the nights he's not there."

Lisa leaned back on a cushion and sighed. "Didn't you understand what being a missionary wife meant?"

"What?"

"You know I love you, but I'm not pulling any punches. The nature of his work *is* being on call, and ready to go when he's needed. He took a whole year out of school to pray and decide if this was God's will for his life. It was the first thing he shared with you when you started dating. It was so important for him to have a wife that shared his calling that he put his feelings for you aside until he found out you were a Christian."

Brooke didn't want to hear it. She wanted Lisa to sympathize with her feelings and be angry with Mitch.

"What do you want him to do, Brooke? It's his job and he's working for the Lord. You know that's not always convenient-"

"That's easy for you to say." Brooke continued to argue her case. "You live in a beautiful home, your husband comes home every night and you don't have to worry if you'll have enough to pay the bills."

"Wait a minute." Lisa shifted in her seat. "It sounds like there's more to this than Mitch being gone."

"I'm not cut out to be a missionary's wife. I hate being poor. I hate being left alone. I want a normal life with a husband that's home every night. I want to do things with my kids and buy them nice clothes. I'm sick of the whole thing."

Lisa understood how difficult it must be with two small children and left to care for them alone. She also knew Brooke had been enamored by the affluent lifestyle of Mitch's parents, and pictured herself living in the same manner. She, obviously, had not given thought to the challenges she would face, and she knew her walk with the Lord had never been a close one. This was definitely something she would have to talk over with Jack before giving any more advice.

"Does Mitch know you're gone?"

"No."

"When will he be back from Colombia?"

"I don't know. Maybe tonight…maybe tomorrow. They didn't know how long it would take to bring them out of the jungle."

"Did you leave him a note or let anyone know where you are?"

"No, I wanted him to know how it feels. To be left alone, without knowing if we would be back."

"You can't do that to him. At least let him know where you are."

"No! That's my whole point. I want him to worry about us for a change."

Lisa sighed. "You're going to have to sit down with him eventually, and tell him how you feel."

"I told him how I feel, just before he left."

"I'm sure you did that in a calm and collected manner."

166

"I was upset."

"You have a prince of a guy. He loves you dearly and he adores his children. I know him too well to think otherwise."

Brooke didn't answer.

"The two of you have to sit down and talk this thing out. You owe it to your children."

"I suppose, but I need to be away from the whole situation for a while."

"You know you're welcome here. We'll do some fun things, get you rested up and then, my friend, you need to talk to your husband."

"I know."

"Now, I think we have talked enough for tonight. Let's get to bed. Don't worry about sleeping in. I'll take care of the kids."

"Oh, you don't have—"

"You need some rest. Besides, Aunt Lisa hasn't had an opportunity to get acquainted with her niece and nephew."

"Thanks, Lisa."

"Now off to bed with you and I'll see you in the morning."

Lisa lay in bed listening to the familiar sounds coming from the bathroom as her husband prepared for work. She needed to talk to Jack before he left that morning. She valued his advice. She was certain he would have better answers than she had managed.

"You don't have to be quiet," she said as he tip-toed through the room. "I'm awake."

He walked over to the bedside to deliver a kiss. "What are you doing awake so early?"

"We need to talk. I need your counsel."

"I had a feeling that this impromptu visit was more than Brooke was saying."

"You're right. She's having a problem being a missionary's wife."

"Truthfully, honey, I'm not surprised." He sat on the bed next to his wife. "Brooke never did strike me as a fully committed Christian. With her, it was kind of a nominal thing."

"Right again. I thought Mitch's strong faith had made a difference, but evidently not." She retold the conversation from the night before.

"Hmm…not an easy problem to solve. We'll have to do some praying over this one. In the meantime, Mitch needs to know his family is safe."

"I agree but she's adamant she's going to show him how she feels."

"Write down their home phone number for me. I'll call from the office." He stood to finish dressing. "I don't care what kind of lesson she thinks she needs to teach him, I'm not going to have him frantic over his family."

"Bless you, I couldn't figure out how I could call Mitch with Brooke right here."

"It would probably be a good idea to let her rest. Why don't you go to lunch and do some girl stuff. It will give her some time to cool down."

"How do you think they can resolve this?"

"I don't know sweetheart, but it's not really ours to work out." He finished knotting his tie and smoothed it against his shirt. "The decisions they make will have to be their own. The best we can do is pray for the Lord to give them wisdom and guide them through this. That is, give Mitch wisdom. I don't think Brooke cares much about what the Lord wants; she just knows what she wants."

"Don't be harsh, Jack."

Jack sat down on the edge of the bed next to his wife. "I know that's not very kind, but it's the truth."

"I'm afraid it is. Brooke didn't cause her parents any problems while she was growing up." Pressing her hand against Jack's knee, Lisa climbed out of bed and reached for her robe. "I guess her parents assumed that because she was in church all her life she shared the same deep faith, and they pretty much let her do anything she wanted."

Jack stood and reached for his suit jacket. "Not having any adversity in your life can leave you unprepared for the curves life throws at you as an adult."

Lisa reached up to pull his face toward hers and kissed him soundly, breathing in his masculine scent. "I'm so thankful for you and your willingness to follow God. How did I get so lucky?"

Jack held her close. "It's me that's thankful my love. Your support makes it easy."

Chapter Twenty-Two

Mitch glanced at his watch…three-thirty. Another half-hour to land, forty minutes to deliver the children, secure his plane, and file paper work. He should be home by five or earlier. The trip and the children kept him preoccupied, but now that it was coming to a close his mind returned to the scene two days before. It seemed so much longer. *What's been going on?* He wrestled with the worry. *I thought Brooke was happy. Has she always been this miserable? Why didn't I see the signs?* He reached up to massage the back of his neck. He was anxious to talk to his wife but his stomach knotted at the thought of picking up their last conversation. *Lord, what did I miss? How did I fail to recognize something so troubling to my wife? Are you trying to tell me something or is this Satan using my family. I need some answers here.*

The familiar land sites came into view and Mitch radioed for clearance to land. With a glance behind at his passengers, he taxied in. They were still in a daze.

"Okay, munchkins." He unbuckled Michael's seat belt and then turned to Denise. "Time to get you to Grandma and Grandpa."

He lifted Denise into his arms and took Michael's hand. Denise clung to his neck with such a grip she nearly cut off his breath.

"It's alright now baby, you're safe." He looked down at Michael. "How long since you've seen your grandparents?"

"Don't know."

"Do you remember them?"

Michael shrugged. "Not really. I think we went to their house for Christmas."

"So you don't really know them."

Michael shook his head and looked down at his feet.

Mitch squatted down to Michael's level and turned Denise around to perch on his thigh. "Kids, your grandparents are wonderful people. After all, they raised your mama didn't they?"

The sadness in their eyes brimmed with tears.

"They're going to love and take care of you, just like they did your mama. I'll bet your grandma has her cookie jar filled and waiting for you." He grinned and gave Denise a squeeze. "You know what? I don't live very far from them. Did you know that?"

They both shook their heads and Michael wiped away tears with the back of his hand.

"That's right. I have a little girl named McKenzie and a baby boy named Conner. I'll bet if I talk to your grandparents we could come see you. McKenzie would like some new friends. Would you like that?"

They both nodded.

"Okay, I'll get their phone number and we'll just do that." He gave them both a tight squeeze. "Now, let's go meet your grandparents."

Mitch pulled into the driveway and saw that Brooke's car was gone. He felt a wave of relief, but disappointment that they were not there. Probably shopping. He unlocked the front door and breathed in the familiar smells of home. He dropped off his bag in the bedroom and went to the kitchen for some iced tea. *Hmm, Brooke must not have made any today.* He filled the kettle and pulled tea bags out of Brooke's oriental tin. His father brought it to her from Chinatown when he made a trip to deliver a stallion for a buyer in Los Angeles. Once the tea was made he put it in the refrigerator to cool and went in to take a shower.

In fresh jeans and tee-shirt, he searched the refrigerator for an easy menu to have ready when she got home. Tuna fish sandwiches were about his speed and a little left-over coleslaw. He set the table, put a sandwich and a scoop of coleslaw on each plate and finished off with a vase holding some of Brooke's roses. He checked his watch again… seven-thirty. *It's awfully late for her to be out.* He looked out the window, half expecting to see her drive in, but was met with nothing but silence. Mitch paced between the kitchen and living room, periodically checking out the windows for some sign of his wife. *Maybe she's gone to Clearwater—of course.*

He reached for the phone and dialed the familiar number. "Hello." He heard the rich accent of his mother-in-law.

"Annie, Mitch here."

"Ah Mitch, how are you doing?"

"Doin' fine. I just got back from Colombia."

"Oh, I did not realize you would be going for a while."

Mitch felt a thud in the pit of his stomach. Brooke was not there.

"Yeah, I wasn't supposed to, but we had an emergency. A couple of our missionaries were killed. Bill and I had to go down and get them."

"That is terrible."

"It was very sad and their children witnessed the whole thing."

"Oh, I am so sorry. Where are the children now?"

"With their grandparents, they live in Deland."

"Bless their hearts."

"Yes...actually, Annie, I was calling to see if Brooke was with you."

"No, she is not. I have not heard from Brooke since Conner was born."

"Well, no need for alarm. I'm sure she's just shopping late."

"I will let you know if I hear from her."

"Thanks, Annie."

Mitch flipped on the TV and watched without interest as his mind raced. He was beginning to get worried. He wandered out to the porch and stood, staring down the street as if to will her appearance. He longed for the sight of her little red car— nothing but a quiet street. The sad part was, he had no idea where to begin looking. He didn't know what she did while he was gone. Going back to the kitchen, Mitch stared at the table he had so carefully prepared. He wasn't hungry but filled a glass with tea to quench his dry mouth. He jumped at the sound of the phone, the adrenaline pumping through his body as he jerked it off the hook.

"Brooke?"

"Mitch...Jack here."

"Oh... Jack...how are you buddy?"

"I'm fine but I'm guessing you're not. Brooke is here, Mitch."

"In Arizona?"

"Yeah, I meant to call you earlier but I got tied up in a late meeting and I wasn't sure when you'd be back."

"What...what's she..."

"It seems you have some problems, friend. Brooke thinks your work is more important than your family."

173

Mitch sank into a chair and sighed. "I had my first indication that something was wrong when I got ready to leave Sunday. Before then, Jack, I didn't have a clue she was unhappy."

"I figured. Brooke can be a pretty complicated woman."

"How did she get there—when—"

"She called Lisa yesterday morning, said you were out of the country and she was on her way to visit. They took a plane last night."

"I can't believe this."

"Yeah, we surmised there was more to it than Brooke was saying, but we figured Lisa could get to the bottom of it. You know how close they are."

"Yeah, I've sometimes envied Lisa. So what does she plan to do? Does she have a return ticket?"

"Yeah, for next Sunday. I believe her car is at the airport."

He raked his hand through his hair. "I don't know what to say."

"I have a suggestion."

"I'm open to whatever you have in mind."

"Lisa is going to do a lot of girl things with Brooke…shopping…going to lunch… kind of calm her down."

"Sounds good." Mitch stood up and began to pace back and forth across the kitchen.

"Lisa told her she needs to sit down with you and talk this out."

"What did she say to that?"

"She knows she needs to, but she was pretty wigged out last night. I don't know if you can manage this but, we have a company plane coming here on Friday. I can arrange for you to hitch a ride. Maybe a change of scenery would help. We'll watch

174

the kids and you guys can spend all day Saturday together. See if you can sort things out."

"That sounds great, Jack, but if you can do that, the plane I mean—how would I get back?"

"Only a couple of guys on board so one more won't make a difference. They'll be going back on Monday with just one passenger. It won't be a problem for all of you to go back together."

"Jack, I don't know how to thank you."

"Glad to do it, Mitch. I'm just sorry I didn't get hold of you earlier."

"I was getting pretty worried." Mitch rolled his shoulders to release the grip of his muscles.

"They're safe and sound. I'll give you a call in the morning with the details for your flight."

"Right. I'll talk to you then and...thanks, Jack."

Mitch hung up the phone and leaned against the wall. The strain of the trip to Colombia, losing friends to a brutal death, the fight with Brooke, and then her disappearance had all taken their toll. He went straight to the bedroom, collapsed on the bed and fell into a deep slumber.

Mitch sat up with a start. It finally registered that the phone was ringing. He jumped out of bed and ran for the kitchen to grab it.

"Yeah." His brain still foggy, he wiped his hand across his face.

"Did I wake you?"

"Jack, I can't believe I slept this late." The kitchen clock showed eleven-thirty.

"Sorry, I wanted to catch you before you went out. You're all set for the flight out on Friday."

"Great, let me get something to write on." He reached into a drawer and scrambled for a pen and note pad. "Okay, go ahead."

"They plan to leave around two. You'll be meeting up with John Wise. He's about six-three, slender and white hair. He'll wait for you by the Delta counter."

"Got it, I'll be there in plenty of time. Tell him I'll have on my flight jacket."

Jack laughed. "I just told him to look for the red hair."

Mitch laughed with him. "Right, not too many of us."

"You can come to the office with John and then go home with me."

Mitch leaned against his palm on the door frame. "Sounds like a plan."

"See you Friday then."

"Right...and...thanks again, Jack."

Mitch ran his fingers through his hair and surveyed the remains from the evening before. Tuna sandwiches sat dried on the plates with the bottoms soggy from the coleslaw. He started the coffee, scraped the plates, and put them into the sink. After a quick shave and shower, he pulled on a pair of shorts and straightened the bed. A cup of coffee in hand, he ambled out to the porch. A dog barked in the distance. It was going to be a hot day and the humidity hung heavy in the air. Their neighbor across the street was working in her flower bed with her two granddaughters, and he gave them a wave. He wandered around to the back yard where Brooke spent hours grooming her garden. Deep purple and white petunias spilled out over the edge of the porch and filled the air with their perfume. McKenzie's toy stroller

176

sat abandoned near the back door. Her doll was carefully bundled inside, damp from the humidity. He set it inside in case of an afternoon shower.

Well, now what am I going to do with myself? Walking through the back door to the kitchen, he reached for the phone and dialed his parent's number.

"Harris Farms."

"Rose—"

"Mitch! How are you doing? How's that boy?"

"Just great, Rose...ah...is Mom there?"

"You just missed her. She had a meetin' and they were going to have lunch. Should be home around three. I can have her call."

"No, I think I'll just run on over for a bit. Brooke is in Arizona with the kids."

"My, it's awful early to be travelin' with that baby."

"Well, you know how close Brooke and Lisa are. She couldn't wait to show him off."

"Honey, you just come on. I'll throw another potato in the pot."

"Okay Rose, see you in a couple of hours."

Roland looked up as his son rode in from the meadow on his horse.

"It's been a long time since you rode him. I don't have much time for riding and he needs the exercise."

"I was just thinking. I should bring Brooke." He swung out of the saddle. "We need to bring the kids over and start them riding."

"I had you in the saddle before you were a year old." His father chuckled. "Your mother was furious." He shook his head. "I told her the best way was to get you in the saddle before you knew how to be afraid."

"It was a good childhood, Dad. I didn't realize how much I've missed it." He removed the saddle and leaned against the fence.

"What's going on? You've got something troubling you."

Mitch sighed, looked down at his feet and shook his head. "It's Brooke, dad. She's unhappy about being home alone while I'm in Colombia."

"Well, son, it's not an easy life for a young woman with two small children to take care of." He put his hands on his hips. "Besides, I imagine she's worried about your safety."

Mitch leaned his arms on the coral fence and stared out at the meadow. "I know, Dad, I just thought she understood. The hardest thing is, she didn't say anything and I had no idea she was unhappy."

"That's part of being married." Roland leaned his arms against the fence with his son. "Women expect you to find these things out. They don't want to have to spell it out to you. They want you to notice that things aren't right."

"How can you do that if they don't tell you?"

"Can't...you just have an understanding with them. When they've got a gripe, they let you know about it."

"Does that work?"

"Sometimes...sometimes you're going to be out on a limb no matter what you do."

Mitch laughed and shook his head. "That's encouraging."

"Just the facts, son. So, what are you going to do?"

"I wish I knew. Jack made arrangements for me to go out to Phoenix on their company plane on Friday. They'll watch the kids while I spend the day with Brooke and see what we can work out."

"You aren't thinking about divorce are you?"

"No way, that never occurred to me."

"Don't be so sure she hasn't. She must've been in quite a state to fly all the way to Arizona."

"I don't think so, Dad. She just wanted to be with Lisa."

"I hope you're right. We love Brooke like she was our own. Don't want to see this family busted apart." He patted Mitch's shoulder. "In the meantime, maybe you should consider whether you're in the right profession."

Mitch shook his head. "I know you were disappointed when I didn't join you in the horse business, but I knew God was calling me to this work."

"Maybe God is trying to tell you something now. Maybe this thing with Brooke is a message that he doesn't want you doing this anymore."

Mitch shrugged. "I don't know. I don't feel like he's telling me that. I'm praying for the right direction and I promise you. If that's what he's telling me, I'll listen."

"Glad to hear it." He ruffled Mitch's hair. "C'mon, I'm sure those women have quite a meal ready for us."

Chapter Twenty-Three

The silence screamed in Mitch's ears as they headed downtown to the restaurant Jack had suggested. His arrival last night was met with little more than civility. McKenzie, of course, had squealed in delight and came running into his arms. Jack and Lisa kept the conversation going, and Brooke went to bed long after Mitch. She spent the night on the far side, her back turned to him. He was desperate to end this madness, but he didn't know where to start. Brooke was like a hostile stranger, and he didn't know how to break down her defenses long enough to listen. The heavy traffic was a blessing. A distraction from the cold indifference of his wife beside him. He pulled into a parking space beside the restaurant and Brooke jumped out of the car before he could come around. They had reservations and the hostess showed them to a secluded table toward the back of the room with a window that looked out on an atrium. "Thank you, Lord for this private spot," he whispered.

Their meal was served and eaten in civil conversation. With the table cleared, they lingered over hot coffee. Mitch knew it was time to plunge into dreaded territory.

"Brooke," he said. "I'm so confused. I don't even know where to start."

Brooke stared into her coffee.

"Honey, I went to the farm this week after I talked to Jack and knew you were safe."

Brooke looked up at him, her brow creased in a frown. "When did you talk to Jack?"

"The night after you came here. I'd just returned from Colombia."

"I didn't want him to do that," she said between clenched teeth.

"Why Brooke? I was afraid something had happened to you."

"That's what I wanted," she bit out, "for you to see what it's like to be left alone all the time and afraid that you won't come back."

"Brooke, why did you keep this to yourself for so long? This isn't something that just came up last week. I had no idea you had any problem with what I was doing."

Brooke stared out the window.

"Do you remember when we first started dating and I told you I was going to be an aviation missionary?'

She didn't respond.

"I thought you were excited about it too. I thought you shared this vision."

"It's pretty hard to share something when you're not involved."

"We discussed a trip for you to go with me to meet Roger and Mary Ann and see the orphanage. I brought back two beautiful little orphans who would love to get to know you."

"You what!" Brooke glared at him. "You brought them where?"

Mitch reached for her hand. "Not Colombian, honey. The kids I brought back to their grandparents. They're in a state of shock and I thought it would help them to spend some time with us and McKenzie."

"Always the good Samaritan to everyone but your family." She pulled her hand away.

"That's not fair, Brooke. My little girl doesn't come running into my arms without a reason. I love her, and I spend more time with her than most fathers."

"When you're home."

"Okay, Brooke, I've begged you to help me understand and you just seem bent on being angry and throwing insults." He raised her chin with his finger and forced her to look at him. "What is it you want, Brooke—a divorce? You want me out of your life? Would that makes things better for you and our children?"

Mitch caught the startled look in her eyes "Well...well...no. I never said I wanted a divorce."

"Then I suggest you begin talking to me like a wife who wants her marriage to work. I've been trying to get you to open up and help me understand. I can't change anything until you explain to me what I've done wrong."

Brooke picked at her fingernail polish, tears brimming as she fought for control. "I...I...feel like we're your left-overs. That your orphans...your missionaries...that flying is your priority and we just get what's left."

"Oh, Brooke, you are my life. Our babies mean everything to me. I don't know how I would go on without you. It's just my nature to reach out to others who don't have what we enjoy in this country. I don't ever want to put them before you." He searched her face for understanding. "But doing my part, to make this a better world, and reach people for the Lord is not just my work. It's who I am."

"I don't think I'm cut out to be a missionary's wife."

"I think that would change if you could see those beautiful children. You'll want to be a part of making a better life for them."

"It's not just that." She gazed out the window again.

"What do you mean?" A bit of panic gripped his stomach. "What else?"

She took a drink of her coffee. "I hate being poor. I don't have time to paint anymore and even if I did, I don't have the money to buy supplies. We barely have enough to buy the kids clothes."

Mitch sat silent for a time. "I didn't realize. I hadn't noticed you weren't painting and I should have. I thought you were involved with the babies and happy with that."

She looked up at him, her eyes slightly softening. "Mitch, painting is to me what flying missions are to you. It's what I am and it's been my life since I was in middle school. Not being able to paint is almost like not being able to breathe."

"Brooke—" Mitch reached for her hands and caressed them with his thumbs. "I'm so sorry. I wish you had said something. You know men aren't very good at picking up on things. Sometimes you just have to hit us over the head." He smiled tentatively.

She gave him a crooked smile, the tears glistening in her eyes. "I thought about it. Truthfully, I didn't realize until just now that it bothered me so much."

"Okay," he said, "this is one thing I can definitely fix. We'll set aside part of my pay each month and designate it for your paint supplies."

She started to protest.

183

"No," he shook his head, "we can do it. We'll just have to make it a priority." He kissed her fingers. "Then when I'm home, I can go with you and watch the kids or you can go by yourself. You can take as much time as you want…all day if you like." He squeezed her hands. "Will that help? Do you see that as a possible solution?"

She nodded her head. "Yes, that would mean a lot to me." She looked up at him. "But that doesn't solve the other problem."

"Alright, let's talk about that. When I go, I'm gone for a week sometimes. But most of the time it's just a couple of days…right?"

"Yes."

"And then I'm home for at least several days. Sometimes a week before I go out again…right?"

Brooke nodded.

"Well, what if I was in a regular job. Wouldn't I be gone all day for at least five days a week?"

"Yes, but you would be home every night."

"That's true but I would also be tired from work. The kids would be in bed before I had much time to spend with them. I'd just crash in front of the TV with my cigar and can of beer."

Brooke giggled. "Right."

"You see, Honey, I do understand that it's hard to be home alone at night with two babies, but I actually spend more time with you in the long run. I don't have to bring home files to work on at night, and I can devote all of my time to my family."

"I suppose."

"So, can we go back home and start over? I promise to try and be more sensitive to your needs, but you've got to let me know when I'm missing it."

She gave him a tentative smile. "All right."

Mitch relaxed a little still hanging onto her hands, unwilling to let go of the progress made. "What would you think about going out to the farm for a few days when we get back? I'd like to introduce McKenzie to horseback riding and we haven't been riding since we got married."

"I think I would like that."

Mitch reached over the table and caressed her cheek, slid his hands into her hair and pulled her toward him to kiss her mouth ever so softly. "I love you lady, and I don't want anything to ever separate us again."

"I love you too." She stifled a sob as she took his hand and hugged it to her chest.

Mitch held her eyes with his. "Now, Mrs. Harris, Jack tells me there is a fabulous art museum just down the street. How about it?"

Chapter Twenty-Four

The familiar pungent smell of hay and horses flooded Brooke with fond memories and happy times, as she pushed open the heavy wooden doors. The sun was just beginning to glow over the horizon and filled the barn with a soft yellow light. Intricate shadowed patterns fell across the floor as the light penetrated the big oak tree outside the barn window. Saddles, bridles and other riding gear were neatly housed on the north wall.

"Hello, Lady." She rubbed the velvety nose of her horse who met her greeting with enthusiasm and a deep throated whinny.

"I'm afraid I've neglected you girl. I got busy raising babies. Wait 'till you meet my McKenzie." She stroked the mare's neck. "Would you like to help me teach her to ride?" Lady Esther bobbed her head and pranced in answer.

They'd come to the farm after a short stop at home to pick up fresh clothes and a few necessities for Conner. The flight back had been pleasant. John Wise, the CEO of Jack's company, put her at ease and he held Conner like a seasoned grandfather. He and Mitch talked comfortably about the favorable aspects of the small jet that propelled them across the country. John was more than a little interested in Mitch's work and the countries where he traveled.

"Hello there." Mitch came up behind her and slipped his arms around her waist. "You're up early. You seemed deep in thought."

She pulled his arms tighter around her. "I was just thinking what a nice man John is, and what a nice friend he might be."

"He is, I was impressed." He snuggled his face into her neck and rested his chin on her shoulder. "Jack has a great deal of respect for him." He pulled away from her and took her hand as if he didn't want to be separated from her for a moment.

"Mitch, did you know the headquarters for Jack's company was here in Orlando?"

"Yeah, that's where Jack interviewed before graduation. The timing was perfect with the new plant in Arizona just opening up. John knew Jack had been raised there and his dad was successful in his own right. It made for plenty of contacts."

"Jack and Lisa seem to have it all together, don't they?" She reached out her hand to her horse and rubbed her nose.

"It certainly seems that way." Mitch hesitated. "That's what I want for us. To know, even during the difficult times, we can count on each other."

Brooke shifted and looked out the window. "That's what I want, too."

"How are we going to get there? What is it they've figured out that we haven't?"

She looked back at him. "I'm not sure. Lisa did a lot of talking and told me things I didn't want to hear."

"I'm sure it's not all you, Brooke."

Brooke laughed. "Don't worry Mitch. I'm not going to take off again if you agree that I have some issues." She reached over and smoothed his cheek. "I've had a pretty selfish attitude. Yes, I've been a bit overwhelmed with two babies and worried about your safety. But I've been pretty focused on myself and what I think I need, instead of counting my blessings."

Mitch waited for the constriction in his throat to release. "I should have been more aware of your fears. The night I came home and you weren't there; I didn't have a clue where to start searching for you. I had no idea what you do when I'm gone."

187

Brooke chuckled. "Nothing very dramatic."

"I'd like to take you to Colombia soon. Mom and Dad said they would watch the kids. I've spoken to Bill and he's fine with it."

"I don't know…I mean how soon?"

He laughed. "Well, it can't be too long from now. If I don't get in some flying, we're not going to be able to make the house payment."

"And our credit card." She sighed. "I'm sorry I went crazy and added to our financial burden with plane tickets."

Mitch shrugged. "Maybe that's the cost for getting us back on track. I would rather be paying a bill than continue the way we were going." He pulled her around to plant a kiss on her forehead and then looked into her eyes. "So, how about it? Would you like to see where your husband goes…meet Roger and Mary Ann?"

She had to smile at him, watching her eagerly with an infectious grin. "I guess I could. You're sure your parents don't mind?"

"Not on your life. My mom is not about to give up the chance to have those babies."

Brooke laughed. "She'll be more than ready to return them."

"Probably but let's take advantage of it while they're still enthusiastic."

"Okay, let's do it."

Mitch pulled her into his arms and hugged her tight. "I love you, and I'm going to keep my promise." He pulled back with his hands on her shoulders. "We're going to have you painting again as soon as we get back."

Brooke's heart swelled with pride as she watched her husband expertly prepare the aircraft for their departure. They were loaded with clothing from a women's mission drive at Bill's church, and the all-important mail that would be distributed to missionaries throughout the country.

"We're cleared for takeoff." Mitch set the aircraft in motion and before Brooke had time to be concerned they were airborne and leveling off.

"Now is the worst part."

"What—?"

He chuckled. "Sheer boredom, with hours of flying and nothing to do." He reached over and squeezed her knee. "Taking off and landing is the fun part."

"That's easy for you to say. I'll take a little of this boredom."

"We'll be flying toward the Gulf around Ft. Myers and then over the coast to South America. We'll actually cross over the western part of Venezuela. Bogotá is not quite the middle of Colombia." Brooke watched out the window at the landscape looking like a quilt with the cities along the Gulf forming the border. It was four in the morning when they left the farm and the drone of the engines soon lulled her to sleep.

"Honey." Mitch roused her from a doze. "We're crossing into Colombia now, and it won't be long before we land."

She looked out the window to see land under them once again and smiled at him. "I'm ready."

Poco had been awaiting their arrival and he grinned at Mitch as they put the luggage in the back. "You have beautiful wife, Mr. Mitch."

"Yes, I do, Poco."

189

As Mitch opened the door for her, he whispered in her ear, "I told you they would love you."

Mary Ann was out of the house before the station wagon came to a stop. She gave Mitch a warm hug and waited for introductions.

"Mary Ann, this is my wife Brooke."

"We've been anxious to meet you, Brooke. You know, as much as Mitch talks about you and the kids, I feel like I know you already."

"It's the same on the other end." Brooke reassured Mary Ann. "I've heard all about you and Roger and the children."

"Come on in." She led them inside. "I have some cold juice and you can get settled before Roger comes in for lunch."

They sat around the kitchen table, lingering over cold tea and conversation. Brooke immediately warmed to Roger. His mannerisms were similar to those of her father. Strong in his convictions but comfortable to sit quietly and listen to the conversation. She knew the warmth of this big man's arms, around those parentless children, brought them love and security. She could see why Mitch loved these two, and felt compelled to do whatever he could to make their task less difficult.

"We'll go over in the morning." Brooke was brought back to the conversation. "I hope you brought a camera," Mary Ann said.

"I did and a bag full of film."

"Too bad we didn't think to bring some of your art supplies," Mitch said. "My wife is one of the best artists you'll ever see. Her work will be in a gallery one of these days."

190

"I don't know about that." She gave Mitch a nudge with her shoulder. "I just love to paint and be creative. There wouldn't be time to complete a painting and I can do just as well working from a photograph."

"So, you'll do paintings of our children?" Roger said.

"The posters that Mitch had in his apartment were heart-stopping. I'd like to do some paintings that are equally as compelling."

Roger's eyes gleamed. "That might be a way to bring awareness to our work here, if you displayed them."

"I'd never thought—"

"There's nothing like children to melt people's hearts," Mary Ann said.

Brooke could feel the excitement. She'd never painted for anyone but herself and an occasional painting for her family. Could she actually do something with a purpose?

"I never thought of using my painting in such a way. I could speak to our pastor and maybe have a display with a message focused on your work here."

"Or even Bill," Mitch said. "He's active in the community and he has lots of contacts in city government."

Brooke couldn't wait to get to the orphanage.

Brooke sat cross-legged on her living room floor and surveyed the display of photographs before her. Dark chocolate-brown eyes peered out of tanned faces framed with silky, thick black hair. They were laughing, saddened, curious eyes all touching the heart of the viewer. Some posed in delight and some were caught unaware as they played with brothers and sisters. All reflected the trauma in their young lives. True to his

191

word, Mitch had come through with a multi-purpose plan. On his days off, he headed to the farm to earn extra money and took the children to spend time with their grandmother. It left Brooke an entire day to devote to her art. Not to over-burden Janet, Brooke occasionally loaded up babies and art supplies and went to the Gulf, to Annie's delight. Brooke could not remember a time when she felt so inspired and content. Mitch had spoken to Bill not long after their return. He was open to the possibilities and suggested that Mitch bring in some of her work. She had also been encouraged to bring a sample to the couples Bible study they had begun attending. Mitch mentioned her project after the meeting one night and learned that one of their members was active in the Orlando Museum of Art.

With ten portraits of the orphanage children finished, she was now ready to begin portraits of the children she had photographed on the streets. The contrast of the two sets of paintings would surely tell the story without a word said. Surveying the photographs, she selected a small boy, perhaps three and dressed in nothing but a shirt too large for him but adequate to cover his bare body. In his hand, he held a stick that he used to stir up a puddle in the street that smelled of sewer. His hair, matted and uncut, hung over one eye and he turned to give Brooke a curious look as she knelt to capture him on film. There was dirt-smudge smeared to the uncovered eye with the back of a dirty hand. Stains and discoloration, from the filth of his surroundings, covered his shirt, his bare feet protruding from underneath. His skin was dark brown from constant exposure to the outdoors, and a sore marked his arm where he had been injured and left untreated in unsanitary conditions. Most predominant were his eyes, huge and black as coal…and empty. Empty of emotion, recognition, fear, or love. He was already numb to the cruel life he had been dealt. Brooke's eyes filled as she recalled that day. She longed to sweep up this little one and carry him off to a better life. But there were so many, she couldn't begin to make a dent. Which is why I need to raise the money for more orphanages she thought as she replaced the other photos in an envelope. She slipped the chosen child into her bag with her painting supplies and headed for her favorite park.

In the months to come, Brooke's project became a success beyond their expectations. With the help of Victor, from their Bible study group, the Orlando Museum of Art had given her three showings. The response had been overwhelming and she was now in demand. They prayed for direction and divided up her earnings to cover her painting supplies, a small portion to add to their budget, and the remainder sent for the support of new and existing orphanages.

It was mid-December and Brooke was nearing completion of another set of paintings to be shown the week before Christmas. The coldest hearts softened during the Christmas season and they were hoping her paintings would command a higher price with an outpouring of generosity. Mitch was on his last run before Christmas, getting gifts, food, clothing and Christmas mail to their friends in Colombia. Between Brooke, her mother and Janet, a large variety of Christmas delicacies from their kitchens had gone to Roger and Mary Ann. They were not living in affluence. The majority of her earnings went to the orphanages, but her work gave them a more comfortable life and she was content. The greatest reward was to realize her dream to paint and be recognized for her talent. The fact that it brought new life to helpless children was the bonus that took it over the top.

Chapter Twenty-Five

Brooke scrutinized the last painting in the collection she would be showing when the phone rang. She grimaced at the interruptions and raced to reach it before it stopped ringing.

"Brooke." Bill's voice sounded heavy on the other end and her breath caught.

"Bill—?"

"We've just had word…we don't have details yet. Mitch's plane went down."

A flash of blinding pain seared through her body and her heart pounded in her throat. "Nooooo—"

"Honey, it doesn't mean he's lost. He went down off the coast of Venezuela on his way back."

"Why—what—"

"We don't know the cause yet. We just know that he radioed the closest airport. He said something about an aircraft coming in his direction and not responding to his communication. We've already got search planes scanning the area and our Atlanta crew is headed for the coast to search on land."

She sank to the floor and leaned her head back against the kitchen door while tears ran down her cheeks.

"Do you have anyone close by? Someone to stay with you?"

"My…parents…are in…Clearwater. The kids…are w…with them."

"Do you want me to call them?"

She couldn't think beyond her husband.

"Brooke, should I come over there?"

"No…no…I'll call them."

"If you're sure. I'll check back with you in a while. I don't want you to be alone."

Brooke didn't answer.

"I'll let you know, first thing...anything we find out."

"Okay."

"Make sure you call your folks as soon as we hang up."

"I...I...will."

"Brooke, God is with him. Just keep praying that we'll find him soon."

Brooke let the receiver drop to her lap and cried out with the wail of a wounded animal. She cried until she was spent and had no more.

"What am I going to do? He's got to be alive...they've got to find him." Mechanically, she picked up the receiver and dialed the familiar number.

"Mama—" was all she could manage as she began to cry again.

"Sweetheart, what is it?"

"Mitch—"

"What about Mitch...Brooke?"

"His...plane went down."

"Oh, Brooke, is he—"

"They don't know yet, Mama. He can't be...he...just can't...be—

"I'll call Papa. We'll be there as soon as we can."

"But—"

"I'll call Emma. She'll take McKenzie and Conner. There's no need to alarm McKenzie. Get yourself busy. Make some tea—and pray, Brooke. We must ask God to protect him."

"Okay, Mama." She hung up the phone, went to the living room, curled up in a chair and waited for her mama and papa.

A massive search, on both land and sea for forty-eight hours, proved fruitless. A cold front came through and heavy raindrops pelted the roof and windows of their home. Ominous, dark clouds rolled across the sky while gusts of wind blew the branches of the large oak tree against the roof. Brooke sat listlessly in the large leather chair listening to the storm and the sound of traffic with tires singing on the wet pavement. Memories flooded her mind. The first Christmas when she met Mitch at the Schoope's, and when he suddenly came back into her life at church. The hours they'd spent talking on the porch of her apartment or in his jeep. The first time he'd taken her to the farm. Their weekend on the beach when she first discovered she was pregnant with McKenzie. What a kind, thoughtful husband she had and how much he loved God. How could God take such a man who was serving him? He couldn't, she resolved. She knew it in her heart. He was somewhere out there waiting for them to find him. She refused to let her mind wander to possibilities and the dangers he might be facing. All of Annie's attempts to persuade Brooke to go back to Clearwater had fallen on deaf ears. She needed to be here, close to her life with Mitch.

Church friends had been calling and coming by with food, words of comfort and prayer. Lisa called several times and was ready to fly out whenever Brooke gave the word. Victor stopped in to pick up her paintings for the show that would go on as planned without her. Even in her numbed state, she was grateful for friends and family who were willing to handle the things she could not.

197

Carl touched his daughter's shoulder bringing her back from her thoughts. "Brooke, we need to take you back to Clearwater."

She began shaking her head in protest.

"I know you want to be here but you have babies who need their mama, and I need to get back to the store. We don't want to leave you alone and we need to get back."

A tear trickled down her cheek. "Papa, what if they call and I'm not here. I just feel closer to him in our house."

Her father pulled her into his arms and held her close. "Honey, if there was any way I could take your pain I would do it in a minute." He stroked her back and held her close to him. "I know how you feel, but it doesn't matter where you are. Mitch will know you are pulling for him." She cried quietly in the strength of her father's arms. "You're babies' need you now and they don't understand what's going on."

"He's coming back, Papa...he's coming back—"

He laid his cheek against the top of her head. "You know we're praying for that. Go in and put your things together while I call Bill to make sure he has our number. I'll tell your mama to get ready and we can be home before dinner."

Brooke pulled from her father's embrace. "All right. I'll just be a few minutes."

Carl looked in their directory and dialed Bill's number. "Bill, Carl here."

"Carl, I was just about to call."

"You have news?"

"Well, not anything great."

Carl's heart sank "What is it."

"They've located Mitch's aircraft in the trees at the edge of a beach in Venezuela. There's no sign of Mitch."

"What does this mean?"

"We're fairly certain that Mitch's plane was shot down. He could be held captive or he could've been thrown from the plane and they just haven't discovered his body. There's the possibility that he was able to parachute to a place where he was undetected. In any case, Carl, it doesn't look good."

"I see." Carl placed his forearm against the door frame for support but kept his voice even to avoid alarming Brooke with anything she might overhear. "We're getting ready to take Brooke back to Clearwater with us. I wanted to make sure you have our phone number. She needs to be with the children and we didn't want to leave them here alone."

"I wish I had better news for you. I have your number right here and we'll be in touch with anything we find out."

"Thanks, Bill, we know you're doing your best." He hung up the receiver and looked up at his wife.

"Carl—?"

He shook his head. "Go ahead and get our things together."

Her eyes filled. "Dead?"

"No. Let's get Brooke home and settled first. Then I can fill you in with the details."

Annie quickly wiped her eyes and went to pack up the few things they grabbed before coming to Orlando.

Brooke's sleep was fitful and, only in the early morning hours had she fallen into a deeper sleep. She awoke with a start and a feeling of alarm as she became aware of her surroundings, and the reason behind it. She slid out of bed and fell to her knees. "Oh, Father, I can't live without Mitch. Lord we were doing so well. I know I was wrong in what I did to Mitch, but

I've been painting for your children in Colombia. Why, why do you punish me? Oh, God, I know I don't deserve your love, a woman who would kill her baby. When will I stop paying for that terrible mistake? Why punish everyone else for what I've done? Please don't take my children's father. Lord, I love him so much. Please, please let him live."

Annie was passing Brooke's door and heard her crying. She found her daughter with her knees pulled to her chest, rocking while she sobbed. Annie went to the floor and pulled Brooke to her breast. When Brooke's crying quieted, she sat back and looked at her daughter.

"Brooke, what do you think Mitch would want you to be doing right now?"

"What?"

"Do you think he would want you to be sitting around as if he was already dead?"

Brooke wiped her eyes with her arm. "No, I guess not."

"Don't you think he would want you to trust the Lord?"

"Yes—"

"And what about his children, don't you think he would want you to be caring for them?"

She nodded her head.

"Your babies are in the kitchen with Papa. Why don't you go down and have some breakfast with them"

"Okay."

"Then you can take them to the beach. There will be lots of shells after the storm. McKenzie will love that, and the fresh air will do all of you some good."

"But what if they call?"

"Do you think we would not come get you? Sitting around here waiting for the phone to ring is not going to bring you news any sooner, and it is causing some alarm for McKenzie."

"I didn't realize."

"My child, do you think she doesn't sense something is wrong. She's old enough to know when you're upset."

"I...I just didn't think. I...Mitch is all I can think about, Mama. I'm so afraid for him. I don't know how I can live without him."

"Shush, shush, you can do all things through Christ who strengthens you, even things you don't believe you can do. Mitch is in the Lord's hands."

Brooke wiped her face with her hands and nodded. "All right, Mama. I guess it would be good for McKenzie. She loves the beach and maybe it will get my mind off of Mitch for a little while."

Annie hugged her again. "Now wash your face and go down to the kitchen with a smile for your little ones and reassure McKenzie that her mother is okay."

Chapter Twenty-Six

$\mathcal{B}$rooke stared through her kitchen window into their backyard. The hibiscus was a bold display of red and salmon pink blossom. Impatiens splashed color along the wood fence surrounding the yard while bougainvillea covered the roof of the garage and boasted a blanket of magenta. It seemed odd there could be such beauty and life continued, as though nothing out of the ordinary had happened. It was over two months since Mitch's plane went down. The coffee brewed beside her as her children slept in the room nearby. Morning sun gave the room a warm glow, promising another beautiful day. Brooke sighed and poured herself a cup of coffee, pulled her robe about her, grabbed her Bible and tip-toed out to the front porch.

A peace came over her as she read from the Psalms. "Thank, you Lord, you've made your presence known to me this morning. Please show me what to do. I need some direction. Give me strength to face the future ahead and do what's right for my children." She gazed out across the front yard and down the street where the oak tree limbs dipped to the ground. Since her escapade to Arizona and the trip to Colombia, they had been happy in their little home. She was enveloped in a kind of serenity, here in familiar surroundings.

Christmas had been dismal with their celebration shrouded in fear for Mitch's safety. For the children's sake, they'd opened gifts with fabricated gaiety and feasted on food that was tasteless in Brooke's mouth. Roland and Janet drove over on Christmas Eve to bring presents for the children and Brooke, but could not be persuaded to stay. Mitch's brother, Peter and his wife Megan were expected in from New York that evening.

Brooke insisted on returning home after Christmas. Jack and Lisa, home for the holidays, made arrangements to bring in the New Year with Brooke. Lisa and Brooke put together a pot of spaghetti and a salad while Jack entertained Conner and McKenzie. Once the children were in bed, they settled in for an evening of favorite old movies. At the stroke of midnight, Jack led them in prayer.

"Mighty God and Father, you love Mitch more than any of us. You know where he is, and your hand is on him. God we can't begin to understand your ways. We only know that you are sovereign. We trust you with Mitch. Whether in life or death, we know we'll see him again. Father, I pray you'll give Brooke strength, peace and wisdom now...and in the days ahead. Help her to care for these precious children that are a gift from you. Lord, we don't know what the next year will bring for this family, but we know that you care...that you care very much. Lord, let others see what a difference you make in the lives of your children. May there be good come from this tragedy that Satan meant for a stumbling block. And it is through these things that we get a glimpse of what you sacrificed in your son, Jesus Christ. Thank you, Lord, for loving us so much."

Jack's prayer brought a great peace to Brooke's heart and the two women spent another hour talking after Jack went to bed.

"Even if Mitch is alive, Brooke, if he's held captive...it could be a long time before his release."

"I'm beginning to realize that, the longer this goes on. It's just that—well, if he's being held hostage, why haven't they demanded something?"

"Who knows what motivates them."

Brooke sighed, grateful for her dear friend to confide her deepest thoughts. "This is why I was afraid for Mitch to fly missions."

"I know you were, but God touched his heart for those children."

"Yes, they won my heart, too. It's just that—"

"Now your children are possibly without a father. Orphaned for the sake of orphans."

Brooke nodded and choked back tears. It amazed her that there were any tears left. She took a deep breath.

"Not knowing, that's the hard part. It would make my decisions so much easier. I don't know, Lisa. I have this feeling he's still alive and out there somewhere trying to get back to us."

"I wish I could encourage you in that but the longer the time—"

"For now, that hope is what keeps me going. I know I have to make some decisions but I'm not ready to write him off yet."

"I would be disappointed in you if you did. Will you keep on painting for the mission?"

"I don't see how I can do anything else. It's almost like keeping Mitch alive by keeping his mission going." Brooke laughed. "Besides, how can I not paint? It's who I am."

Lisa leaned over and squeezed Brooke's hand. "Yes, it is. I always knew you would be famous someday."

Brooke was brought back from her reverie by the sound of little feet.

"McKenzie, Mama's out here." She laughed as the curly head popped around the screen door. "Come here my beautiful girl, come sit with Mama."

McKenzie ran to her, crawled into her mother's lap and snuggled up in her arms. Brooke kissed the top of her head.

"Is Conner awake?"

McKenzie nodded.

"What's he doing?"

"Sitting in his bed, playing wiff his toy."

"Would you like to go for a picnic today at the park?"

McKenzie's eyes grew wide. "I can go on the swings?"

"Yes, of course. You can go on all the things in the park."

"But not the spinning wheel." She shook her head vigorously. She got sick to her stomach when Mitch spun her around, and she was adamantly opposed to ever venturing on that piece of equipment again.

Brooke laughed. "No, not the spinning wheel. I won't put you on the spinning wheel." She gave her a squeeze. "C'mon, let's go get Conner out of bed and make some breakfast. Then we'll go to the park."

McKenzie jumped from her lap and ran ahead. Brooke was headed for the kitchen with Conner on her hip when the phone rang.

"Now who could that be?" she said to Conner and he grinned as he bounced in her arms.

"Hello."

"Brooke, Vic here."

"Oh, hi Vic. What's up?"

"I need to stop by for a bit if you're going to be home."

"We're headed for the park, but it will take us a while to get ready. What time did you plan to come over?"

"I'm ready to leave now; I can be there within the hour."

"Sounds great. I'll see you then."

205

Brooke was certain it had something to do with her paintings. She quickly dressed and made the children's breakfast. She knew her show had gone on but hadn't spoken to Vic since Mitch's disappearance. She was just cleaning jelly from McKenzie's hands and face when she heard him calling through the open door.

"We're in the kitchen, come on in." She went to the door to greet him, not too far from keeping an eye on Conner in his high chair.

"How are you doing?" He gave her a hug.

"I'm doing better," she said, glad to see their old friend.

He tossed his briefcase into a chair and tousled the top of McKenzie's head.

"Hey 'Kenzie." He reached down for her and tossed her in the air. McKenzie squealed in delight while Conner kicked his legs and pounded his table top. Vic held McKenzie in his arms. "How's my girl?"

"We're going to the park."

"You're going to the park. What are you going to do there?"

"Going on the swings, and the slide, but not the spinning wheel." She shook her head for emphasis.

"Not the spinning wheel." He laughed. "I don't like the spinning wheel either."

Still holding McKenzie, he reached into his briefcase and handed Brooke an envelope.

"This is from your last show. It's a sizable amount, Brooke. People are recognizing and buying your work."

Brooke's jaw dropped as she pulled out a check for thirty-four thousand, five hundred dollars. "Oh—"

"I know you planned for most of this to go to the orphanages, but I think you should consider keeping a good portion for yourself."

Brooke looked at him, not sure what to say.

"I know you're hoping Mitch will return, we're all praying for that. But in the meantime, I'm sure you have expenses."

"Well, the Missions Group in Atlanta has been sending some."

"But not nearly enough and I doubt they will be able to continue that indefinitely."

"Roland has been helping out too."

"That's good but, as much as you don't want to, you've got to start thinking about how you are going to manage if they don't find Mitch. You have great family support but you'll to want to stand on your own eventually."

Brooke gazed out the window, not wanting to hear what he was saying but knowing there was truth in his words.

"You might consider branching out in your subject matter. People recognize your name and, at this point, you will easily sell anything you choose to paint."

"What do you mean?"

"Well, instead of painting only Colombian children, begin painting other subjects like the farm where Mitch's parents live or the gulf...whatever interests you. I love your painting of the water lilies."

"Oh, I could never sell that. It's Mitch's favorite."

"You don't need to, Brooke. Just do some things that are similar. Your own children would make beautiful subjects. Then the money that comes in from the Colombian paintings can continue to go to the ministry, and your other works can provide you with an income."

Could this be God speaking to her? She wrestled with the thought before answering. "I suppose I could. It just seems so final. Like I'm closing the door on my life with Mitch."

"Not at all, you'll make him proud for the way you've taken care of your family until he returns."

She looked at the check again. "Let me think about this Vic. I need to pray and ask God what He wants." She took a deep breath. "I've been asking God to give me wisdom and show me what I should do. Maybe He's giving me an answer."

With Vic gone, she slipped the envelope into her purse and began making a small lunch for their picnic. She would run to the bank and deposit her check for safe keeping until she could determine how it would be spent. In the meantime, she had promised her daughter a nice day and she intended to keep that promise. McKenzie missed her papa and there was no way to explain his absence. She couldn't tell her that Papa was in heaven. They didn't know that for sure. She would surely be confused when her Papa walked in the door one day.

"Lord, there isn't anything about this that's easy." She loaded up the car. They deserved a day of fun, and she was going to make sure that nothing interfered.

Chapter Twenty-Seven

It was a good message in church and sweet fellowship with friends. Vic and Ruth offered to take them to lunch and Brooke thankfully accepted the offer. It was always difficult to go home on Sundays without her beloved husband. Sitting around black iron tables under the shade of large old oaks, they leisurely sampled a variety of Greek delicacies. Small gyros, stuffed cabbage rolls, marinated cold salmon and a salad of tomatoes, olives and cucumbers seasoned with fruity olive oil and vinegar. With a small tray of fresh fruit and cheese to finish, they had discussed the details of her next show. She'd found a new excitement in combining her painting efforts to accomplish both the mission and support for herself and her children.

Now, stretched out on the couch, Brooke reveled in the luxury of a Sunday afternoon nap while her children were resting. She had barely dozed off when the phone rang. She raced to answer before the children were wakened and her hour of quiet dissolved.

"Hello," she spoke softly.

There was nothing but static on the other end. Great, all she needed was a prankster.

"Hello!"

"Brooke—" she heard the faint but unmistakable voice. Her legs wilted beneath her and she slid down the door frame to the floor. Tears welled. "Mitch, you're alive!"

"Yes honey, I'm very much alive."

"Where are you—what—are you okay?"

"I'm not the best I've ever been but they tell me I'll live. I've been held captive—got away—rescued by fishermen." The static continued and broke up his conversation.

"Oh, I've prayed and prayed. I knew in my heart you were still alive."

"I love you, Babe. I can't wait to get home."

"When are you coming?"

"I need you to call Bill—give him—phone number—the information he needs to pick me up in Caracas."

"Is that where you are now?"

"Staying with some good people—saved my life—wanted to call you first Brooke—didn't want you—second hand."

Brooke swallowed hard.

"Call Bill for me?"

"Are you kidding? I want you home as fast as he can get you here."

"Me too—" The static threatened to cut them off. "Write this number."

Brooke scrambled for a pen and paper and took down the information.

"Listen, honey—you everything—get back. I can't—this phone very long."

"All right, I love you Mitch."

"Love you too."

Brooke's hands trembled as she dialed Bill's number.

"Betty, this is Brooke. Is Bill there?"

"Why no dear, he's on his way to the airport. He's taking a flight out this afternoon."

"Oh no, I have to reach him. I got a call from Mitch—he's alive."

210

"Praise the Lord! When did you hear?"

"I just got off the phone with him. He asked me to call Bill and give him the information so he can pick him up in Caracas."

"I'm sure you can reach him at the airport. Do you have the number of the office there?"

"Let me just check...Yes, I have it. I'll fill you in on the details later."

She dialed the number and listened for the ring...two times...three times...five times...

"C'mon Bill, you can't be gone yet." She was about to hang up when a voice, out of breath, came on the line.

"Yeah?"

"Hello, I'm Brooke Harris. I've got to talk to Bill."

"He was taking a flight out this afternoon. I don't know if he's still here."

"Please! I've got to talk to him, this is an emergency!"

"Hold on."

Brooke paced back and forth as far as the cord would allow. "Please Lord, please. I've waited three months for this, don't let Bill be gone."

"Hello."

"Bill, Mitch is alive."

"Brooke?"

"Yes. Mitch just called me. He's in Caracas and he needs you to bring him home."

"In Caracas? Is that where he's been? Is he alright?"

"I don't have all the details. We had a bad connection and he couldn't talk long. The only thing I know is that he's been held captive and managed to get away. He mentioned some fisherman had rescued him.

211

Bill laughed. "This is the best news I've had in a long time! Where do I pick him up?"

"I've got a phone number to call and I guess they'll give you the details."

"Wait a minute, let me grab something to write on…okay, go ahead."

Brooke repeated the phone number she had so carefully written down.

"I want to be at the airport when you get there. Bill. How will I know?"

"I'll radio in far enough ahead for someone to give you a call."

"Do you have any idea?"

"Well, as long as we don't have any red tape, I imagine we'll be back here by tomorrow, maybe early afternoon."

"Tomorrow! I thought I would see him tonight."

"I don't see how we can make it any sooner. By the time I get down there, it will be too late to head back. After what happened to Mitch, I don't like the idea of a night flight."

"Bill, let me go with you."

"I don't know Brooke."

"Please, Bill, I've got my passport. Remember when I went to Colombia with Mitch? I've waited for three long months. I want to see him today."

"Well, it's against my better judgment."

"Bless you! I'll call a friend to stay with McKenzie and Conner. I'll be at the airport as soon as possible."

"You've got time. I'll need to get a replacement to take the run I was getting ready to make, and I'll need to file a new flight plan."

"Thank you so much. I promise I won't be a problem."

Brooke dialed again, "Mama Susanne."

"Brooke, honey."

"Mama Suzanne, Mitch is alive."

"Oh! Bless your heart that's good news."

"I need a big favor."

"Of course sugar, what do you need?"

"I'm going with Bill to pick up Mitch in Caracas, and I need someone to keep McKenzie and Conner."

"Don't say another word darlin', I'm on my way. You just get yourself ready and don't worry about a thing. We'll be here waiting when you bring him home."

Two more calls to make. She hated to take the time but she couldn't leave without letting their mother's know.

"Janet, I've just heard from Mitch."

There was silence on the other end.

"Janet?"

"Yes—" she choked.

"He's in Caracas, some fishermen rescued him."

"Is he alright?"

"He sounded tired, but I think he's okay. We couldn't talk long and our connection wasn't good."

"Thank you Jesus. When—?"

"I'm flying down with Bill this afternoon. He said that, barring any red tape, we should be back by tomorrow afternoon."

"What about the children?"

"I've called Mama Suzanne and she's on the way over."

"Of course…but we want to be there when you arrive."

213

"We'll radio ahead and someone will call you in plenty of time."

"I just can't believe it, after all this time."

"I know." Both women were in tears. "I've got to call Mama and get to the airport."

"All right honey, we'll be waiting. Just bring him home."

The hum of the engines droned on in the small aircraft as it headed north with its precious cargo. Sitting next to her husband, she clung to his hand, afraid to sleep in the event she'd wake and find it all a dream. She watched him sleeping, studying every familiar line in his face, now thin from poor nutrition and care. His auburn hair was nearly strawberry blond from the sun and his skin was tanned to a golden brown. A tear escaped as she recalled their reunion.

Luis met them at the airport. They zigzagged through narrow streets before pulling into an alley and parked outside a wall that surrounded a modest home. Luis jumped from the car to open her door.

"You come." He smiled broadly and led them indoors. Luis was obviously a romantic and anxious to present his surprise. She found Mitch stretched out on a small couch. She quietly knelt beside her sleeping husband and kissed his forehead. Mitch's eyes fluttered open to see his wife smiling at him with tears running down her cheeks.

"Brooke—how—what—?"

Closing his arms around her and pulling her to himself he cried, unable to speak. Stroking her hair, he whispered in her ear, "How I've dreamed of this day. I love you so much. I can't believe you're here."

Brooke was beyond controlling her tears. "I love you so. I couldn't wait for Bill to bring you back."

"I know, I'm so sorry, I couldn't let you know."

"I would wait for you forever."

They were oblivious of the bleary-eyed group that watched their reunion. Suddenly remembering, Brooke pulled away from Mitch. "There's someone else here who's really glad to see you."

Bill came forward, his eyes glistening with unshed tears. Mitch slowly got to his feet and Bill pulled him into a hug and slapped his back. "Hey buddy, it's sure good to see you alive and kickin'"

"Bill, sure appreciate you coming to get me and bringing the love of my life."

He turned to the group still waiting in the room. "I want you to meet some fine folk here. I guess you've met Luis and this is his wife Maria, their sons Andres and Herrera. I owe my life to them." Everyone smiled and shook hands.

"What happened, Buddy?" Bill pulled up a chair next to Mitch who was still clutching Brooke's hand as she sat close to him on the couch.

"I was shot down, Bill. I didn't get a clear view of the aircraft but it was evident he was chasing me. Whether I was mistaken for someone else, I don't know but they were determined I was going down. As soon as I knew I was hit, I got into my parachute and got out of there. I was in the drink for a couple of hours when a speed boat came along to fish me out. It turned out to be part of the group that shot me down. They hauled me off to the jungle where I was kept under constant guard. They tried to get a name out of me. I guess they were looking for someone to hold up for ransom. I refused to give them anything,

215

and I guess my wallet was lost while I was in the water. After a while they pretty much left me alone except for a single guard. I managed to slip out one night and they either considered me a lost cause or I outmaneuvered them. Anyway, when I came out on shore, Luis and his family were there fishing. Fortunately, Luis speaks a little English and I managed to explain my situation. They hid me in their boat until that night and then moved me here to their house."

"Amazing. God's hand has sure been on you." Bill wiped a rough hand across his face. "So what's your status? Are you okay to leave?"

"Thanks to Luis, you bet I am. He's called the authorities and got me cleared to go. I guess you guys made such a ruckus looking for me, they didn't want to provoke any kind of incident. They didn't give me much of a runaround."

"Considering what happened to you, Mitch, I didn't really want to do a night flight. Is there a place we can stay and leave first thing in the morning?"

"Here," Luis gave them a broad smile. "You can stay here and tomorrow I take you to the airport."

The accommodations were tight but the fellowship and celebration were warm as Brooke became acquainted with the family who had saved the life of her precious Mitch.

Chapter Twenty-Eight

Mitch was regaining strength every day. His breath came hard as he walked the hills of the farm, but the view at the top was worth it.

He sat down to take it all in. "How you have blessed me, Lord," he whispered as he gazed at the natural beauty of his childhood home. The blue sky was softened by billowy, white clouds touched with hues of grey, pink and yellow as the sun began it's descent into the horizon. The meadows were an intense green and the trees vibrant with color in the warm glow of the afternoon. Splashes of yellow flowers bobbed their heads in the breeze.

He had some difficult decisions to make. Even in the midst of being shot down, he didn't think about leaving the mission field. Brooke, on the other hand, was adamant he find other employment. She argued that his mission wouldn't be abandoned as long as she was painting for the support of the orphanage. He was so proud of how she'd coped with his capture, and established herself in the world of art. His wife was not only beautiful; she was a survivor and a fighter. *Do I have a right to put her through more anxiety?* He stretched out on his back, laced his fingers behind his head and gazed at the glorious sunset before him. The sun, now a bright red-orange, spilled out over the clouds in fingers of brilliant hues. He filled his lungs with the cool fresh air.

"How can anyone doubt you, Lord, with so much beauty around us?"

He knew he had other career options. His father showed signs of aging, even more pronounced since his return. But, as much as he loved this place, making it his life's work just didn't feel right. Curiously, he'd received a phone call from Jack a few days ago.

"Mitch."

"Hey buddy."

"You gave us quite a scare."

He collapsed into a chair, glad for a conversation with his friend. "I know. Thanks for being here for Brooke."

"We didn't do all that much. I wish we could have been there longer."

"She told me about your New Year's. It meant a lot."

Jack chuckled. "We're just glad you're back in one piece." Jack paused for a moment before speaking again. "Besides being glad to have your sorry hide back, I have a question for you. Do you plan to continue flying for missions?"

Mitch sighed. "That's a decision I'm struggling with."

"You remember our CEO, John Wise?"

"Sure, nice fellow. We had quite a visit on the way home from Arizona."

"Apparently you made quite an impression. He heard about your rescue and asked me if you'd consider flying for him."

Mitch hesitated. *Where was this going?* "What about the pilot he has now?"

"Had a heart attack last week. He has to give up flying."

"Tough! Hard for a pilot to hang it up."

"That's what I was thinking, buddy. I don't even have to ask how Brooke feels about you going back."

Mitch laughed. "You're right on there, and she's got my mother backing her up."

"Thought this might be a compromise she could live with."

He rubbed his forehead. *Another possibility?* "It's certainly something to consider."

"I know you're not into the materialism thing but the pay would be substantial."

He stared out the window. *Could this be God opening doors?* "I've been praying for the Lord to show me what to do. Brooke has been a champ but—"

"Yeah, there's a limit. I know this is a tough one for you, my friend. I just thought it was worth throwing out there. I'll be praying for you to know the right way to go."

Reflecting on that conversation, Mitch prayed. *Is this your answer, Lord.* He knew he couldn't ask any more of Brooke. *Maybe you're offering me this position. You know my heart, Lord, and you know my wife's limitations.* The sun was barely peeping over the horizon as Mitch headed back to the house. *I guess I can find a mission field where ever I work as long as I keep my eyes on you.*

Walking up to the farm in near darkness, he could see lights coming from the barn. He stuck his head in the door and called out. "Hello, anyone in here?"

"Back here," his dad called back.

He found his dad in the stall with Brooke's mare, Lady. "What's up?"

"She's getting ready to foal and things aren't going right." His dad's expression told Mitch he was concerned. "Reed is on his way. Wouldn't you know he'd be in town when she decided to start?"

Reed was the resident veterinarian who lived on the property. As a teenager, Mitch spent many all-nighters with him and, at one time, considered the profession. Mitch squatted down and brushed the mare's neck to calm her. She seemed to relax under his touch and they sat back to wait for the next wave.

The two men sat quiet for a while, but Mitch knew he needed to talk about his future. "Been thinking about what I'm going to do with the rest of my life."

"That right."

"Guess it's pretty obvious that Brooke isn't going to tolerate any more trips to South America."

"Can't say that I blame her, son." He felt the mare's belly as she whinnied. "I'd say that's pretty much the way we all feel. We thought we'd lost you for sure."

Mitch grimaced. He hated the ordeal he knew his family had been through. "I know. It was hard for everyone."

His father's eyes met his. "So, what have you decided?"

"Well, I had an interesting call from Jack." Mitch picked up a piece of straw and wound it around his finger. "His CEO would like to talk to me about going to work for him, flying his Leer jet for meetings and travel."

Roland sighed. "I was hoping you would settle down here."

He felt his throat tighten. *Why couldn't he just give in and do this for his father?* "I know you were, Dad, but I'm just not ready to take this on full time. I love flying too much. But, I would have more free time to help you out."

His father's face was heavy with disappointment. "I would appreciate that. This business is beginning to wear me down."

Mitch watched his father for a while. He moved slower and his eyes told the story. With his dad's mortality staring him in the face he knew he couldn't delay any longer.

"Dad, there's something I need to ask you."

"What's that?"

Mitch shifted his weight to look directly at him. "Well, Dad, I don't know for sure...I mean...has there ever been a time when you prayed and asked God to forgive your sins and come into your heart?"

Mitch saw a mix of emotions flash across his father's face before he lowered his head. "No, son, I haven't and it has been on my mind ever since the phone call that your plane was down."

"Why then?"

"I was afraid if I didn't see you again in this lifetime I wouldn't see you in the next."

Mitch scooted closer to his dad. "Wouldn't you like to make sure that you will?"

Roland looked up at him.

"Let's pray right now, Dad. Let's secure your place in heaven right here and now."

The two men bowed their heads and Mitch placed his hand on his dad's shoulder.

"God, you know I've been pretending all these years." Roland started. "And I've never asked you to be my savior. Well, I'm asking now. I'm asking you to forgive me for the way I've sinned against you and for the way I've fooled people into believing I was a Christian. I do believe you came to earth to save the world and I'm asking you to be my Savior. And Lord, thank you for this son of mine. Amen."

The two men hugged while they laughed, moisture filling the lines around their eyes. "Why didn't I ask you about this a long time ago?"

"Probably because I was too stubborn to listen. I had to almost lose you before I came to my senses."

"What's going on?" Reed stepped into the barn. "Did she foal yet?"

"No, you've got a long night ahead of you."

"Let's take a look and see what she's doing."

Roland patted Reed's shoulder. "Now that you're here to take over we're going up to the house for some dinner. Can I bring you something to eat?"

"Naw, I grabbed something when I got home. From your message, I figured I would have my hands full when I got here."

"I'll be back out to help you." Mitch slapped Reed on the back. "Don't want anything to happen to Brooke's horse."

"Thanks, I can use the company. Looks like this is going to take a while."

They pulled on to Interstate 4 after their first social event at the home of John Wise, Mitch's new boss.

"What did you think?" Mitch said.

Brooke grinned. "Their house is gorgeous. I can't even imagine living like that."

"That too, but what did you think of Mallory and the rest of the group?"

"I like Mallory," she hesitated for a second, "and most of the others were nice enough."

"But not all—"

"Well, I'm afraid I didn't impress Summer very much. She looked like she'd swallowed a bug when I told her you used to fly missions."

Mitch busted out laughing. "I'm afraid we're going to run into that. These are not Christian people and we'll have to consider this our new mission field."

222

"I felt just awful. Like I had blown it for you."

"Hey, hey, sweetie, whether Summer approves of us or not, it won't make any difference to my job performance." Mitch patted her knee. "More importantly, we don't have to be ashamed of loving God and serving Him. If they have a problem with that, I can always take over the farm. I'm not desperate for this job."

Brooke bit her lip. She didn't want to discourage him right out of the gate. "I guess you're right. I was just concerned about making a good impression for your sake."

He reached over and squeezed her hand. "Honey, anyone who's not impressed with you is just not worth my time or worry.

Brooke gave him a crooked smile. "You're just prejudiced."

Chapter Twenty-Nine

With both children fed and busy playing, Brooke started the laundry and began cleaning the breakfast dishes. Oh for a maid, she thought, remembering their evening at John and Mallory's. Mitch left that morning to take John and several members of top management to Phoenix. He would be gone several days and staying with Jack and Lisa. Brooke was a bit melancholy that she couldn't be part of their reunion. At least she'd be able to start a new project. Since her last show, she'd thrown herself into being a full time wife and mother. She looked forward to a new challenge. She grabbed a towel to dry her hands, and started to check on the children when the phone rang.

"Brooke, Mallory Wise."

"Oh! Mallory." A charge of fear ran through her. Did she blow it already?

"I'm playing tennis at the club this morning and I wondered if you could meet me for lunch afterwards, my treat."

"That would be wonderful but...I'll have to see if I can get someone to watch McKenzie and Conner."

"No need for that. There's a nursery for our members with small children. How does twelve-thirty sound?"

Brooke had to remind herself to breathe. "That sounds wonderful."

"I'll meet you in front of the club. Do you need directions?"

"Ah...yes." Brooke reached for the pen and notepad she kept close to the phone. "Okay, go ahead."

Mallory gave her directions as Brooke grappled with the awesome idea that she had been invited to lunch with her husband's boss's wife.

"I'll look forward to it." Mallory said.

Brooke stood, holding the phone, her mind in a whirl. What do I wear? Oh my gosh. Lunch with Mallory Wise. Oh, Lord, please don't let me blow this for Mitch.

Brooke basked in the opulence surrounding her. She and Mallory sat at a linen covered table, being served by an attentive waiter. It was a golf and tennis club and their table gave them an unobstructed view of the meticulously landscaped course.

"I must confess," Mallory said, as they finished their meal. "I had an ulterior motive in asking you here today."

Blood drained from Brooke's face, what had she done wrong?

"I was with Olivia the other day and she took me to her sister's home to show me one of your paintings."

"Oh—"

"You're a talented young woman."

Brooke's cheeks flushed. She was still uncomfortable with the notoriety of her work. "Thank you, but I'm afraid I get more pleasure from my work than anyone. I'm completely consumed when I'm working on a project."

"It shows, but let me tell you my idea. Our twenty-fifth anniversary is next month and I was thinking it would be lovely to have a portrait of John and me as a surprise for him."

"What a lovely idea, but how would we accomplish that without him knowing?"

"I have a photograph of the two of us while we were in the Greek Islands. Could you paint from that?"

"Of course. All my paintings of the Colombian children are from photographs. It makes it easier, actually. I don't have to deal with the subject sitting still."

Mallory laughed. "Quite right, and John would be far too restless." She pulled a photograph from her purse. "Do you think you can work with this?"

Brooke took the photograph and studied it. "This is beautiful." Brooke looked over the photograph at Mallory. "Did you want me to include the background, or just you and John?"

"What do you think?"

She was quickly drawn into the excitement of this new project and her creative senses were in full gear. "Well, it really depends on whether you want it to be formal or more casual."

"Hmmm...I believe, more casual. It was a wonderful trip for both of us with lots of special memories."

"Then let's include the background." Brooke's smile spread warmly across her face at the romance involved. "You can relive your memories every time you look at it."

"I can't tell you how much I appreciate this Brooke. I'll certainly pay you well, and I hope it's not an imposition."

"Not at all, I'll consider it an honor."

"No, consider it a special gift to a very grateful friend."

"Hello my love." Mitch was calling from Jack and Lisa's. "I called earlier but you must have been out."

Brooke could barely stand still. "You'll never guess where."

Mitch laughed. "I give up, where?"

"Mallory took me to lunch at the tennis club."

"Whoa, moving up in the world are we?"

"She's very nice, Mitch. Not anything like I expected."

226

"I'm glad you two are getting along so well."

"You'll never guess what else," she said with a large grin on her face, while she swung the phone cord around her finger.

"Nope, I still give up."

"She asked me to do a portrait of her and John. But you've got to keep that a secret," she hurriedly added. "She's giving it to him for their twenty-fifth anniversary."

"Wow, that's great, honey."

"I hope so. I can't tell you how nervous I am." She sat on a kitchen chair and stood just as quickly. "I mean, I'm nervous, and I'm excited. I've never been commissioned to do a painting before."

"So, what do you call all the paintings you've sold through the museum?" He laughed. "I have the utmost confidence in you, sweetie. You've already proven what a fabulous artist you are, and I knew it before the rest of the world."

How she loved this husband of hers. "Just keep telling me that, love. I need to hear it."

"You've got it babe." He made the sound of a kiss in the phone. "Now, I thought I would say hi to the kids and then I have orders to hand this phone over to a certain young woman who is threatening me if I take too long."

"I know. Lisa and I have hardly talked since you got back."

"I love you, Babe. I'll give you a call tomorrow night.

Brooke dove into her new assignment and used every free minute to work. Within two weeks she was ready to deliver it to Mallory. With inside information from Mitch, she knew John would be in New York for the day. She called Mallory as soon as she felt comfortable that John had left for the airport.

227

"Brooke, my dear, lovely to hear from you."

"I've finished your portrait, Mallory. I thought, since John is in New York today, it would be a good time to bring it over."

"Wonderful idea. I have a tennis commitment but I'll be back by one."

"Perfect."

"Come for lunch and bring the children. I so enjoy them." With help from the maid, Brooke managed to bring her children, and the rather large painting, to the sunroom. A table had been set for lunch. French doors opened up to the pool where wicker furniture and lush green plants created a tropical feel.

"I can go swimming." McKenzie declared. She had become an expert swimmer with their visits to the farm.

"Not today. We didn't bring your bathing suit and Mama needs to talk to Mrs. Wise."

"Please, I can swim in my shorts."

"McKenzie, listen to me. We're not going swimming today. If you continue to ask, Mama will have to take you back home."

"What's this?" Mallory surprised them. "McKenzie, you're not leaving already are you? We haven't had lunch?"

McKenzie looked up sheepishly and shook her head.

"Come along." She extended her hand. "We've got a chair all set up with some big cushions so you'll be up high with us."

McKenzie grinned, pleased at her special treatment, as the maid brought out a high chair for Conner.

With the children settled, Brooke pulled out the painting. "I hope you like it. I was pleased with the way it turned out."

Mallory's face lit up. "Brooke, this is wonderful. It's everything I wanted and more."

228

Brooke let out the breath she hadn't realized she was holding. "I'm glad. I wanted it to be special."

"Indeed it is. John is going to be so surprised." She turned from the painting and smiled at Brooke. "I would be prepared for a lot more work, my dear. Once my friends see this, they are going to be scrambling for a piece of your talent."

With lunch cleared, Brooke and Mallory visited comfortably, sharing their backgrounds and the courtships of their husbands. McKenzie was being entertained in the kitchen making cookies while Mallory held Conner, now asleep on her shoulder.

"I envy you Brooke," Mallory said as she stroked Conner's head.

She was caught completely by surprise. "Why would you envy me?"

"John and I always wanted children but they never came. You have a real treasure in your babies."

Now what should she say. "I didn't realize. I mean, not everyone wants children. I just assumed—"

Moisture glistened in the corners of her eyes. "Many people make the assumption it's our choice."

She was saddened at this woman's loss and wanted to bring her some comfort. "I'll share mine. How about that?"

"That's so sweet." She smiled as she patted Conner's back. "I'll hold you to that."

They sat quietly for a time while Mallory rocked Conner. Then as more of a thought than conversation, she said, "I've never been able to understand how anyone could abort a baby."

Brooke's heart stopped.

"I mean, if you don't want a child, give it up for adoption."

229

"Well...I guess...sometimes there are extenuating circumstances. They don't want anyone to know—"

"Brooke, surely with your missionary background, you're not defending them. After all, we're not living in the puritan ages. How difficult would it be to tolerate a few months of embarrassment?"

She was cut to the core. How could such a lovely day suddenly bring her ugly past crashing down around her? Accusing her once more of her murderous act. "Of course."

She kissed Conner's curly head. "Just look at him. How could anyone destroy something so perfect?"

Brooke barely spoke above a whisper. "You're right, there's no excuse. You have no idea how special my children are to me."

"I'm sure I don't, but I wish I'd had the opportunity."

"Oh, I didn't mean—" she stammered. She reached for a way out of her bumble. "Why didn't you adopt?"

She sighed. "John was afraid to take that chance. He didn't feel he could accept another man's child as his own."

That night, Brooke tossed in her bed with the afternoon's conversation playing and replaying in her head. *How anyone could abort a baby...surely you're not defending...for a few months of embarrassment.* No matter how hard she tried, the words kept slamming back into her brain. *Would this never end?*

Chapter Thirty

March, 2000

City lights were shining with the promise of glitter across the skyline, still showing in the dusk of early evening as they sped along the Cross-Town. Brooke gazed out the window of their Mercedes looking for a distraction from her troubled thoughts. The sky was ablaze with shades of pink, orange, blue and gray as the sun slipped slowly into the horizon. Florida skies displayed the most amazing sunsets. In the midst of this spectacular display, a small gray cloud hung so low it appeared as if you could reach out and touch it. That in itself was not unusual. She had seen many low hanging clouds, but this one was detached and set apart. Alone and suspended like a sad, lost lamb in the midst of all this beauty. *That's what I feel like, alone and suspended in the midst of this beautiful life. I don't know where I belong anymore. I'm not part of Mitch's world and I've lost the world where I used to belong.* She tried to shake the disturbing thoughts.

"What a beautiful sunset."

"Hmmm…" Mitch responded. She knew he never saw the beauty of nature from her perspective, alive and waiting to be reproduced on canvas. But he used to appreciate it as God's handiwork. He barely noticed his surroundings anymore or her for that matter. *When did they grow so far apart? Granted his work took him away too much but it had always been that way. At least he'd been actively involved with his family.*

The children, for all practical purposes were gone too. McKenzie had graduated from nursing school and was now working at Memorial. She was still living at home but, between work and friends, it was rare when they connected. She tried to ignore McKenzie's interest in becoming a missionary. Brooke wrote it off as an effort to please a young doctor who intended to go to India. Conner was away at Princeton with a major in business. *Ah, Conner, my beautiful young man.* He was brilliant and handsome like his father and would go far under the wing and influence of John Wise.

Mitch pulled into the circular drive of their opulent home to drop Brooke off at the front door and drove on to the garage. Inside, Brooke secured the lock on the door, absently dropped her bag into one of the chairs in the entry and headed for the kitchen. She started for a glass of wine and then thought otherwise. There had been enough to drink at dinner she decided, and put on some tea instead. She heard Mitch come in from the garage and go down the hall to the den. He would be there the remainder of the evening watching some kind of sports. Perhaps reading would be a distraction from her gloomy mood. She took a tray with the teapot and cup up to their room, changed into pajamas and settled into the chaise with a book she had purchased on a whim while shopping that afternoon.

She began reading. *"It was a cold rainy day in the south of England as Lisa stepped out of the local bakery shop for the long walk home…"* *Lisa,* she thought, *we were so close. How I would love to share a cup of coffee with you. Like the many we shared when we were in school.* She smiled to herself, fondly remembering those days. Lisa had been there for her so many times. Her teenage pregnancy and the years of remorse, her encounter with drug-using friends, her courtship with Mitch and Mitch's escape from death. She sighed. *Lisa, how shoddily I've treated you when you've been nothing but my best*

232

friend. She remembered their last conversation. It was preceded by a call from Emma.

"Brooke, I need to talk to you about something."

"What is it Emma? Is there something wrong with Mama or Papa?"

"Well, nothing serious. It's just that…well, I can really see Papa slowing down and not looking so great."

"That's to be expected, Em, I mean, he is getting older."

"Of course it is…my point being…well, Brooke…I…uh…I guess I'll just have to come right out and say it. You don't come over to see them much anymore. They miss you Brooke, and Papa, well he just looks sad that he doesn't see you or his grandchildren. Mama is heartbroken."

"That's not entirely accurate; I was over there last Easter."

"Exactly, Brooke. You haven't visited them since last Easter."

"Look, it's not easy for me. Between all the kid's activities and the hours that Mitch works. Not to mention the hours I have to put in with my painting. I mean…I have three people waiting for portraits now."

Emma sighed. "We all have busy lives. I don't know what's happened to you. It seems like we're not good enough for you anymore."

"That's not fair. Just because Mitch has been successful and we have a nice home—"

"Brooke! I didn't call to fight with you. I just thought I could make you understand how Mama and Papa miss you. Someday, they'll be gone and you'll be sorry you didn't take the time."

Brooke heard the phone click in her ear. Her blood soared to her head as she started to redial Emma's number and then

233

realized she didn't remember it. She grabbed the phone directory, stabbed in the numbers and broke one of her newly manicured nails. Pacing in her kitchen, she waited for a response…one…two…ten…She slammed down the phone, yanked open the refrigerator, and poured a glass of wine. Her fingernails drummed on the counter as she contemplated her next move. Grabbing the directory again, she punched in Lisa's phone number.

"Hey, Lisa."

"Brooke?"

"Yeah, don't sound so surprised."

"It has been a while."

What? Has everybody got a grudge here? "Don't you start in on me too."

"Hey, I just answered the phone. What's got you in such a huff?"

She sighed. She needed to pull herself together. Lisa would understand and she needed an understanding friend right about now. "Sorry, Emma just called me and I'm a bit upset and hurt."

"What was that all about?"

"Oh, you know, my schedule is filled with all the kids' activities. Mitch is only home on weekends and I've got more paintings to do than I can keep up with."

"Sounds pretty much like the schedule most people keep."

She knew she could count on Lisa. "Exactly."

"So what's the problem?"

"Emma called to nag me about not spending more time with Mama and Papa. According to her, I'm the reason that Papa is not looking so good. It's easy enough for her; she lives in the same town." She took a sip of her wine and waited.

Lisa was silent on the other end. "Are you still there?"

"Yes...I am."

What's going on here? "You agree with her?"

"Sorry, I talked to Mama yesterday and she pretty much told me the same thing."

She slammed down her glass and started to pace the length of her kitchen. "What am I—the family member to gossip about?"

"You know I'm going to give it to you straight."

Brooke didn't respond.

"I know your life is busy. That's the way it is these days, but Mama said your parents are really hurt. McKenzie and Conner don't even know who they are anymore."

"They're teenagers," she raged. "At this age they don't think about anyone but themselves."

"They don't seem to have a problem spending time with John and Mallory. That's all they talk about when they visit your parents."

This was too much. Now her friends are a problem? "Well, you know how John and Mallory spoil them, especially Mallory."

"So where does that leave their grandparents. They don't feel like they can compete. All Conner and McKenzie are interested in is what you can buy them."

"What's wrong with wanting your children to have a better life than you did?"

There was a hesitation on the other end. "I can't believe you said that. You make it sound like you were raised in the ghettos."

She stumbled over her words. "I just want them to have every opportunity, to fit in the right crowd."

235

"So what's wrong with the youth group at church? I can't imagine where all this is coming from. It seems to me you've left all the important values behind and run after the materialistic dream."

"That's not very kind. Just because we've seen some success—"

She could hear that Lisa was straining to keep it under control but she didn't care. How dare they all gang up on her?

"There's nothing wrong with success," Lisa continued, "if you get your priorities right and don't leave out people who are really important."

This conversation was becoming impossible. "I'm not leaving anyone out," she almost screamed.

"Really? When was the last time you called me?"

"Well—"

"Exactly. I've left messages on your phone and you've never called back. Clearwater is not that far away and I can't imagine how your parents would feel if they heard you talking about your poor upbringing." Brooke was silent. "I love you, Brooke, but you're not the person I grew up with. Something's happened to you. One of these days you'll regret the way you've treated your parents if you don't listen to what we're trying to tell you."

How right Lisa had been and what a cost she'd paid. When her mother suffered a fatal stroke, Brooke was never sure if she was able to hear her tears and confessions of regret before she slipped away.

"Mama?" McKenzie stood in her doorway.

"Kenzie." She pulled her legs up and patted the end of the chaise. "Come talk to me." McKenzie plopped down, cross-legged in front of her mother. "What brings you home so early, especially on a Friday night?"

"I've got an early morning. I decided to get some rest."

How she loved this beautiful daughter of hers. "So, tell me what's going on in your life?"

She tilted her head and grinned. "Just the most wonderful guy I've ever met."

"Oh, I see." Brooke smiled, remembering those first days of getting to know Mitch. "You've met the first Mr. Right."

She frowned. "Not the first, Mom, the only."

"I stand corrected. So who is this Mr. Wonderful?"

"Remember, I told you about Joel, the guy I met over spring break? He's the one who's doing his residency and wants to go to India as a missionary."

Brooke felt that old uneasy feeling of her daughter being drawn into missions. With all the young men out there, why did she have to be interested in this one? "You told me he was at Memorial. I just didn't realize you were so serious."

"It hasn't been easy. When you're in a residency, there isn't much time for anything else. Fortunately, we've been working the same shifts. We've managed lunch and dinner. That is, when he gets dinner."

"A pretty demanding life, McKenzie. It takes a great deal of understanding and sacrifice when you're married to a doctor. Look at Meredith. She drowns her loneliness in alcohol every night."

"I'm aware of the demands, Mama. I work with it every day. But there's a difference with Joel. He's a wonderful Christian man." She smiled. "He reminds me of Papa when we were young."

Brooke gazed off. "Yes, your papa was a wonderful Christian man. I thought I could follow him anywhere."

"Mama, is there something wrong with you and Papa?"

Brooke jerked back. "Oh…no…just settling into old age I guess." Her smile fell short.

"You're only forty-five, that's hardly old age."

"I guess not but somehow I feel old."

"Mama, I've noticed, you don't go out with Mallory and your friends like you used to. Is there something really wrong?"

In spite of her efforts to contain it, a tear slid from the corner of Brooke's eye and rolled down her cheek. She took a deep breath to release the lump in her throat. "Mallory seems to have lost interest in my company. She has a new protégé to coddle." She gave McKenzie a watery smile. "I'm afraid I got my priorities all wrong."

"But, you've been very successful with your painting."

"For what, child? It hasn't made me happy like I was when I painted for the Colombian mission effort. Everything I went after—it all seems so shallow and meaningless now."

"Don't say that! You've given Conner and me every opportunity."

Brooke patted her daughter's arm. "Maybe I did some things right."

"You did lots of things right, Mama."

"What I regret most is the way I treated my family and I'll never get over your grandmother." She stared out the window to their vast garden now lit with lamps and small lights around the edge of pathways. "I shut out my best friend, Lisa." She turned back to her daughter. "Lisa stood by me through some of the darkest days of my life, and I let that relationship go for what I thought was a better life."

McKenzie reached out to hold her mother's hand. "Maybe you could restore that friendship, I mean, if you were that close."

"Perhaps." She gave her a slight smile.

"Mama" she said hesitantly. "I know you and Papa don't go to church anymore but I'm going to a women's seminar tomorrow. Why don't you come with me?"

"I don't know, McKenzie—" A bit of fear gripped her heart.

"Mama, I think it's what you need." She squeezed both of Brooke's hands.

She was desperate for an excuse. "But, I haven't registered—"

"I know the lady who put this together. I can call her tonight and I know she'll let you go." She squeezed Brooke's hands again. "C'mon, Mamma, we haven't spent time together in ages. It'll be fun. Please, I want you to go."

Brooke laughed, how could she deny her? "You're impossible." She reached out and tousled her daughter's curly head. "I never could tell you no."

McKenzie hugged her mother. "I'm going to call right now. It's going to be great fun."

239

Chapter Thirty-One

Birds, singing outside the window, stirred Brooke as she stretched under the covers. She could hear Mitch in the shower and she relished this time to slowly wake. *Why did I tell McKenzie I would go with her today? It's been so long I won't know anyone.* She smiled thinking about McKenzie's enthusiasm. *I can't disappoint her.* Slipping out from under the covers, she went to her closet to survey her choices. She selected a pastel-pink, silk suit and laid it across the bed. Mitch came into the room as she was gathering the rest of her things.

"You're up early. I can't imagine Mallory doing anything before noon."

She flinched under her husband's harsh comment. "I'm not going with Mallory." She closed her dresser drawer. "McKenzie invited me to go with her to a women's seminar at church."

Mitch gave her a mocking look and towel dried his hair.

The look hurt. "What? You've never seen me go to a women's seminar?"

"Not lately, it's not the kind of thing Mallory would approve."

Brooke knew the insult was earned. She'd made a career of meeting Mallory's expectations to the point of sacrificing everything that got in the way, including her husband.

"I'm afraid what I do is not of much importance to Mallory anymore. I've been replaced."

His face softened for a moment but he replaced a reply with a shrug. Brooke knew he had, long ago, given up trying to compete with Mallory. Undoubtedly, a part of him felt smugly justified that his wife had been dumped as easily as she had dumped everyone else, including their marriage.

"I don't believe this program will be over until late tonight. Do you want me to leave you something for dinner?"

"I'll be golfing all day. I can manage. I'll eat at the club."

She picked up her things and headed for the shower.

Her stomach knotted as she stepped into the foyer of their old church. So much had changed since she and Mitch first began here as a young couple. It was a small membership of about three hundred in those days. With the growth in the area, a new sanctuary had been built to accommodate ten thousand. Christian concerts and women's seminars were a common occurrence and they filled the sanctuary to capacity. No chance of embarrassing explanations to old members in this crowd.

"Brooke?" She turned to see Kathy from their old Bible study. "It's so good to see you," she said as she reached out and gave her a warm hug. "Elizabeth," she called to another of their friends and waved her over.

Before Brooke realized what was happening, she was surrounded by old friends. Friends who had stood by her during her horrific wait for Mitch, when he'd been captured in South America. Her heart surged with the love she was extended and her fears melted. Of course they would welcome her without reservation or judgment. She had forgotten that about Christian women.

McKenzie stood by with a wide grin on her face.

"McKenzie—over here. We saved you seats," a friend called to her.

McKenzie waved back as she maneuvered her way through the crowd and stopped numerous times for hugs along the way.

"Katie." She gave her friend a hug. "Great seats! You must have been here all night."

"Actually, we did bring our sleeping bags."

"Really." McKenzie's eyes grew wide.

Katie laughed. "Just kidding, girlfriend, you are so gullible."

"Guilty as charged." she threw up her hands.

"I take it this is your mom."

"Oh sorry, this is my mom, Brooke." She threw her arm around Brooke's shoulder and gave her a squeeze. "This is Katie. We went on the Colorado trip during spring break. We've been best buddies ever since."

"I'm pleased to meet you." Brooke gave her a warm smile. "And thank you for saving these wonderful seats."

"Truth is, a bunch of us came early to set up and we were allowed in before the doors opened. They let us stake out a row for everyone when we were finished."

"Looks like we're here just in time." McKenzie pointed to the stage. "Here comes the praise team."

They took their seats and the hum of the crowd began to subside when the praise team leader called for everyone's attention. As the music started, everyone came to their feet, clapping and singing in celebration. Brooke felt washed new; this is where she belonged.

It was the last session before dinner break. Brooke had enjoyed the speaker and listened intently as she wound up her message of the day.

242

"Have you discovered that no matter how close your friends, they can't be everything you need? When you're in crisis, feeling insecure and experiencing pain, there is no human being who can be all you need them to be. God is our unending source. He will never turn away or fail us. We'll have all kinds of trials, but God has a plan—one that is vital in developing us to be used for His greater purpose. In our aloneness, in our times of rebellion, when we feel we've gone too far for God to possibly forgive or love us...there he will be waiting...wooing us to him. You can trust him..." she ended in a whisper.

"Let's pray. Father, how we thank you for all these ladies who are earnestly seeking you. I pray that, as you speak to hearts, each one will reach out to you...for salvation...for restoration...for direction and guidance. May we be in your will, Lord. May we search your word and your ways, may we trust you with the innermost secrets of our lives. Bless hearts and be with us for the remainder of our time here today. Thank you for what you are doing in so many lives. We love you precious Jesus...Amen."

Katie had been accurate in describing their place for dinner as a Mexican hole-in-the-wall. Brooke dug into a huge Taco salad, heaped with sour cream and guacamole. She didn't know when she had enjoyed a meal more. The lively conversations of McKenzie and her friends gave her a new perspective. She laughed at their antics and stories until her sides were sore. With quick service they got back in plenty of time for the evening session. Katie swept McKenzie off to get the hand-outs for the next speaker, while Brooke took advantage of the time to freshen up. She was combing her hair when she heard someone behind her.

243

"Brooke?" She turned around to see Victor's wife, Ruth, smiling back at her.

"Ruth." The two women immediately went to each other for a huge hug.

"It's so good to see you, Brooke. You're as beautiful as ever."

Brooke blushed, never accepting the reality of her beauty. "You're too kind. How have you been? What's Victor doing these days?"

"He's still working at the museum. You know how he loves that."

"And he's so talented. He's an immeasurable asset to them you know."

"Well, I've always felt that. He's also working on a project in Lakeland for a fund raiser."

How had she left this life behind? "Interesting, when will that be?"

"The show's in two weeks but he's over there now, making sure it all comes together perfectly."

Her heart tightened at all the years lost with Victor. "He's good at that. I miss working with him." Brooke sighed. "I miss those good times."

"Maybe you could help him on this project. He'd love to see you and he always valued your insight." Ruth caught herself. "That is if you have time, I'm sure you're busy."

Such regret pounded through her. These were some of the important people she had set aside. Did she dare think she could re-establish their special relationship? "As it turns out, I'm not. I would love to work with Victor again. Maybe I could give him a call."

Ruth's face lit up and Brooke could see she was pleased. "Better yet, why don't you join us for lunch after church tomorrow? He could give you all the details."

"I would love that, but let me check with Mitch. I'll give you a call and let you know."

Ruth reached out and squeezed Brooke's hand. "Victor will be so pleased to see you again. It was a joy for him to promote your work."

"He was a good friend in a desperate time in my life." She gave Ruth another warm hug. "I'll call you first thing in the morning."

Brooke floated into the sanctuary, anxious for whatever was next. She met McKenzie in the auditorium and they settled in as the next speaker was introduced.

"My topic this evening is one that's difficult to hear about and one that most Christians are largely ignorant. I'm talking about the legalized murder of innocent children called abortion."

A wave of fear moved through Brooke's body and constricted her breathing.

"Since 1973, after Row v Wade, there have been over forty-three million babies who have lost their lives to abortion. That's three times the population of this state of Florida. Forty-three percent of women in this country have experienced an abortion. I know—because I used to be a baby-killer."

She paused and looked out at the crowd. "I was introduced to the lucrative business of abortion by a friend who owned a clinic and invited me to be a partner." She came out from the podium and leaned toward the audience. "If you believe that abortion clinics are there to help women in distress—you believe a lie. If you believe that they will counsel women for other options—you believe a lie. If you believe that they care what happens to these women. You—believe—a—lie."

"Abortion is all about money, was always about money, always will be about money. I became a millionaire making women believe that I was concerned about their lives." She paused and came back to the podium.

"Partial Birth Abortion. What does that mean to you?" Her eyes scanned the audience. "That they are only partially aborted? I continue to be amazed at how many people in this country, Christians even, who are totally ignorant about this cruel and murderous act. Let me explain." She leaned her arms against the podium and scanned the audience again. "A baby, clear up to the ninth month, is turned around in the birth canal and brought out breach, face down—that's important. Because...before the head is freed from the mother, a sharp instrument is plunged into the back of the baby's skull and the brains are sucked out." Gasps and cries of horror were heard throughout the audience. "Yes...yes...and those babies feel every bit of the pain." She walked out from the podium again. "Now, how would sucking the brains from a child save the life of a birthing mother? And do you realize how many women used to die from a breach birth...are still dying from a breach birth? There is nothing about a breach birth that can save the life of a mother."

She put her hands on her hips. "I thank God for a president who put an end to this murderous event and shame on any member of Congress or the Senate who voted against that bill." The audience exploded into applause. "Let me interject here that the risk of a mother's life in her pregnancy amounts to only six percent of the abortions performed. We are concerned about the mother and her child. Abortion clinics are not."

246

She walked to the side of the podium and rested her arm against it. "In the span of about five years, I became a multi-millionaire by telling young women I cared about them. But all I cared about was the money they were going to put in my pocket. I would tell them whatever was necessary to make sure they went through the procedure." Her voice softened. "It wasn't until a young Christian woman came to our clinic one day that my life took a drastic change.

"Two of our counselors called in sick and so I needed to fill in. I call them counselors when in actuality they were simply salespeople. This sweet young girl was the daughter of a pastor. She was devastated…filled with guilt at the thought of disappointing her father and bringing him embarrassment.

"Well, of course, I seized on the idea of what I thought would be a judgmental man who would condemn his daughter to a ruined life. I assured her that we could take care of her problem without anyone knowing, and that her self-righteous father wouldn't have to know a thing."

She walked around again to the front of the podium. "I will never forget the look on her face as she put me in my place. 'My father's not like that.' she shouted at me. 'He's a gentle loving man who loves God and he loves me.' She ran from my clinic." She paused and put her hands behind her back. "I'd had other sweet young girls in my clinic before. I have no explanation but that God sent that young girl. I couldn't get her face out of my mind and it haunted me for days.

"Later that week, her father came in and asked to speak to me." She chuckled. "I thought, here it comes now. The wrath of God is going to come down on me today." She shook her head "But that's not what happened. He told me that his daughter had

247

come home and confessed what she had nearly done. After a lot of crying and hugging, they had made arrangements for her to go live with an aunt in California where she would be home schooled until after the baby was born. It would be adopted by a childless couple in his sister's church." Tears glistened in her eyes. "And then...he began to tell me about Jesus...how much Jesus loved me."

She wiped her eyes. "I'm not going to tell you that I gave my heart to Jesus right then and there. I was stubborn and, let's face it, we were talking about a multi-million dollar business. But the face of that young girl would not leave my mind. I began attending that pastor's church, always in the back pew of course, until Jesus finally got hold of my heart. I walked that aisle to proclaim him as my savior."

The sanctuary was still with every woman's tear-filled eyes trained on the speaker. "I've used every dime I made in those abortion clinics to promote the Pregnancy Crisis Centers and it will never be enough to compensate for the thousands of lives I took." She waited, looking out over the audience. "David tells us in the Psalms that God knew us before we were born. That he formed us in our mother's womb. God calls us wonderfully made and that he already has a plan for our lives.

She paused and shook her head. "In the state of Florida, it is a punishable offence to disturb...just disturb a turtle's nest. We can be put in jail for killing an alligator. We have bumper stickers and license plates telling us to save the manatees, the whales, the baby seals...and yet...it's a woman's choice to kill her baby human. At eighteen days, their hearts are beating. It's not just tissue. What kind of society have we become that we murderously rip babies from their mother's womb?

She walked down the steps to come closer to the audience and spoke in a tender voice, "I know...there are many, many of you who have used a clinic like mine. In a time of fear and desperation, you listened and trusted those who would do you harm. Maybe you've made your peace with God...maybe you haven't. Many of you have that secret hidden in your heart and it has eaten you alive. I'm here to tell you that if God can forgive me for the lives I've taken, he can forgive you. Will you come tonight and let him take your burden.

"Maybe you have another stronghold in your life that you need to release to him. Maybe you're here tonight and you don't know Jesus, but you'd like to. Maybe you know him, but you've strayed away and your heart is longing to be right again. I'm going to pray for you right now and then Melissa is going to sing. If you have a burden on your heart that you would like to lay to rest...if you would like to trust Jesus as your savior and be set free...I want you to quietly leave your seat and come up here to the front. We have counselors waiting to help you. Come...don't live with this burden another day... don't say no to Jesus...He's waiting for you."

A sweet voice began singing...*Amazing Grace...how sweet the sound...*

Brooke's hands shook. Her legs were unstable and felt like stone underneath her. Women were walking down the aisles by the hundreds. Her mind was a blur as she found herself in the midst of the movement going forward. She was met by Candice, the speaker that she had enjoyed so much. Her eyes met Brooke's and she took her hand to lead her into the prayer room. Candice put an arm around Brooke and waited for her to begin.

249

"I...I...had an abortion when I was eighteen." Candice waited. "I've prayed for God's forgiveness...so many times...but it just keeps coming back to haunt me." Brooke broke down in sobs.

Candice handed her a tissue and held her close. "Could it be that God has forgiven you, but you haven't forgiven yourself? When God forgives, he doesn't even remember the sin, so it can't be him who is bringing it to mind. But we do remember and Satan will take every opportunity to remind you. The last thing the enemy wants you to believe is that God can and does forgive you. He wants you to feel unworthy."

"How...how can...you...understand. You haven't ...lived w...with this torment...I've felt...my whole life."

Candice waited for a moment, and then gently took her hands. "You're wrong, I know exactly what you've lived with." Her eyes held Brooke's. "I was the victim of a brutal rape. I was in the hospital for two weeks recovering from stab wounds. I was horrified when I discovered I was pregnant from that terrifying experience. Everyone encouraged me to end the pregnancy. My parents weren't Christians and it didn't take much to persuade me." She shook her head. "That was not a solution. I didn't forget the rape and I had continual reminders of what I'd done."

Brooke's eyes widened. Someone who really understood...someone who knew.

"My baby kicked...right after they injected the saline solution. That was probably him feeling the pain. How could I do such a thing?" She shuddered and continued to weep.

"We can't go back, and we'll always have sorrow for what we've done, but we don't have to let it rule over us. God can use

250

us in a mighty way to keep other women from making the same mistake. You can overcome Satan's hold by helping others to avoid what you've gone through. There's no question that God forgives you. Don't let this handicap you to the point that God can't use you."

"No one knows...only my best friend...not my husband...my parents..."

"God will give you a way." Candice smiled encouragement.

"I can maybe work as a counselor, but I'm not ready to tell anyone. I haven't even been going to church and I've left God out of my life for years."

Candice hugged her shoulder. "You've made the first step. Just ask him to take over and use you in any way he sees fit. Do you live in the area?"

"Yes, in Winter Park."

Candice reached into her pocket and handed her a business card. "I live here in Orlando. Whenever you need someone to talk to, call me. We can have lunch and spend some time together."

Brooke took the card and slipped it into her pocket.

"Let's pray before you leave."

Brooke gave her a watery smile. "I'd like that."

Chapter Thirty-Two

With the early dawn cloaked in shades of gray, Brooke slipped quietly from their bed without disturbing her husband's sleep. She had plans to surprise Mitch and McKenzie with a nice breakfast of French pastry, coddled eggs and fresh coffee. It was something, regretfully, she had neglected for many years. Busy with her dough, she didn't see her husband leaning against the kitchen door frame.

"What are you doing?"

"Oh! I didn't see you there." She glanced back at Mitch giving him a hopeful smile. "I thought I would fix us a nice breakfast and then we could go to church with McKenzie."

Mitch poured himself a cup of coffee. "That must have been some meeting yesterday."

She turned to face her husband. "It was, Mitch. It confirmed what I've been thinking about lately. About how badly I've messed up. I've been looking for happiness in all the wrong places."

He leaned his back against the counter and studied her. "I'm glad for you Brooke but—"

"I saw Ruth yesterday," she hurried on hoping to curtail any protests he might have. "Vic is working on a charity project in Lakeland. She thought Vic could use my help and invited us to lunch after church."

Mitch held his hand over his eyes and then drew it down over his face before looking up at his wife. "Brooke, I'm glad you've found some new direction but you can't expect me to just drop everything. I have a tee-time with a foursome this morning.

It's too late to get a replacement. Besides, I'm not much interested in—"

"I remember a time when you wouldn't miss a Sunday. Serving the Lord was everything to you."

"Well you certainly changed that, didn't you?" He set his cup on the counter and strode out. "I need to get ready."

Brooke bit her lip. *He was right. She was responsible.* For a year or more, Mitch took their children to church while she was off with Mallory and her friends. It was for a good cause she thought; charity benefits, but always on a Sunday. Then she got the kids involved in tennis and tournaments were always on Sunday. Mitch held strong until he was tired of fighting. She couldn't remember when they had totally stopped going to church but she knew her insistence on pleasing Mallory, instead of God, had taken them down a selfish and disastrous path.

"Breakfast?" McKenzie popped into the kitchen. "This looks great and I'm starved."

"I thought we could have breakfast together and go to church this morning but your father has an early tee-time."

McKenzie hugged her mother. "Don't be discouraged. I've been praying for you both for a long time. He'll come around."

"I hoped we could go to lunch with Vic and Ruth, to talk about the charity art show." She turned back to her pastry, laying it on a baking sheet to put into the oven.

"I can go with you. Joel won't be off until three this afternoon."

"I don't know McKenzie." She glanced back at her daughter, doubt coloring her expression. "It was one thing to go to a women's seminar but everyone will be asking about him."

"Tell them he had plans that couldn't be cancelled."

"I…I…don't—" She wiped an errant tear before it could make its way down her cheek.

"Mama." McKenzie hopped up on one of the stools next to the kitchen bar. "You're going to have to take the lead. He'll never come around if you sit home. Besides, this can work out perfect. I'll go to lunch with you and then I can take you to meet Joel."

Brooke gave her daughter a tentative grin. "I would like to meet this young man who has captured your heart."

"Alright then, let's dig into this breakfast and get ready for a fun day."

Brooke was exuberant following the morning services. She'd seen many old friends and the warmth of Christian fellowship filled her heart with a new expectation. McKenzie followed Vic and Ruth to the restaurant in her little BMW. It was a lovely afternoon and they shared a shaded table outside on a patio enhanced with blue skies and a soft breeze. They finished their meal and visited over fruit-flavored tea.

"So, you want to hear about our project in Lakeland?" Victor asked. There had been so much catching up to do during their meal that the subject had yet to be discussed.

"I would." She was eager. "I'm ready to get involved in something worthwhile." She'd already confessed her multitude of mistakes and misguided priorities over the years. Victor and Ruth were understanding and suggested she move on.

"Well, it's for the benefit of a Pregnancy Crisis Center and all the proceeds will go toward the purchase of a machine to do sonograms. They've had tremendous success convincing mothers to have their babies by using the sonogram. Once the

254

mother actually sees her baby…that it's a real living baby…well it's almost a done deal."

"I've seen that at the hospital." McKenzie said. "I've been working in neonatal care and it's just amazing. Sometimes they're sucking their thumbs. You see them stretch. There's an immediate bond."

"I can see the benefit from that. I'm sure there wouldn't be the numbers of abortions if this had been available years ago," Brooke added, as she struggled with the thought of another confession.

"Exactly but these machines are very expensive. That's why the drive for funds."

"So how does the art show come into play? What's the game plan?"

"There's a large park around the lake right downtown. It's frequently used for events, and it's perfect for an art show."

"And the artists?"

"From the local Christian college. The art department assigned the project and their students will receive a grade with the understanding that their work will be donated."

"What's the subject?" Brooke asked, thinking it would be babies and children.

"That's left up to the student but they're aware of what the project will fund."

"Hmmm…how would you like some pictures of babies…something like Ann Geddes, but in oils instead of photographs?" Brooke's old enthusiasm was taking hold. "Have you seen her work?"

"I'm not sure—"

"She photographs very young newborns and puts them into flowers and unusual settings. They're quite striking."

Ruth's eyes lit up. "I've seen them at the mall during Christmas season. They had a whole calendar of them."

Victor grinned. "That could be quite a seller. I'd be thrilled with anything you can bring me."

"And if you don't mind, I'd like to help set up the show."

"Blessings galore." Victor laughed. "I'm headed for the Pregnancy Center tomorrow if you'd like to go. I can introduce you to the ladies there."

"Sounds delightful, will we have an opportunity to see—"

McKenzie glanced at her watch and interrupted. "Mama, I need to go."

"Go ahead, honey." Ruth patted McKenzie's arm. "We can take your mother home."

"Would you mind 'Kenzie? I'd love to meet Joel, but this is quite important."

"It's fine, Mama." She kissed her mother's cheek. "Maybe I can bring him by this evening."

Brooke squeezed McKenzie's hand as she left. "We'll plan on it, honey."

Brooke heard the television in the den as she returned from her afternoon with Vic and Ruth. Mitch was settled in for the evening watching a game, she surmised. She went upstairs to their room, pulled on some jeans, a soft cotton sweater and scooted her feet into a pair of soft fuzzy slippers. She sat down on the end of the bed not sure what to do next. *Pray*...the thought came to mind. She swung around and kneeled beside the bed.

256

"Lord, I've been so wrong. I've ignored you and my husband. I went my own way. I know you've forgiven me but how do I get Mitch to forgive me?" *Wait*...the thought came. "I know it's not going to happen overnight but what can I do to convince him that I've changed?" *The fruit of the spirit...kindness...earn his trust.*

"Oh yes, Lord. It's been so long since I've been kind to him and it'll take even longer before he trusts me, won't it?" She knew the answer without even asking.

Mitch would have had his usual lunch with his friends but she was sure he hadn't eaten anything since. She hurried down to the kitchen. Something light. She searched the cabinets and refrigerator. There was chicken—maybe chicken salad sandwiches. She and McKenzie had barely touched the pastries. Some fresh cantaloupe cut up in small dishes, and some mint tea. She was happy with her menu. She arranged a tray with his meal and headed down the hall to the den.

"I thought you might like a light dinner."

"Uh... thanks." He sat up straighter in his recliner to balance the tray. Brooke went after her tray and snuggled into a chair near Mitch.

"Who's winning?"

"Lakers, up by ten."

"McKenzie might bring her young man by this evening."

"That right." Mitch's eyes remained fixed on the television before him.

This was so hard, like talking to a stranger. But she had to hang in there. "I've never met him, have you?"

"No, I don't believe I have."

257

"I'm sure you would remember, from what I'm told. They seem to be quite serious."

"Bound to happen at her age."

"He's the one she met on spring break in Colorado."

"I remember that."

Brooke was out of conversation. She decided to remain quiet and allow her husband to watch his game. Maybe just being here with him would send a message.

Brooke jumped as the phone rang. Mitch picked it up and answered while Brooke listened to his side of the conversation.

"Yes, she mentioned that to me...that's understandable...another time...you go ahead and have fun...yes...I'll tell her...love you too."

"That must have been McKenzie."

"Yes, her friend was called in for an emergency. Big pile-up on I-4 She's going on with the singles group for game night and pizza."

She slumped in her chair. It could have been a way to spend a nice evening without all this tension. "That's disappointing; I was looking forward to meeting him."

"The life of a doctor is pretty demanding."

"I-4 is getting so bad. You take your life in your hands just getting on, especially over there by Disney."

"I avoid it as much as possible."

"I guess I'll be on it tomorrow. I'm going with Vic to Lakeland and check out the site for the art show. It's a fund raiser for a sonogram machine at the Pregnancy Center."

"That right." Mitch's attention was now caught by the final seconds of a close game. With the final buzzer, Mitch got up and stretched. "I'll be leaving for Chicago tomorrow. I won't be back until late Wednesday."

"Will you be here in time for dinner?"

"Not likely."

She knew he wanted to leave the room but if she could just keep their conversation going. "Vic was disappointed he didn't get to see you. They wanted to know if we could get together at their place."

"I doubt I'll be home much of the week."

"What about next week?" Brooke knew she was pushing but she looked hopefully at her husband.

Mitch collapsed back down into his chair. "Brooke, since when do you not remember that my time is not my own. I don't know what I'll be doing next week." He rubbed his brow in defense of this unwelcome conversation.

"Well, what about the weekend? We could go to church and then do lunch—"

Mitch shook his head and looked at his wife. "What is it you want? You've spent all these years running after Mallory and leaving me out of your plans. Now all of a sudden you want me to go to church and lunch. What's this all about, Brooke? Now that Mallory has cut you off you need some company? I can't just turn it on and off again according to your whim."

Brooke squeezed her eyes shut willing herself not to cry. Looking down at her hands rather than face Mitch she said, "I deserved that, every bit of it. I know what I've done and I'm sorry."

"Well, maybe that's a start, but I'm just not ready to jump back into this relationship like nothing has happened." He turned back to the television and began switching channels.

Brooke sat in silence, wooden and feeling the scorn deep in her soul. The tension was thick and she couldn't decide what to do next. She was miserable just sitting here. But if she left, would he take it as a sign she was resigned to going back to the way it had been? Finally, unable to stand it any longer, she stood quietly and told him, "I'm going for a walk."

"Fine," he said without looking up.

Chapter Thirty-Three

Gloom settled over their bedroom like a shroud as Brooke dialed Mitch's cell number. He would recognize the number and she prayed he wasn't so angry he wouldn't answer.

"Yeah."

"Mitch, I've had some bad news."

"One of the kids—"

"No, it's Papa, he has cancer." Her throat constricted and she choked back the tears.

He sighed. "How bad?"

"Throughout his body, they're not going to do treatment."

"No treatment?"

"No point. Emma says the treatment would be worse than the cancer. He has three to six months."

"I'm so sorry, Brooke. I can try to get someone to fill in for me."

"No, save it for later. McKenzie and I are driving over tomorrow morning. We'll probably stay the night."

"Stay as long as you like. I'll just be home for one evening."

"I'll have to see. I'll let you know."

"All right, let me know if there's anything I can do."

She took a quick breath to hold back sobs that threatened. "Call your parents for me…and Mama Suzanne. I'm not sure I can do it."

"Sure, I'll call as soon as we hang up."

Oh, to have the comfort of her husband's arms around her, but his concern would have to be enough for now. "Okay, I'll be in touch."

Brooke found her mother's kitchen bare. There were only a few cereal boxes, some milk, a loaf of bread, and a package of lunch meat in the refrigerator. It was evidence of how her father had been living since his wife's death.

Her father pushed the door open to the kitchen. "Sure smells good in here."

After a trip to the market, Brooke had dived into baking and preparing a supply of food for her father after she was gone.

"Papa." She smiled at him. "I've got fresh coffee if you'd like."

"Sounds good." He eased himself into the chair and winced. It was the first time she'd seen evidence of the deadly disease that was ravaging his body. She poured two cups of coffee, put one in front of him and slid into the chair across the table.

"This kitchen smells like it used to, when your mama was alive." His faded eyes sparkled in remembrance of his beloved Annie.

"She was a wonderful cook." Brooke tried to keep it light.

"And she was careful to pass it on to her daughters."

"Yes, she did." Brooke said, thinking that she had failed to do the same with McKenzie.

"So what's going on in my little girl's life these days?" He patted her arm that rested on the table and then left his hand there.

"I talked to Victor this Sunday after church. I'm going to do some paintings and help him put on a benefit art show for the Pregnancy Center in Lakeland."

His eyebrows rose. "Sounds like quite a project."

"They're raising funds for a sonogram machine to show mothers that they have a live baby. Most of them decide against abortion afterwards."

"Sounds like a pretty important machine. Do you have all your paintings done?"

"No, I haven't even started."

"Then you need to be home so you can get to work." He patted her arm again and reached for his coffee cup.

"It's all right Papa, I want to spend some time here with you."

"I appreciate you coming and fixing me dinner. You know I'm always glad to see you." He laid his forearms on the table, sighed and looked up at her. "There's nothing to be done to keep me on this earth, and I wouldn't want it either. I miss your mama."

Brooke's eyes filled.

"I know it's hard for you kids," he continued. "And I'm sad for you, but don't you understand, honey, I'm going to be with Mama."

Brooke's heart was filled with regret. Why didn't she listen to what Emma and Lisa were trying to tell her? "I'm sorry for the way I've treated you and Mama—"

"Shush now." He stood and pulled Brooke into his arms. "Your mama and I never stopped loving you. Someday we're all going to be together and that'll be for eternity, honey."

Brooke held him tight with her arms around his waist and cried into his chest. "What am I going to do without you, Papa? You always make things right."

263

"You're going to go on with that fine husband of yours. You'll always have the memories of the times we've had together."

She nodded her head and sniffed.

"Now, I'm going to watch a little news while you finish up dinner."

"Okay, Papa." She pulled away and wiped her face with her apron.

"I'll send in McKenzie," he called over his shoulder. "It's time you get that young lady in the kitchen and teach her how to cook like Mama."

Mitch waited in line for his turn to take off from the Atlanta airport. It had been a routine week with the exception of two phone calls from Brooke. First that her father was dying from cancer and the second to see what time he would be home so she could have dinner ready. He'd seen a change in Brooke, and her effort to reconnect. Mitch felt numb. He would have given anything for this attitude-change years ago, but Brooke had chosen her own path. First she'd altered his life insisting that he leave the mission work he loved. Then she dumped him for her own pursuits and agenda. Mitch felt more than numb. He gripped the yoke in front of him. He was angry.

"Forty-four thirty-five…you're cleared for takeoff." Mitch was an excellent pilot and his passengers always privileged to the smoothest takeoff and landing. Now at cruising altitude, he allowed his thoughts to return. We used to be so much in love. I would have done anything for her. But I wasn't enough for Brooke. She wanted fame and wealth. He heaved a heavy sigh.

But what kind of man am I that I let all of this get so out of control?

At least he had done something right. In spite of his loneliness, he'd never been unfaithful. Not that the opportunity hadn't presented itself. The men that he shuttled back and forth were usually out in the evenings and many times in the company of young women. On one occasion, when he was feeling particularly down, he'd consented to go with them. Unknown to him, he was the victim of a set-up, and found himself paired off with a young woman, not much older than his daughter. Before the evening was over, the others had gone their separate ways, leaving him and Jillian to themselves.

"Jillian," he started. "I'm a married man and I didn't realize I was being paired off tonight."

"Yeah, Becky set me up too." Her eyes looked wide with fear over what Mitch expected.

"How about a cup of coffee and then I'll get you a cab home?"

Tears filled her eyes. "Thank you, I was so afraid. I didn't know how I was going to get myself out of this."

"You know, Jillian, I think the Lord was looking out for both of us tonight."

The Lord…Mitch was brought back to the present. When was the last time he gave the Lord credit for anything? He wiped his hand across his face. *I accuse Brooke of being off track but I can't say I've done such a great job. Maybe I could go to church with them this weekend. I don't know…lot of people to face…we'll see.*

Mitch pulled into his space in the garage and waited for a few minutes before getting out of his SUV. He never looked forward

265

to coming home anymore. The house was either empty or may as well be. McKenzie was usually gone. Now, he was uncertain what he would face. One thing he did know, he needed to support his wife through her father's illness. After all, he would be hit pretty hard if it was his dad and she'd already lost her mother. Whatever their problems, he felt bad for her. He grabbed his overnight bag from the back and headed into the house. From the hall he could hear his wife and daughter chattering and laughing and there were tantalizing smells coming from the kitchen.

"Well, what have we here?" Mitch stood in the kitchen doorway.

"Papa." She ran over to give him a kiss. "Mama is teaching me the family secrets."

"Secrets?"

McKenzie laughed. "Grandmere's recipes, so I can carry on the family traditions."

"I see. And would this be for anything in the eminent future?"

"Not yet, Papa, but it doesn't hurt to be prepared."

"No, it doesn't. Your mother was taught well. I was spoiled with her cooking."

Brooke watched the interaction between father and daughter and smiled.

"How's your dad, Brooke?" He asked tentatively as he slipped onto a kitchen bar stool.

"He's doing well for someone in his condition." She leaned against the counter and folded her arms. "He wants to frame my paintings for the show we're doing in Lakeland."

"He can do that?"

266

"I protested but you know how he is. Said he wasn't going to waste time in front of the television."

"Amazing." He shook his head and then rubbed the back of his neck. "Do I have time for a shower?"

"We'll be another twenty minutes."

"That works." He slipped off the stool and headed upstairs.

The conversation over dinner was the most pleasant they'd had in years and Brooke savored the time together as they lingered over coffee. As usual, McKenzie's cell rang and she excused herself, talking as she headed upstairs.

"I'm really sorry about your dad. I'm surprised you didn't stay the week."

"I would have but he didn't want me to." She fought the constriction in her throat. "He said I needed to get home and work on my paintings to save all those babies." She leaned on her forearms on the table. "He's actually looking forward to the end of his life because he doesn't want to live without Mama any longer." She looked down at her plate. "He said he felt sad for us but we'll all be together one day and, right now, he just wants to be with Mama and Jesus."

Mitch was silent.

"It's crazy." She gulped back the threat of tears. "I went over there to help him and he helped me instead. I was glad I went."

Mitch nodded. "We should have known he would be like this. It exemplifies the life he's always lived."

"Yes, he was the pillar of our home. It's probably better that Mama went first. She would have been financially set but I don't think she could have made it without him."

There was a moment of awkward silence between them. "Well," Mitch finally stood. "I can help you clean up here. It seems our daughter is gone for the evening."

"No, that's okay. You go ahead and relax. You've had a long day. I'll be done in no time."

Mitch hesitated, shrugged and then retreated to the den.

Why didn't I accept his offer, she screamed at herself? At least I would be spending time with him. You are so stupid. She finished up the dishes and walked down the hall to the den.

"Would you like a dish of ice cream or maybe some coffee?"

"No thanks, I'm fine," he said without looking up.

"I think I'll go up and read. I'm a bit tired from the trip."

"Right," was his only answer.

Her steps were heavy as she walked upstairs and into her room. An opportunity to connect and she'd blown it. She was grateful for his concern over her dad, but she was so hoping for a show of affection. Even to hold her in his arms in sympathy. But, she reminded herself, we didn't get this way in a day or even a week…it's going to be a long road back.

Chapter Thirty-Four

Brooke put in a couple of pieces of toast and cracked eggs into a bowl. McKenzie grabbed a bagel on her way out to a seven o'clock shift, and she'd called to Mitch in the shower that she was fixing breakfast. He came in just as she was finishing their omelets. He poured their coffee as she filled their plates and set them on the table.

"What are your plans today?" he said as he poured cream in his coffee.

She spread some jam on her toast. "I'm going to paint all day. I have one finished but I'm running out of time so I need to get another one started."

"Sounds like you've taken on quite a project."

She gave him a shy smile. "I couldn't resist the subject matter."

He took a drink of his coffee. "Well, that's good, I guess."

"Actually, I'm going to do some more shows at the museum. Whatever the profits, I'll give to the center. The sonogram machine is very expensive and this show is only a start."

"I'm sure they'll appreciate that." He dug into some more of his eggs.

She took a sip of her coffee. "Where do you go today?"

"Phoenix, just an overnighter. I'll be back Friday afternoon."

"So you'll be with Jack and Lisa."

Mitch gave her a puzzled stare. "Brooke, Jack and Lisa haven't lived in Phoenix for a year."

"They haven't?" Brooke set her coffee cup down. It was another slap in the face with the reality of how out-of-touch she'd been.

"No, Jack got a promotion and they've been living in Orlando." He wiped his mouth with his napkin and took another bite.

"Why haven't we seen them at parties and things with Mallory and John?"

"They don't participate. They're involved in their church."

"Oh...so, have you seen them since they moved?"

"Jack flies back to Phoenix once in a while and we visit. We usually go over to his parents for dinner.'"

Brooke's mind was reeling with guilt, her unfinished omelet forgotten. "I didn't realize—"

"Jack said Lisa left a message but you haven't returned her call." Mitch concentrated on his plate as he finished off his eggs and the last bit of toast.

She had no answer. Lisa hadn't mentioned where she was living when she called, and Brooke hadn't bothered listening to the number Lisa left. She'd been in a rush, running in to change clothes and go out again.

"Thanks for breakfast," Mitch was saying as he grabbed a last gulp of coffee. "I need to get going."

"Okay." She hoped he would bend down and give her a kiss on the cheek. He reached for his jacket.

"See you Friday."

"See you Friday...have a good flight," she said as she began gathering dishes from the table.

Brooke threw herself into her painting, for therapy as much as the need to get finished. The news that Lisa had been living in the same town for a year was another addition to the snowball of Brooke's sins. She was beginning to dislike herself as much as

Mitch did. How could she hold anything against Mallory? She'd been doing the same thing for all these years. She was lucky she had anyone to talk to. *Lord what a mess I've made.*

At three in the afternoon, she stepped back and surveyed her work. She was pleased. It was exactly what she had been striving for. She walked into the kitchen to put on a pot of tea and decide on something for dinner for her and McKenzie. That was, assuming McKenzie would be here for dinner. She'd scarcely had the thought when the phone rang.

"McKenzie, I was just thinking about you. Will you be home for dinner?"

"That's why I was calling. Joel has a seven-thirty dinner break. I'll grab something with him and, after I stop by the mall, I'll be home."

"All right then, I'll just grab something left over."

She had to be thankful for the effort McKenzie was making to spend time with her. They'd been like passing ships all these years. *At least I did something right with my daughter.* With McKenzie becoming a problem in her high school years, Brooke readily agreed when her friend invited her to the Christian retreat over spring break. As unsettled as she was about McKenzie's enthusiastic ideas of following this young man into missions, it had been worth it. She'd found a love of Christ and a new attitude. *Give it time and she'd give up this mission nonsense.*

With a cup of fresh coffee, she sat down to rest, only to wrestle with thoughts of Lisa. Did she dare call? Would Lisa's reaction be the same as Mitch? She took a deep breath and reached for the phone, her stomach churning as she dialed Mama Suzanne.

"Brooke, honey, how's your daddy?"

You could always count on Mama Suzanne. Brooke felt tense muscles begin to relax. "Actually, he's doing fairly well."

"I was so sorry to hear. I just couldn't believe it."

Brooke sighed." I know but he's ready. He misses Mama."

Mama Suzanne's voice softened as she spoke about her best friend. "I know he does. There was never another woman for him after he met her in that French café."

"They had something very special."

"Yes, they did. Now, tell me about yourself." Her sparkle was back. "I heard you were doin' real well with your painting."

How could she be so sweet? It was more than she deserved. "I wish I could say the same for my personal life. I've made some poor choices, Mama Suzanne," she choked out.

"Now, now," she soothed. "We've all done things we wish we hadn't."

"Do you think Lisa will still talk to me?"

"Of course she will," Mama Suzanne encouraged. "You just go on and give her a call. You girls need to be together again. There's nothing like best friends."

She punched in Lisa's number. Her palms were sweaty and her tongue felt twice its size as the phone rang several times.

"Hello?"

"Lisa."

"Yes?"

"This is Brooke."

"Brooke?"

"I know, I don't have any right to call. I wouldn't blame you if you hung up but, please don't."

An edge of reserve tinted Lisa's voice. "How have you been?"

She took a deep breath. "Better, now that I'm getting my head on straight. I know I've hurt a lot of people."

Silence filled the receiver for such a long time, she thought Lisa had hung up. When she finally spoke, her voice softened a bit. "Yes, you have, but I guess realizing it is a good start. What are you doing these days?"

"I'm helping Victor with a show in Lakeland. It's a benefit for the Pregnancy Crisis Center."

"I didn't think you were working with him anymore."

"I went to a women's seminar last weekend. I ran into Ruth and she suggested he could use my help."

"Was that the seminar with the awesome lady from the abortion clinics?" Lisa asked tentatively.

"Yes...it was."

"I was there." Lisa sighed heavily. "I'll bet that was tough."

"It was, but I'm glad I went. The Lord was already working on me and the conference just finished it off."

Warmth was absent from their conversation. Brooke felt the bitter sting of a lost friendship as the disquieted silence expanded into a canyon of sadness.

"Lisa, I owe you so much, and I've treated you so badly."

Another long silence. "Yes you have, but you're still my friend."

Brooke wiped away the tears that threatened. "Lisa, I don't deserve you."

"No, you don't but I'm willing to mend fences. I've missed you Brooke."

"I've missed you too. I just didn't realize how much."

"Brooke, I don't mean to cut you off but I need to pick up the boys at school. Maybe we can go to lunch sometime?"

Brooke collapsed to the stool in relief. "I would love that so much. The show will be finished the weekend after next. How about the following Monday?" She reached for her calendar to note the date.

"As far as I know, that'll be okay. I'll give you a call and we can set a time and place."

"Thank you." she brushed the tears from her face that were now in free fall. "I love you."

"I love you too, Brooke." Her voice also hinted at tears. "I'll see you soon."

The mountain that had been sitting on Brooke's shoulders, lifted as she hung up the phone. She knew they would not pick up where they'd left off any more than she had with Mitch. It was going to be a journey, but it was a start. Brooke refilled her cup and headed for her studio.

A smile slipped across McKenzie's face as she contemplated Joel's arrival. He was just finishing up with a patient, and she managed to signal her intentions to meet him in the cafeteria. She was rewarded with a grin of pure pleasure, his dark eyes sparkling at the sight of her. It was a quiet time of day with most of the staff gone back from their break. They would have the place almost to themselves.

Joel slid into the chair across from her. She leaned across the table for a quick kiss. It was still a wonder that this handsome, loving guy was interested in her.

"Rough day?" she asked.

"Not too bad, how about you."

274

"We lost a baby this morning, a preemie. There were too many complications and he just couldn't hold on."

"You can only do your best, my love." Joel reached out and placed his hands on her arms. "It's always in God's hands."

"I know." She looked out the large window to the landscaped grounds. "I just feel bad for the parents; it's so hard."

"You can't let it get you down." Joel stood and planted a kiss on her forehead, "I've got to eat, babe."

They opted for the meatloaf as the better of the selections and returned to their table.

"How's your grandfather?"

She grinned. "Amazing."

"How so?"

"He's so ready. My grandmother died almost two years ago and he's lost without her."

"How's your mother handling it?"

She took a sip of her soda. "She was pretty devastated to begin with but, after spending time with my grandfather, she's doing much better."

He loaded a fork full of mashed potatoes and gravy. "Were they close?"

"They were a close family when Mama was growing up." She scrunched up her nose. "The Mallory thing, you know." She'd confided in Joel about her concerns for her parent's relationship and described how Brooke's obsession with Mallory had sucked the life out of their family.

"Hmmm." he nodded.

"But you know." She pointed with her fork while she swallowed a bite. "Mama is making a real effort with Papa. We came home from Clearwater and I helped her fix dinner. We actually sat around the dinner table and talked. It was great. When I left this morning, she was up fixing his breakfast. I'm really encouraged."

He took a large drink of his iced tea. "I'm glad, honey. Just don't get your hopes up too soon."

McKenzie stopped eating and looked up at Joel. "What do you mean?"

He rested his arms against the table next to his plate. "From the way you've described it, there is a chasm between them, largely your mother's doing."

She nodded.

"Don't expect your father to just turn on the charm and affection." He resumed eating his meal. "We're not built that way. It takes time to heal, even when you're a Christian."

"I suppose you're right. They just seemed to be getting along so well at dinner last night. Mama wants me to call my brother to see if he will come home for spring break."

Joel gave her a quick look as he ate another bite. "How do you feel about that?"

"I understand Mama is trying to be a family again, it's just that Conner—"

"Is not into family right now?" he finished for her.

"No, he's not. He's been John Wises' protégé for so long. Since he was in grade school, John has been telling him how he would go to Princeton. He kept track of his grades and the classes he took. He was priming him to follow in his footsteps."

"How did your father feel about that?"

She shrugged. "As I remember, he thought it was amusing when Conner was younger and I suppose, flattering that John would take such an interest. As Conner got older and John was

276

so instrumental in guiding Conner's decisions, Papa tried to steer Conner away from such worldly goals."

"And—" Joel stopped eating to wait for her answer.

"Mama, of course. She was absorbed in their lifestyle and saw it as Conner's opportunity to be as successful as John."

"Ouch!" He shook his head.

She grimaced. "Yeah, she's got a lot of making up to do."

"So does Conner ever come home?" Joel finished his meal and took another drink of tea.

"He was home at Thanksgiving and Christmas. He spent most of his Christmas vacation working in John's office and running around with his friends."

"That's pretty typical 'Kenzie." He pushed his plate aside and leaned back. "He's young and out on his own for the first time."

"I suppose, but I'll give him a call at the frat house tonight."

Joel checked his watch. "Time for me to get back." He took one last drink of his tea.

She looked at him with a pout. "It goes too fast."

"I know." He pulled her up from her chair and slung his arm around her shoulders. "I'll walk you to your car. Are you headed home?"

She reached her arm around his waist. "After I stop by the mall. I need to pick up some makeup."

Dusk was moving in softly with shadows stretching across the hospital parking lot. As they reached her car, Joel pulled her into his arms and held her close.

"Hmmm...you feel good," he breathed into her ear.

McKenzie's arms went around his waist as she snuggled into his chest and relished the day they could be together forever.

277

He pulled away slightly and slipped his fingers into her hair. "You be careful driving home."

"I will." She placed her hand on his face and smiled up at him. "Give me a call when you get off?"

"That might be pretty late—"

She pressed two fingers against his mouth. "I don't care. Call me on my cell and it won't disturb Mama."

"You got it." He lifted her chin and kissed her tenderly. "Now go. You're too much temptation and I need to get back to work."

McKenzie grinned; pleased with the effect she had on him. It was definitely mutual.

Chapter Thirty-Five

McKenzie came through the kitchen, "Mom?"

"In here," Brooke called from her studio.

She stopped at the door. "Oh, Mom! It's breathtaking."

Brooke turned to her daughter with an appreciative smile. "You really like it?"

"It's a message all on its own. They are a gift from God."

"Hmmm..." Brooke turned back to examine her painting. "I guess you're right. I had thought of it as them being in God's hands."

"That too, mom, this is beautiful." She came up behind her for a closer look and placed her hands on her mother's shoulders.

Brooke patted McKenzie's hand. "Thank you. I needed that affirmation." She started putting her brushes in the cleaning fluid. "How about iced tea? I'm ready for a break."

"Have you had dinner?"

"No—"

"Mom, you can't do that. C'mon, I'll pour the tea and you get something to eat."

Brooke fixed a sandwich while McKenzie chattered about her day.

"We lost a preemie this morning."

"Oh, that's sad." Brooke set her plate on the bar and walked around to perch on a stool.

"Yeah, they were young parents. They were pretty broken up."

She took her glass of tea from McKenzie. "It must be devastating."

"I can't imagine how awful. I stayed with her for a while, and asked if I could pray for her." She pulled a stool around to face Brooke as they talked "She seemed a little uncomfortable but she agreed." McKenzie paused for a sip of tea. "So, how's the show going?"

Brooke swallowed a bite of sandwich. "Vic and I will be going back over next Monday to finalize all the details. I imagine he'll be over there on Friday but I won't go again until Saturday morning."

"Unless things change, Joel is supposed to have that Saturday off. Maybe we'll drive over, and we can all have lunch."

"That sounds lovely. I don't know if I'll be able to take much time for lunch, but I'm sure I'll be able to visit for a little bit."

"Is Papa going?"

"If he is, he hasn't mentioned it." Brooke shook her head. "Perhaps you and Joel could invite him to go with you."

McKenzie grinned. "Excellent idea. I'm sure Joel would be up for that. He's been anxious to meet both of you."

"They'll be giving tours at the Pregnancy Center as well as having representatives at the show with all kinds of literature."

McKenzie shook her head. "How can they do it?"

"Well, they're very committed to the cause." Brooke paused before taking another bite.

"No, I mean the women who get abortions. How can they murder their own child?"

Brooke stared into her plate wondering if she had the courage to tell her daughter that she was one of those women. "Many of them are so very young." She looked up at her daughter. "They don't make clear decisions. They're worried about telling parents and some of them have been raped. I saw a young couple come out of the center while we were visiting. Their eyes were lowered from embarrassment and they hurried through the room to get outside. My heart went out to them. That's what this is all about. Helping them make better decisions."

"I still can't understand it." McKenzie frowned as she flipped her hair behind her shoulder.

"Don't be so quick to judge, sweetheart, until you've walked in their shoes."

"It's not for the rest of their lives, but it's the end of their baby's life. As long as I live, I will never understand how someone could do that."

Brooke sighed. Apparently she would not be confessing tonight or any other night to her idealistic daughter.

Conner sat at his desk just finishing his calculus assignment. He loved anything to do with math; it just clicked for him. Dr. Lee, his calculus professor had been gently prodding him to consider an engineering degree rather than business. It was flattering and there was a longing to investigate the possibilities. Still, what would he say to Mr. Wise? If it hadn't been for his influence, Conner doubted there would have been an acceptance letter from Princeton.

"Hey, Red." His frat brother stood at the door. "One of your ladies on the phone."

Conner had gained quite a reputation as a ladies man with his handsome features and bright blue eyes. He'd melted the hearts of many young women on campus.

"Who?" He didn't move from his chair, annoyed at the interruption.

"Didn't say." He leaned against the door frame and grinned. "Just wanted to know if Conner was here."

Conner shoved out of his chair, brushed past the brother and headed down stairs. He really didn't have time for this. He still had to start that book for English Lit.

"Conner here." He collapsed into a well-worn chair.

"Hey, this is your big sister."

"McKenzie?"

"Yeah, surprise, huh."

"No kidding, what's up?"

"Mom and I were talking and I wanted to know if you're coming home for spring break."

"Not if my plans work out. Looks like I'm going to be invited to Tahoe for skiing with Tom Wooster and his family."

"I know it's a lot to ask but, I think you should come home."

"Why, for gosh sakes, no one's home. Mom's with her friends, Dad's out flying or golfing, and you're off working or with your friends." He raked his hands through his hair.

"I know that's the way it's been, but things are changing around here. Mom's painting for charities again and it's not the same, Conner." McKenzie paused. "Besides, Grandpapa has been diagnosed with cancer."

Conner jumped up. "When did this happen?"

"We found out Monday—"

"Gee thanks! You're just now calling me?"

"Cool down." McKenzie was growing impatient. "Mom was devastated," she explained. "We drove over there Tuesday and spent some time with him."

"So, when does he start treatment?" Conner sat down again on the edge of the chair.

"He's not, it's gone too far. It's an aggressive cancer and all through his body. He'd rather have quality life for the time he has left."

There was a long pause. "I'll think about it." He threw himself back into the chair. "I hate to pass up Tahoe."

"Conner! He's only got three to six months to live."

"All right, all right, I hear you. Maybe…I'll see if I can come for a couple of days and then fly out to meet them in Tahoe."

"Gee, Conner; don't put yourself out for your family," McKenzie huffed in at her brother's callous attitude.

"Just following the family tradition, big sister," he shot back. "I haven't noticed anyone breaking their necks to even call me."

She sighed. "You're right, but give us a try. I think you'll see a difference, and besides, it's not Grandpapa's fault. He's so proud of you, Conner, and it would mean a lot to him."

Mitch came in the back door. "Hello."

"In the kitchen, Papa."

Mitch found his daughter red faced as she bent over the oven basting a chicken.

"Where's your mother?" He set his travel bag down and tossed his jacket over the back of a bar stool.

"I have her locked in her studio." She closed the oven door. "She's been working like a slave trying to get her paintings done so she can take them with her on Monday. You should see the first one, Papa. It will give you goose bumps. It's so awesome. I think it's her best work ever."

"Do I have time to check it out before dinner?" Mitch reached out to hug his daughter.

"Give me another fifteen minutes and we'll be ready to eat."

283

"By the way, when did you become such an expert in the kitchen?"

McKenzie grinned. "Not so expert yet, Papa. Mama got me started and I've been running back and forth with questions ever since."

"I'm sure it will be quite tasty. I'm looking forward to it." He gave her a squeeze and patted her back.

Mitch knocked softly on the open door of Brooke's studio to avoid startling her. When Brooke was engrossed in a painting, she was oblivious to everything around her.

She looked up. "Mitch!"

"I heard you've done your best work ever." Mitch walked over, stopping short of touching her, and examined the painting on her easel. It was a tiny infant, sleeping on his stomach in the center of an open rose. "Interesting."

"This isn't the one McKenzie was talking about." She pointed to the corner. "It's over there."

He walked over to the other painting and stopped cold. Out of billowy white clouds and blue sky were the extended arms of God with his hands cupped to hold a tiny sleeping infant. He stared, unable to take his eyes away from the tiny baby as he remembered Conner cradled in his arms right after birth. He checked the moisture forming in his eyes and turned to Brooke.

"McKenzie is right. This is your best work ever"

"Thanks, that means a lot to me. It's been a long time coming."

"Yes, well, it's the truth." He looked back at the painting. "It's beautiful. It should fetch a fair price at the show."

"I hope so."

284

He saw the longing in her eyes but the old wariness held him back. "Are you at a stopping point?" he asked as he headed to the door. "I believe our daughter is about ready for us."

"Yes." she looked down at the brush in her hand. "Just give me a minute to clean up."

As he turned to leave the room, he could see her shoulders sag and a tear escape down her cheek. He felt bad but he just wasn't ready. Too much had been lost between them.

Chapter Thirty-Six

Sunlight streamed into the bedroom as Brooke roused from a deep sleep. The bed-side clock showed eight-thirty. Mitch lay on his back, hands behind his head, staring at the ceiling.

"Aren't you playing golf?"

"I got a substitute for this weekend."

"Oh…" She pulled herself up to a sitting position, fluffed up her pillow and leaned against it.

He rolled over to his side, put his elbow into his pillow and propped up his head with his hand. "I was thinking about going to the farm."

"I see." Brooke nodded, trying not to sound disappointed.

"I've been thinking a lot since we heard about your dad." Mitch glanced over at Brooke. "It could have easily been one of my parents."

"Yes, I suppose you're right." She pulled up her knees and hugged her covers.

"Anyway, I thought it would be good to go spend some time with them." He picked at a thread on the blanket.

"I know they would love that."

Mitch swung his legs out and sat on the edge of the bed. "Would you like to go with me?"

Her heart leapt in her chest. "I'd like that Mitch. I'd like that a lot—" Then stopped as she remembered. "Oh, but I told Papa I would be over tomorrow afternoon." She slid her legs down and pulled back the covers. "He's going to frame my pictures for the show."

Mitch turned around to look at her. "We could still do that. We can drive over from the farm. I'd like to spend some time with your dad."

Brooke slipped out of bed and reached for her robe "That would be grand. I know he'd be glad to see you."

"I'll give my folks a call after I shower."

"What about breakfast?" She tried to appear calm in spite of the excitement she could barely contain.

"Just coffee. We can run through McDonald's on the way," he called from the bathroom.

Brooke fairly flew down the stairs. It had been years since she and Mitch had spent a weekend together. No need to worry about McKenzie, she would have a full schedule. She went back to their room with two steaming mugs and began to pack.

They found Janet in the kitchen as she put an apple pie in the oven. "You made good time." She went over to hug them both. "My, it's good to see you. How's McKenzie?"

"In love." Brooke laughed.

"Is it serious?"

"Well, she thinks it is but we'll have to see. We haven't met him yet." Brooke dropped her purse and sweater on a bar stool.

"No?" Janet put her hands on her hips.

"He's a doctor, a resident I should say, at Memorial," Mitch said as he leaned against the kitchen counter. "You know what kind of schedule they have."

"And how about Connor?" Janet put a pitcher of tea in the refrigerator.

"He seems to be doing well and keeping up his grades." Brooke surveyed the kitchen. "What can I help you with?"

"Not a thing." Janet held up her hands and shook her head. "I've got some sandwiches ready for lunch. I'll throw on a pork roast and a mess of green beans after a while."

"I can do the beans," Brooke insisted.

"I'm fine." Janet patted Brooke's shoulder. "Why don't you and Mitch ride out to the north pasture? Roland is out there working on a fence that's down from that freaky storm we had last week."

"If you're sure—"

"I'm sure. You both look like you could use some of our good fresh air."

Brooke sat in the saddle of her horse. She was quite the old lady now. Mitch's horse, Red, was now gone but he'd claimed one of his many sons. Thunder was a spirited horse and loved to take off when given free reign. He and Mitch had bonded on their first ride. Brooke and Lady were content to amble along but Thunder stamped and snorted anxious to be off.

"Mitch, go ahead." She gave him a knowing smile. "I know you are both itching for a run."

"You sure?"

"Go on," she urged him. "Lady and I will enjoy the scenery and we'll catch up to you in the north pasture."

Mitch grinned, leaned forward and gave Thunder a nudge in his sides. He hollered over his shoulder. "Don't be too long...." and they were gone.

The gentle breeze, blowing the Spanish moss in the trees, felt fresh against Brooke's face. Tiny flowers of purple, white and yellow blanketed the pasture ahead of her. She could hear the cry of a sand crane and was rewarded with the sight of a pair, their baby close between them. They seemed to have no fear of

288

humans, even with their young. The young one was comical looking with a large body dressed in golden yellow fuzz. She pulled Lady up and watched the little family for a while. They gave her a curious look and went on about the business of filling their bellies.

Brooke found the men just finishing up and gathering their tools as she rode into the clearing. Three new posts stood erect in the ground with bright barbed wire stretched between them. Roland gave her a big wave as she rode up. She swung out of her saddle and went to him for a hug.

"Hey girl, you're looking pretty fine." Roland hugged her long and firm.

"You're not looking so bad yourself." Brooke gave him a kiss on the cheek.

"I see you took your time and didn't get here to help us with this fence."

She laughed, happy to be back in their usual teasing. "Looks like I timed it just right."

"That you did," he said with a twinkle in his eye. "That you did."

Brooke loved the special place she held in his heart since the first weekend Mitch brought her to the farm. He turned back to the two hands, now loading the truck with their supplies.

"We'll see you back at the house." He waved and grabbed the reigns of his horse. "I imagine we better get on back. Janet will be waiting lunch."

After lunch, Mitch and Roland left for town while Brooke and Janet cleaned up the lunch dishes. That chore done, they filled gasses with iced tea to sip out by the pool for a visit.

"So, McKenzie is in love." Janet leaned back in her chair and smiled.

"Um hmm...madly," Brooke shook her head and grinned.

Janet gave her a knowing look. "I remember a little blond who came here to visit and left with stars in her eyes."

Brooke laughed. "I was just thinking about that when we drove in. I was so nervous."

"Nervous, what on earth did you have to be nervous about?" Janet propped her legs up on a stool.

Brooke rolled her eyes. "Mom, I did want to make a good impression."

"You know Roland fell in love with you that first weekend. Good thing Mitch proposed because there wouldn't have been anyone else measure up in his dad's eyes."

Brooke's heart ached for all the years they had lost. "I'm afraid I've taken all that for granted." She took a deep breath to release the tightening in her chest.

"Honey, we all have regrets." Janet reached over and patted her arm.

Brooke looked into the soft loving eyes of her mother-in-law. An uncontrollable urge came over her...*did she dare? She must start somewhere.* "Mom...there's... something I did...many years ago." She stopped and shook her head...*how can I do this...* but something kept tugging at her.

"What is it honey?"

"When I was a senior in high school, I was dating this guy...one night...well, we went too far."

"You're not the first one and you won't be the last," Janet reassured, "it happens."

290

"That's not all." She shook her head. "I broke it off with him because I was so ashamed. Then I found out...I...was pregnant."

Janet remained quiet.

"I was scared to death. I was getting ready to go off to college and Lisa found me a doctor."

"You were young," Janet almost whispered. "There are lots of girls who find themselves in that situation."

"But, they didn't take the way out that I did. I had an abortion, Mom." By now Brooke had lost her battle to hold back her tears and they trickled down her face. Janet moved over to Brooke's lounge chair, sat on the end, pulled Brooke into her arms and rocked her.

"Child, you're only human."

Brooke rested her head against Janet's shoulder and felt the comfort of a loving mother. How she wished she had done this with her own mother.

"Does Mitch know?" she whispered.

"No," Brooke breathed. "Lisa is the only one."

Janet sat back and brushed Brooke's hair from her face. "He needs to know if you're going to have the kind of relationship the Lord planned."

"I don't know." Brooke shook her head. "Things are not so good between us right now."

"I know that, Brooke." Janet sighed.

"You do?"

"We've seen the distance growing between you for years."

"It's my fault too." Brooke fell against the back of her chair. "I've been chasing after...who knows what, fame, fortune...empty stuff."

"Maybe you were trying to fill that hole in your heart. The one your baby was supposed to fill." Janet squeezed her hand.

Brooke gave Janet a startled look. "I...I never thought of that!" She brushed an errant strand of hair behind her ear. "Maybe you're right. I've never been able to forget it. There are constant reminders, even though I was sure God had forgiven me."

Janet nodded. "There's a reason I understand that, Brooke."

Brooke frowned as she searched her mother-in-law's face.

"I was nineteen, Roland was still in college. We got careless just like you did."

Brooke listened, covering the shock of what she was hearing.

"Oh yes. It was even more shameful in those days. Roland and I wanted to get married but his father had plans for his son. He wasn't about to allow our foolishness to interrupt that."

"What did you do?"

"My parents whisked me off to Boston to live with my aunt until the baby was born." She looked out over the yard. "They told me it was a little girl. All I saw was the top of her head covered in red hair." She looked back at Brooke. "When McKenzie was born, I felt like God had given me back my little girl." Unshed tears glistened in Janet's eyes.

Brooke reached out to lightly touch Janet's arm. "Did you ever try to find her?"

"Years later, after Mitch was born. We tried for several years, but records had been lost in a fire and it was the end of the road." She reached for Brooke's hand. "I pray, all the time, that she's had a happy life."

"At least you know she's alive." Brooke assured her quietly.

292

"Yes, I do. Abortions were not readily available then. I don't think I would have done that but I'll never know for sure." She looked at Brooke. "You need to tell Mitch. I know he was an idealistic young man but he's had some time to see life. You'll always have that between you if you don't share it with him."

"I'll have to think about it. Maybe when we're not on such shaky ground." She reached out and pulled Janet into a hug. "Thank you for sharing with me. It helps a lot."

Mitch and Brooke pulled out of her father's drive. It had been a lovely visit with Papa, Emma and Richard. They'd driven over after church. She wondered how Mitch felt about the services. Maybe it was a good way to ease back. Janet didn't have a clue that she and Mitch had stopped going to church and she was certain Mitch was not about to bring her up to date.

"Hungry?" He glanced over at her and smiled.

"Yes, I am. I knew if we ate dinner with Papa we wouldn't get out of there until late."

He chuckled. "That's what I figured. Would you like some seafood?" He waited at a stop sign for her answer. "We haven't been to the coast in a long time."

"How about that place at John's Pass, it's early and we should be able to get right in," she offered, eager to extend the quality time they'd spent together.

Brooke breathed in the salt air coming from the open window of the restaurant. The coast would always be home and her place to find peace.

"Remember the weekend we came here, when you were pregnant with McKenzie?"

She laughed. "And I thought I had the stomach flu."

"That was a nice weekend." He smiled as he wiped the condensation from his glass of tea.

"One of the best." She waited for the server who had returned to take their orders. "I never tire of the ocean," she added when they were alone again. "It's so calming to the soul."

"I never thought of it that way but I guess it's because I didn't grow up here." He took a sip of his tea. "The farm does that for me."

"You're right; it has the same effect. Did I tell you about the family of sand cranes I happened on, after you and Thunder took off?"

"No. I don't believe you did."

"I heard them before I actually spotted them. There were two adults and a baby. I've never seen one that young before." She laughed. "He was all golden yellow fluff and he looked so comical because he was so big."

"I've only seen a few myself; they are funny looking."

They finished their meal and Mitch ordered cappuccinos. "By the way, did I hear you say that you're going to Lakeland tomorrow?"

"Yes, it's our final trip over before the show."

"What time are you leaving?" He frowned.

"Around ten-thirty or eleven." Her eyes lit with excitement at his interest. "Vic is going over earlier so I'll take my car. We have a luncheon meeting with the events director and then we'll mark off the layout around the lake."

"Is there any way that Victor can handle this by himself?"

"I don't know." A shot of alarm hit her stomach.

"I guess you've forgotten that we have a meeting with the accountant at three." A tinge of sarcasm edged his voice.

"Oh, I didn't realize." Brooke struggled to remember Mitch mentioning that, but hesitated to contradict him. "I thought you were flying out tomorrow," she finally managed.

"We need you there to help us out with your records, Brooke. You've got a lot of paperwork and it's hard to tell what is charity, and what is purely profit." As a final punch he added, "Your expense records are pretty haphazard too."

"I know." She sighed and aimlessly stirred her coffee. "I'm not an organizer like you."

"That's why we need you there. I scheduled it for tomorrow because I knew I wouldn't be going out until Tuesday. It's hard for me to get a week day in town."

"I did promise Vic—"

"Brooke, this is something we need to get done." A frown creased his brow. "Frank is a busy man and if we cancel, we'll be lucky to get another appointment before our taxes are due." He tossed his napkin on the table. "His wife Jenny is going to meet us afterwards for an early dinner."

"Mitch," she struggled to make him understand. "You didn't tell me this—"

"You've just forgotten." His harsh tone sent a charge of fear through her body.

"Perhaps I did," she said in a hushed voice. "I'll just go to the luncheon and start back in plenty of time. I can be on my way by one-thirty."

Mitch shook his head. "That's pushing it but I guess it will have to do." He signaled for their check. "You ready?"

"Yes." she hung her head and reached for her purse.

They rode home in silence with Brooke aching inside for the way their lovely weekend had ended. She helped him with the bags when they arrived home and he put her paintings in the back of her car.

"Would you like some iced tea…or coffee?" she said as they walked inside.

"No thanks," was his only reply. After taking their bags upstairs he returned to the den and turned on a game.

Brooke sighed. "Why did it have to end this way, Lord? It was going so well." She trudged up the stairs to their room to unpack. Back to square one.

Chapter Thirty-Seven

It had been a miserable day. Showers pelted on and off with drizzle in between. Their luncheon had gone well and they were satisfied everything was covered for a good show. Brooke told them goodbye and was on her way by one-thirty, as she'd promised Mitch. She took 98 to pick up I-4. As she crossed Memorial, the traffic came to a standstill. She was blocked in, and unable to take a different route. She sat fuming as she crawled toward her entrance to the Interstate with her time clicking away. As she neared her exit, she could see that a lane was closed causing a bottleneck. Finally out of the congestion and on her way, she checked her watch. Half an hour was lost and her stomach tightened. She would have to risk a ticket to make up time. A few miles west of Highway 27 the skies opened up and she was caught in a blinding down-pour. There was no way around it. Mitch would have to be called. Her hands trembled as she searched for his number on her cell.

"Yeah."

"Mitch?"

"Brooke, where are you."

"Mitch, I'm sorry I'm on I-4…almost at 27. It's pouring down rain and I can barely see what's in front of me."

"You should have made allowances," he growled in irritation.

"I left on time, Mitch. Traffic was backed up on 98 and it took me half-an-hour to get to the turn-off."

"I explained to you, we need you there for this meeting."

"I don't know what else to do. I'll just have to meet you at Frank's office as soon as I can get….AHHHHH! Mitch—"

The crunch of metal and glass assailed Mitch as he listened, stunned at what he was hearing.

"Brooke...Brooke...talk to me!" The phone was silent. "Oh Lord...No!" His anger suddenly melted. Frozen in fear, his adrenaline pumping, he dialed 911.

"My wife..." he struggled with a brain that would not communicate with his tongue. "I was on the phone with her...she's been in an accident."

"Sir, can you tell me where she's located?"

"She's on I-4 going east...somewhere near 27. I was talking to her and I heard the crash."

"Hold on and let me get someone dispatched to that area." Mitch heard the dead space of being put on hold. "All right sir, they're on their way."

"If she is seriously injured...where will they take her...what hospital?" He paced back and forth desperate for answers.

"I would think Haines City would be the closest."

"I'm headed there...tell them I headed there." He started toward the door.

"Sir, wait. Where will you be coming from?"

"From Winter Park."

"You won't be able to get though. The traffic will be jammed."

"I can't just sit here. It's my wife." He waved his free hand frantically.

"What's your name, sir?"

He hesitated wondering how his name could be of any help. "Mitch...Mitch Harris."

"Okay, Mitch, give me your phone number. I don't usually do this but I'll call you as soon as I find out where they're taking her. Will you wait for me to call?"

"Yes…yes…thank you, I'll wait." He raked his hand through his hair, tossed the phone aside and sank to the bed beside him. Holding his head in his hands he cried, "Dear God, please take care of her…please don't let her die." He wept bitterly for his wife and what they had lost in their marriage. *How did I let it slip away? She's been trying to get it back, why did I have to be so stubborn? Why was I too proud to meet her half way? He knew he could have rescheduled. He just wanted to make a point…wanted to be the boss. Wanted to punish her for all the years she'd ignored him. What if he never got the chance to tell her that he still loved her…ever again?* He threw his face into the pillow and let out a groan that came from his gut. "Please God…please don't let her die…please don't let her die…"

Exhausted from his grief, he pulled himself up from the bed to finish changing from his golf clothes before they called. The phone rang just as he pulled his shirt over his head.

"Mitch?"

"Yes." His body tingled with fear at what the news might be.

"This is Becky with 911. They're airlifting your wife to Memorial in Orlando."

"What's her condition?" He almost shouted.

"I'm sorry, that's the only information I have."

"It can't be good if they are airlifting her there."

"I don't know. It might be because they can't get through the traffic."

"Thank you." He released the air from his lungs not realizing he had been holding his breath. "Thanks for letting me know, you're a kind woman."

"You're welcome sir and I hope she'll be alright…I…I'll be praying for her."

"I appreciate that Becky." Mitch hung up the phone and ran his fingers through his hair. At least she was going to Memorial. He could take the back streets and make better time. Maybe McKenzie would be on duty. She would be on top of it and let him know what was going on. Shoving his feet into a pair of loafers, he bolted down to the garage. He was in his SUV in seconds, his body and mind on autopilot. *What about Brooke's family, no…better wait until I get there. No point in alarming them until I get the whole picture.*

He strode through the doors of emergency and scanned the area for someone behind the reception desk. "My wife…they're bringing my wife."

"Her name, sir?"

"Brooke…Brooke Harris…they're airlifting her from I-4."

She picked up the phone. "Let me check." She asked a few questions and turned to Mitch as she hung up the phone. "Second floor, sir, the doctor will meet you there."

The smell of alcohol assailed his nostrils and made him light headed. He had to hold on…had to get to Brooke. He punched the button for the elevator and waited. The light indicated it was going up. "NO! Down! I need you to come down!" At the second floor he walked towards the nurses' station.

"My wife…Brooke Harris…they're airlifting her from I-4…"

"Mr. Harris," a young nurse smiled at him. "Doctor Ramsey is with her right now. He'll speak with you in a moment. You can wait for him over there in the room to your left."

"Mr. Harris?" Mitch was out of his chair in one jerk. "I'm Doctor Ramsey. I'll be taking care of your wife."

"How is she—?"

"We're preparing her for surgery. She has trauma to the head…appears to be a couple of broken ribs and a collapsed lung, her right leg is broken."

The color drained from Mitch's face, he was speechless.

"Let's sit down over here?" The doctor led him to a couch and sat down beside him.

"Her head and lung are our greatest concern at this point. We'll have to see how serious that's going to be. There may be more internal injuries. We'll know more once we get into surgery. It'll be at least two to three hours. Is there someone we can call?"

"My daughter…she's a nurse here."

"McKenzie?"

Mitch looked up and their eyes held for a moment before he could speak. "Yes—"

Dr. Ramsey visibly slumped and shook his head. "I was hoping there was no connection."

"You know her?"

"This is not exactly the circumstances I intended for our meeting. I'm Joel…Joel Ramsey."

"'Kenzie's doctor?"

"Yes sir." He glanced at his watch. "She should be getting off her shift about now. We were going to meet for dinner. I'll

301

have someone call." He stood and put his hand on Mitch's shoulder. "We have an excellent staff here. We'll do everything possible for your wife."

Mitch sat, staring up at the ceiling. *Brooke, we had such dreams.* He lowered his head to his arms, crossed against his knees and prayed, "Lord, how did we get so far off track. I know I should have kept my family in church. Please hear me Lord, I know I've failed you, and my family but please don't take my wife. I love her Lord. I don't want to lose her."

"Papa?" McKenzie's voice was hushed as she reached out to touch her father's shoulder.

He raised his head and stood to pull his daughter into his arms. "McKenzie I don't know what I will do if I lose her." The tears now flowed unchecked. "I can't lose her."

"We can't think that way, Papa." She held him tight. "We've got to believe she'll be okay."

He gazed at his daughter, so mature in her faith, and collapsed back to the couch. "What can you tell me? Did they give you any information?"

"Nothing more than they told you." she sat down beside him. "But Joel is the best. She's in good hands, Papa and she's in God's hands."

"You're right. I've been praying" He was at a loss for more words.

"Have you called anyone?" She touched his arm gently.

Mitch sighed and shook his head. "No, I just got through talking to the doctor. I didn't want to call before I knew something."

"We need to call Conner."

"I'll call John and see if someone can go up after him."

302

"I'll call Aunt Emma and Nana." McKenzie paused. "Papa, what was Mom doing on I-4?"

"She was coming back from a meeting in Lakeland." He glanced out the window remembering his ugly words to her just before her accident.

"Oh that's right, I forgot she was going over there today."

"This is my fault." His eyes filled again. "I insisted she get back for a meeting with our accountant. She was trying to get back in time…I was angry at her." He dropped his head to his hands.

McKenzie pulled her father into her arms. "Papa, you don't know why this happened. I-4 is treacherous any time of day. Joel said a semi pulled onto the interstate right on top of her."

Mitch shuddered. "I was on the phone with her. I heard it but I didn't know what happened."

"Papa, God probably put you on the phone so you could get them to her right away," she argued.

Mitch wiped his face with the sleeve of his shirt and gave his daughter a sad smile. He was doing Brooke no good in this condition. "You'd better make those phone calls. They will all want to be here and they'll have a distance to travel. I'll see about getting Conner here."

Chapter Thirty-Eight

McKenzie silently slipped into her mother's room. Joel was checking her vital signs and recording her progress on the chart. He was off duty, but he'd opted to keep watch for her family's sake. He looked up and smiled as McKenzie came toward him, laid down the chart and took her into his arms.

Brooke had a severe laceration on the side of her head that resulted in swelling of her brain and a coma. They had purposely kept her in an induced coma until the swelling was relieved. She had two broken ribs. Her right leg with a clean break had been set and cast. A chest drain had been inserted to allow the air to escape from the chest cavity. She was on oxygen for the first fourteen hours but had held her own since removing the mask.

McKenzie looked up at the man she loved and who had saved her mother's life. Brooke hemorrhaged an alarming amount of blood and, had it not been for Joel's skill as a surgeon, she would have been lost. Now, it was a matter of waiting to see if she would come out of the coma and what damage might have been done.

"How's she doing?" She whispered to not disturb her sleeping father in the chair at her mother's bedside. He'd kept constant vigil since her surgery.

Joel ran his finger down the side of her cheek and then took her face in both of his hands and kissed her forehead. "She's doing very well for what's she's been through. We're not completely out of the woods yet, my love, but I'm optimistic," he whispered back.

A tear trickled down her face. "I'm so glad she went with me to the women's seminar. She went forward, and she was just radiant when she came back. I pray it's not her time." She buried her face against his chest. He held her tightly, brushing her hair back and kissing the top of her head. She'd been strong for her father but it was these times, when she could lean on Joel, that she let her emotions take reign.

He squeezed her tight. "I know baby, I know, but God is in control, and he'll give you strength for whatever lies ahead."

She nodded her head and wiped her eyes. "I know and I thank him for bringing you into my life. I'm so grateful for you."

"You're not such a bad deal either, lady." He lifted her chin with his finger and kissed her lips softly.

McKenzie managed a smile. "I'd better tell my grandparents and Conner. They asked me to let them know how things are going. I'm worried about my grandpapa. He looks exhausted but he won't leave. Thank goodness he and Aunt Emma have been able to sleep over at Mama Suzanne's, but he insists that Aunt Emma bring him back here every day.

"It's about time for dinner. Why don't you suggest they go get something to eat and a little rest?"

"Good idea. Papa needs to eat too."

"Go take care of your grandparents. I'll wake up your father and suggest he go with them."

"He won't leave my mom I'm afraid." She watched her father in exhausted slumber.

"I'll convince him, and I'll stay with her until he gets back."

McKenzie stretched up on her toes to kiss him on the cheek. "You're too good. I'll send them off and we can both wait here with her."

"Agreed, but only if you let me take you to dinner afterwards." He swung his arm around her shoulder and led her to the door. "You need to keep up your strength too, my love."

"That sounds like a deal I can't pass up."

He kissed her gently as she left the room.

"Mr. Harris." Joel gently wakened Mitch.

Mitch's eyes flew open. "Is she—?" He looked over at Brooke.

"No sir, nothing yet."

He shook his head. "I'm so afraid she won't wake up."

"It's not enough time to be alarmed. She took quite a blow." He reached out and squeezed Mitch's arm. "Sometimes that's how God works his miracles, by keeping her quiet while He heals her body. She's doing fine." He squatted in front of Mitch. "Mr. Harris, your family is going to your house to get something to eat. Why don't you go with them and maybe get a shower and shave?"

"But I—"

"You don't want your lovely wife to wake up and see you in this condition do you? I'll stay right here with her and McKenzie will be here too."

"But what if—?"

Joel patted Mitch's knee. "You need to keep up your strength for when your wife wakes up."

He rubbed the stubble on his chin. "All right...if you're sure." He struggled out of the chair. He hesitated as he reached the door and looked back at Joel, "you've got my cell number, right?"

"Yes sir, I'll call if there's any change."

Joel was gazing out the window when McKenzie returned and slid her arm around his waist. He smiled down at her and put his arm around her shoulder.

"Nothing new, she's still resting."

"We never know, do we?" McKenzie stared out at the manicured grounds. A magnolia tree showed off large blossoms amid dark green leaves.

"Know what?" Mitch mused as he watched the traffic moving in and out of the hospital.

"How long we have." McKenzie sighed. "Mom was so excited about getting back into her charity work." She glanced up at him. "I wish you could see the painting she did for the show next weekend. It is her best work ever, even Papa said so."

"What's it like?"

"It's a picture of God's arms reaching down from heaven with a tiny newborn cupped in His hands."

"Mmmm...sounds amazing." He casually kissed the top of her head.

"It is. God really spoke to her on that one." She leaned her head against his chest.

"That's what we all are you know, in God's hands."

"I know, even Mama."

"She's a beautiful woman, McKenzie."

"Funny, I never got the impression that Mama thought of herself as beautiful. She's always seemed...I don't know...kind of down on herself."

"How's that?"

"It's not something I can explain. It's just that, she never seemed to feel like she'd done her best. Nothing seemed to be enough, she was always striving."

"You mean a perfectionist?"

"I suppose so, but maybe more like trying to find the thing that would make up for what she was lacking." She shrugged. "Maybe it was just my perception."

"She did get away from the Lord. Could be, she was trying to fill that vacuum."

"You're probably right." She looked up at him. "Can I get you anything?"

"I could use something to drink, maybe a coke to hold me over?"

"You've got it. I'll be right back. I need to give Lisa a call too. I promised to keep her posted."

Joel walked back over to Brooke and checked her vitals once again. He was exhausted from his regular schedule and keeping vigil over Brooke. He collapsed into the chair beside her and leaned his head back to rest. It had been almost eighteen hours since he'd had any sleep. What a twist of fate that he should be the attending physician for McKenzie's mother. McKenzie…he had been attracted to her that first spring in the Colorado Mountains. What a breath of fresh air. She was so vibrant, full of life and so excited about what God was going to do in her life. They'd lingered by the fireside after the others left the Bible study, and talked long into the night. It was then he shared his call to serve as a missionary. He'd never been so comfortable in sharing his dreams. He knew he was falling in love with McKenzie, but he held back his feelings, knowing that he had a long road ahead of him. He'd trusted God. If McKenzie was to be a part of his life, the pieces would fall into place.

"Oh!" Joel's eyes flew open to see Brooke now staring at him in alarm. He jumped to his feet and went to her bedside. She

308

started to cry. "Mark...I'm so sorry... I'm so sorry about the baby."

Joel took her hands in his. "It's alright Mrs. Harris, you've been in a bad accident."

Brooke frowned and tried to shake her head. "Mark—" she tried again.

"I'm Doctor Ramsey. You were in a car accident and you've got a bad gash on your head." He smiled at her. "But it looks like you're going to be just fine."

"Oh!" A wave of clarity washed across her face. "You're not Mark" She squinted and searched his face. "You're eyes are blue—"

"Mrs. Harris" Joel frowned at her seeming recognition. "Do I look like someone you know?"

Before she could answer, McKenzie came in the door. "Mama?"

Brooke looked from Joel to McKenzie and back again.

"Mama, it's me...McKenzie." She hurried to her mother's bedside.

Brooke reached up and touched her cheek. "McKenzie...what—"

"You were in a terrible accident, Mama, and you've been in a coma," she gently rubbed her mother's hand.

"Oh! I'm late to meet Mitch—" alarm crossed her face.

"It's okay Mama, Papa has been here with you the whole time. He went to get something to eat."

Brooke laid her hand across her forehead and closed her eyes. "I disappointed him. I was supposed to be there."

"The meeting was postponed, and Papa's not mad. He just wants you to get better; we all want you to get better."

Brooke's hand slid from her forehead to the pillow and brushed the bandage on her head. She reached out to feel her head again, "What's—

"You've got a pretty big gash on your head, but Joel is the best. Once your hair grows back, you'll never know it was there."

"Joel?" She frowned at her daughter.

"I'm Joel Ramsey, Mrs. Harris. I took care of you when you were brought in from your accident."

Brooke looked back at him. "I'm sorry...I don't understand."

"It may take a while for your memory to completely return and the Lord may keep some of it from you forever...kind of a shield for your protection."

"So...I was in an accident?"

"A pretty nasty one," Joel said. "A semi ran into you."

"I remember it raining and I was talking to Mitch."

"Don't try too hard to remember all of the details. The most important thing is to concentrate on getting your strength back. It will come."

Joel looked at McKenzie. "We'd better call your papa. He wouldn't leave until I promised I'd call with any change."

Mitch was on his way back to the hospital. Conner was driving and Roland in the back seat, when his cell phone rang.

"Papa!"

"What's wrong?" Alarm hit like a punch in his stomach.

"Nothing, Papa, it's time to celebrate." McKenzie giggled. "Mama just woke up."

"Is she...does she—?" Mitch was afraid of the answer.

"She doesn't remember the accident but otherwise she's doing great."

"We'll be there in a few minutes."

Mitch dropped his phone into his jacket pocket, held his head in his hands and cried. All the days of holding it in for Brooke and their family broke loose.

"What—what is it, Dad?"

It was a moment before he could speak. "Your mother's okay...she's...awake."

"Man! You scared me to death." Conner relaxed against his seat.

"That's great news, son." His father reached forward to squeeze his shoulder. "I'll call your mother."

Mitch leaned back against the seat, closed his eyes, and prayed silently. *Thank you, Lord, you've given me back what I don't deserve. Forgive me for leaving you out of my life. You have my undivided attention.* He wiped his eyes with his hands. He felt a cleansing in his heart that had weighed him down for years.

Chapter Thirty-Nine

Joel pulled the stethoscope down to his neck after listening to Brooke's lungs. "You're coming along nicely, Mrs. Harris. I don't see any reason to keep you any longer."

"That's welcome news. These two weeks have seemed an eternity."

He laughed. "Not exactly the Ritz."

"I'm more than ready to be in my own bed, not that everyone hasn't been terrific."

"I'm sure you are." Joel sat down on the stool next to the bed and was quiet for a time before speaking. "Mrs. Harris, there's something I need to ask you."

Brooke held her breath. She'd been tormented with the fear he would tell McKenzie what she'd said coming out of the coma.

"Mrs. Harris, when you first came out of the coma you...well, you mistook me for someone else. Do you know someone that looks like me?"

Brooke gave a nervous laugh. "You look quite similar to a boy I dated in high school, but you don't have the same last name." She dismissed the matter with a flip of her hand.

Joel gave her a startled look. "But, I'm adopted, Mrs. Harris. He might be my father."

Brooke's stomach lurched and she quickly looked away from him.

"You see, my natural mother was very young and I guess frightened that she was pregnant." Brooke's eyes darted back to him and he held her eyes with his. "I was aborted...and I lived."

Brooke's mind reeled. She didn't want to hear anymore. She looked out the window.

Joel stood, put his hands in his pockets and walked toward the window. "I've had wonderful Christian parents. My mother was the nurse who assisted in the abortion. It was the last one she ever participated in. What I know about my birth mother is very sketchy. She left the hospital before I was discovered alive. All we know about her is that she used the name of Jennifer Rogers."

Brooke gasped and fought to hold back the tears.

He turned back to Brooke and watched her reaction. "Do you know something Mrs. Harris? Do you know who my mother is? It's so important to me."

"No...no...I have no idea. It's just so sad, what happened to you." She reached for a tissue and wiped her eyes.

He came toward her. "But the man you dated, maybe he knows, since I look so much like him."

"Well, not so much." She dismissed the idea with a shake of her head. "I was confused. I'm sorry Joel, I can't help you."

Joel's shoulders slumped. "I was so hoping you could help me find my parents. I'm very much in love with your daughter, Mrs. Harris, and I wanted to come to her without a shaded past."

"Sometimes things are better left alone." She barely spoke above a whisper. "You might be very disappointed in what you find. Better to be happy with the life you've been given."

Joel left to finish his rounds after helping Brooke move to a chair in her room. She was stunned. Her baby had lived. But he was in love with her daughter. The thought twisted in her heart. She should be thrilled to learn that her baby had lived. She hadn't murdered him. He was here...but... She wrestled with the joy and the pain of it. This relationship had to end, but how was she going to convince McKenzie? Brooke jumped as the phone rang.

"Hello, my love." She warmed to the sound of her husband's voice. He'd been at her side until finally returning to his flight schedule that Monday.

"Hi, yourself." She smiled, pulling herself back together. "I have some good news."

"I'm up for that."

"Joel says I can go home."

"Today?" Mitch's concern laced his voice.

"He said there was no reason to keep me. I'm progressing nicely."

"What about first thing in the morning," he pleaded. "I won't be home until late."

"Well...McKenzie—"

"Not on your life." He protested. "I'm bringing home my princess and waiting on her hand and foot."

She giggled. "I guess I can tough it out another night."

"That's my girl." She could see his winning smile and those sparkling turquoise blue eyes that had grabbed her heart so many years before. "I'll see you first thing in the morning. I love you, babe."

"Love you too, Mitch," she said soaking up the restored love she thought she had lost.

Mitch stretched under the covers and slowly opened his eyes. Their bedroom flooded with sunlight and the pungent aroma of a dozen pink roses he'd purchased for her homecoming wafted through the room. It was the best night's sleep he'd had since Brooke's accident.

Thank you Lord, for my wife and the second chance you've given us. It had become his morning ritual, since Brooke came out of her coma, to acknowledge and thank God before he got out of bed. Brooke would be ready at nine this morning. Joel wanted to check her one more time before her release. *What a fine young man you've brought our McKenzie, Lord.* He and Joel had spent a considerable amount of time together over meals and coffee while Brooke was recovering. It was apparent the two of them were deeply in love, and Joel shared his missionary calling to India.

"It's been so clear to me that God is taking me in this direction." Joel's enthusiasm lit up his eyes.

"I completely understand." Mitch nodded, remembering those days of dating Brooke, and sharing his passion for missionary aviation.

"I'm certain that McKenzie feels a call on her own life." Joel wanted Mitch to understand his concern for his daughter. "It's important to me that He is calling her and she's not just following me."

"I believe you're right." Mitch agreed. "She's never wavered since she was in high school and I couldn't be happier."

"I hope I'm not overstepping myself here," Joel added cautiously, "but I don't get the feeling that Mrs. Harris shares your enthusiasm."

"No you're not, and you're right on." Their eyes met and held. "You have to understand that Brooke spent almost three months not knowing if I was dead or alive when I was captured in South America. It was a grueling time for her."

"Understandable." Joel nodded. "I imagine it was a frightening experience for you."

"You know, I had no fear. I knew if it was my time, I would be in the presence of God."

"You weren't afraid?"

He chuckled. "Of course, I had a wife and two babies at home. I didn't know if I would ever see them again. Either through carelessness or indifference, I was able to escape and got to the coast. A family of fishermen was at the shore and they hid me until dark, and took me back to their home."

"Whew! What an experience."

Mitch chuckled. "Amazing what God can get you through. That's why I'm not afraid for McKenzie."

Joel gave Mitch a quick glance. "Sometimes I'm not so strong when it comes to her."

"Never take your eyes off God, son. No matter how difficult things get or how much your life seems out of control. He'll see you through anything even if you were to lose McKenzie."

"I don't even like to entertain that thought." Joel shook his head." I guess I should tell you that, with your blessings, I'll ask McKenzie to be my wife in the near future."

Mitch slapped Joel on the shoulder and grinned "I can't think of anything that would make me happier, except taking my wife home, that is."

Mitch pushed the door ajar and stopped at the conversation inside.

"Well, thank you very much, Doctor Ramsey. I appreciate what you've done for me and perhaps we'll see you again sometime."

"Thank you Mrs. Harris…but …a …I do want to see you again for a follow-up."

"I don't think that will be necessary. I'll just schedule an appointment with our regular physician. I think he can take it from here." She smiled her dismissal, very much like Mallory would have handled domestic help.

"All right, Mrs. Harris, you can have his office send for your records. I've signed the release and you can go home anytime." He turned to leave.

"Hello, Joel." Mitch gave him a warm smile. "You're letting her go with a clean bill of health?"

"She'll need to be checked a couple of times to make sure her lung is functioning properly. It'll be good for her to be up and about but no strenuous activity for a few weeks," Joel answered in a very businesslike manner.

"I'll see to that, and we'll be seeing you around." He winked and slapped his shoulder as he leaned into his ear. "McKenzie is home learning culinary skills from her grandmother."

"Thank you." Joel nodded.

Mitch went to his wife, pulled her into his arms, and kissed her long. He pulled back and looked into her eyes. "What was that all about? Weren't you a bit formal with the love of McKenzie's life?"

"Mitch, she's so young she doesn't know what she wants yet. She has a lot of life ahead before she ties herself down to one young man,"

"Brooke, it's not for you to live her life. Honey, she's got her feet on solid ground and besides, I highly approve her choice." He frowned." What's your objection to him?"

"Please, Mitch, I'm excited about going home. Let's don't spoil it with a dispute over McKenzie's love life, okay?"

"Okay, sport, let's get you home so I can start spoiling you."

Mitch spent the entire weekend doting over her every need. They had gone to church, in spite of his reservations. McKenzie had managed to give her a shorter haircut and pull some of the thickness over to cover the place it had been shaved. Brooke insisted that Janet take time off from the kitchen and Mitch took them out for lunch. It was the same restaurant where she had gone with Ruth and Vic. It seemed like years ago.

"This reminds me of the country club in Ocala," Mitch said as he watched his beautiful wife across from him.

"That's exactly what I thought. That's why I wanted to bring you here." She gave him a knowing grin.

He gave her a wink. "We'll have to come here for dinner some time and do a little dancing under the stars."

The rest of the afternoon was spent lounging by the pool until Janet brought out sandwiches and lemonade.

"How about a little TV?" Mitch helped her out of her chair. "It's getting a little cool and I don't want you to be chilled."

She hugged his neck. "I could get used to this."

They'd just settled in the den when McKenzie called from the back door.

"Hello!"

"We're in here, 'Kenzie," Mitch said.

"Look who got the night off." McKenzie came in with Joel in tow.

"Joel," Mitch jumped up and extended his hand. "Come in, we're just lounging around, watching a little TV. Have a seat."

"Hello, Joel," Janet gave him a hug and then hugged McKenzie. "I was just about to get us some peanut butter pie and coffee."

318

"Sounds yummy, I'll help you, Nana." McKenzie followed her grandmother to the kitchen.

Brooke sat wooden in her chair and stared at the television. This was like another bad dream that wouldn't end. Mitch sat next to Joel discussing the Masters while Brooke took side glances at Joel. He was handsome, as handsome as his father and an exact replica except for her blue eyes. The thought sent a shock wave through her body. *My blue eyes...my papa's blue eyes...oh, Joel,* she cried out silently.

"Here we go," Janet and McKenzie came in with trays of pie and steaming cups of coffee. Brooke was silent while Janet and Mitch made Joel welcome. As McKenzie got ready to take Joel back, Brooke looked up. "Don't be too late, McKenzie."

McKenzie's jaw dropped. "Mom, I'm not fifteen."

"I know, dear, but you have work tomorrow...I just—"

"I'll send her right back, Mrs. Harris. I have an early morning myself."

Brooke sighed as the two young people left and turned back to the TV, but not before she caught the puzzled looks on Mitch and Janet's faces.

Within a couple of weeks, Brooke convinced Janet she was well enough to be on her own and immediately dove into her painting. Although Victor had encouraged her to go easy, she felt the need to get enough for a show and money coming in for the sonogram machine.

"Mom! Where are you?

"In here, McKenzie, in the studio," she called back.

McKenzie bounced in. "Mom, what are you doing? You're supposed to be taking it easy." She planted her hands on her hips. "How long have you been at this?"

"Long enough." She patted her daughter's cheek. "Ready for some lunch?"

"Sure."

"Something light; how about a salad?"

"Perfect! I've been eating too much with Nana here. I'll fix it." She held up her hands. "You sit."

"I'll fix iced tea and then I'll sit." Brooke stood to stretch her body.

Brooke enjoyed their lunch with McKenzie chattering away. They hadn't spent time together since her accident and she loved her daughter's company.

McKenzie picked up their dishes and put them in the dishwasher.

"Well, I'm off. I'll be eating dinner with Joel." She grinned. "Can I trust you to rest now?"

"I'll be fine, but don't you think you're spending an awful lot of time with Joel?"

"What do you mean?" McKenzie stopped short.

"Well, you're young, sweetie, and you're neglecting your other friends."

"What is it, Mom?" McKenzie was getting defensive. "Why don't you like him?"

"I didn't say I didn't like him." Brooke tried to be casual and laughed lightly.

"Mom, when we came over Sunday night, you treated him like he had some kind of contagious disease." McKenzie's volume rose slightly.

"McKenzie, I did not." Brooke met her tone.

"Yes, you did, Mom." McKenzie insisted hotly. "I noticed it in the hospital and I just contributed it to your accident. You were rude that night; it was obvious to everyone. I felt so bad for him."

"McKenzie, I just hate to see you tie yourself down." Brooke felt herself losing ground but kept on in spite of the warning signals going off in her heart. "You have the rest of your life to get married. You need to live a little."

"Mom, I've been to college, I have a career, I have lots of friends and I don't need to live a little." McKenzie patience was fast coming to an end. Her mother's accident was not an excuse for her behavior.

"How much do you know about him? Have you met his parents?"

"His dad died several years ago. His mother is a lovely person. I've known Joel for several years and we've been talking and emailing ever since we met in Colorado." McKenzie stood her ground.

"But, that doesn't show you anything more than what he wants you to know." Brooke was desperate to resolve this problem without telling the truth. "Besides how can you really know about his background when he's adopted?"

"What?" McKenzie's face turned as red as her hair.

Brooke realized the minute it was out of her mouth that she'd said too much. "Well, I guess you didn't know as much about him as you thought."

"And how did you know?" McKenzie shot back. "Have you been digging the archives, trying to find some dirt?"

321

"McKenzie, that's enough! He volunteered the information. I mistook him for someone I used to know when I was coming out of the coma, and he thought I could help him find his parents."

"Let me tell you something Mom, Papa and Nana, and the whole family, think he's a great guy. I love him and he loves me. With or without your blessing, I'm going to marry Joel and I don't care who his natural parents are. I know all I need to know about him and he will be my husband." McKenzie swiped at her tears with her hand, grabbed her purse and stormed from the room.

Brooke sank into her chair and put her hands over her face. Defeated in her attempts to protect them, she cried for her two children.

Chapter Forty

Joel opened the door to his apartment where McKenzie stood, eyes red from crying.

"Honey?" she went to his open arms, buried her face in his chest and breathed in the scent of him. Never would her mother separate them. Joel held her tight, rubbed her back and kissed the top of her head.

"Wanna tell me about it," he soothed.

"I had a fight with Mama." He pulled her inside and led her to the couch. With his arm around her she rested against his shoulder while he gently rubbed her arm. They sat silent for a time.

"About me," he finally said with a sigh.

McKenzie sat back just far enough to look into his eyes without moving from his arms. "I don't understand it, Joel. She's never been like this with anyone I dated and I've dated some real self-centered jerks." She emphasized the "jerks."

Joel brushed her hair back from her face and kissed her forehead.

"She says I'm too young to know what I want and I need to live a little. That is so stupid and I don't care what she says."

Joel placed his finger across her lips. "'Kenzie, we'll have to resolve this with your mother if we're to have a future together."

"It doesn't matter, Joel. No one is going to come between us. We've prayed for God to show us if we should be together and he's opened all the doors."

"Except this one." He looked down at her.

"Don't say that." She shook her head. "Please don't say that."

"Sweetheart, family is too important. We won't be happy with your mother rejecting me. We've got to find out why."

"I wouldn't care—"

'Kenzie, you say that now but you're close to your mother and eventually you would resent me."

"Never—"

"Maybe your father can help." He paused and studied the wall across from them. "I agree that her claim of you being too young is just an excuse. There's got to be more to it."

"She was fine with it before her accident."

"I spent quite a bit of time with your dad while she was in the hospital and he told me about his missionary work in South America."

"Yeah, he loved it."

"He also told me your mother's concerns over your call to missions."

"I know."

"Maybe that's her objection to me. She believes I'm the reason you want to go to India and if she discourages this relationship, you'll give up those ideas."

"I won't do that." McKenzie shook her head emphatically. "God has called me clear as day."

"I know that, honey, but she doesn't." He reached up for a long curl by her face and wound it around his finger. "It was after our trip to Colorado, where we met, that you told them you wanted to be a missionary." He leaned over and kissed her forehead. "I guess our job is to convince your mother I'm not the force behind it."

He pulled her into his arms and they held each other in silence for a time. Still in his arms, her cheek against his chest, she looked up at him. "Joel…?"

"Hmmm…" His eyes were closed, enjoying the closeness of her.

"When Mom and I were arguing, she told me I didn't know anything about you because you were adopted."

Joel sighed. "I hoped she wouldn't tell you that before I had the opportunity."

"But why didn't you tell me before?" She leaned back to look into his face.

"I hoped that I could find my parents before I told you. I've been trying for several years but there wasn't enough to go on. I thought I might finally get an answer when your mother came out of her coma, but it was another dead end."

"What made you think that?" McKenzie frowned.

"I was resting, had my eyes closed, when your mother came out of her coma. I heard her gasp. I looked up at her and she started to cry. She kept calling me Mark…and she was sorry about the baby."

McKenzie's eyes were wide as she listened.

"Finally she gave me a funny look and said, 'you're not Mark, you have blue eyes.'"

"Mark who?"

"That's what I asked her the day before she left the hospital."

"And?"

"She said it was an old boyfriend from high school and that I looked quite similar but we didn't have the same name. I pressed her and told her I was adopted and he might be my father."

"What did—?"

"She said we didn't really look that much alike. I was probably better off leaving things alone and that I didn't know what I might find."

McKenzie sat up straight "That's strange. Why wouldn't she want you to find—"

"There's more 'Kenzie. My mother didn't just give me up for adoption. She tried to abort me."

"What!" Anger filled her face.

"It's true."

"Then how—" McKenzie couldn't grasp what she was hearing.

"They used to do abortions with saline and a lot of us lived." They called me a miracle baby. All the surviving babies they knew about had a lot of problems. They suffered from burns, had problems with their lungs and development, and had mental and physical handicaps."

"But you don't."

"I know. Mom said God had his hands cupped around me to protect me from the saline. All I had was a small burn on my knee. Besides, the process went especially fast for her. She barely made it to the hospital in time."

"God reached down and cupped you in his hands…just like mom's painting," she whispered. "But why didn't they give you to your mother when you lived?"

"She didn't know." He ran his finger down McKenzie's cheek. "She used a fictitious name and left the hospital without anyone knowing before they found me."

"Found you?" McKenzie frowned.

326

"Yeah, the clean-up lady heard me putting up a fuss in the garbage can."

"Joel," she gasped.

"The facts, honey. Aborted babies were just disposable tissue."

"Horrible." McKenzie's shivered.

"They tried to contact her with the phone number she left, but it was a pizza parlor."

"How cold."

"McKenzie, we don't know the circumstances." Joel placed a finger against her lips. "We have no idea why she felt compelled to do this. My mom was with her and she said she cried out in regret." He lifted her chin with his finger. "I don't have any anger towards her. I just want to know who I am and maybe some medical background." He touched his lips to hers.

"You are too good. I can't imagine doing something like that to my child."

"There wasn't as much information available in the seventies. Don't condemn her until you know her circumstances."

McKenzie leaned her head against Joel's chest. "I love you more than ever."

"I love you too, sweetheart." He pulled her close and rubbed his palm against her back. "Maybe we can talk to your papa and see if he can't help us resolve this problem." He gave her a quick squeeze. "In the meantime, you wanna go to Barnie's for a latte?"

"Yeah, and a late movie. I don't want to go home before I know Mama's in bed. I don't feel like facing her tonight."

Brooke dialed the number to the farm.

327

"Brooke, I was just wondering how you were doing."

"Not good, Mom." Brooke leaned her head into her hand.

"Your lung?"

"No, nothing physical." Brooke sighed.

"What is it, honey?"

"Remember what I told you when Mitch and I came over for the weekend?"

"Of course—"

"He didn't die."

"What do you mean? Who didn't die?"

"My baby." she stifled a sob.

"How—"

"I don't know. Some of them lived through the abortion. I left the hospital before they knew."

"Honey, that's wonderful! How did you know?"

"He found me. It's...Joel."

Janet sucked in a breath, "'Kenzie's Joel?"

"Yes."

"Oh, Brooke, how bittersweet. It makes sense now, why you were so distant."

"What am I going to do, Mom?"

Janet waited a moment before answering. "There's nothing else you can do honey, it has to be told."

"I thought if I could discourage McKenzie and get them to go their separate ways."

Janet gave a big sigh. "You know that's not going to happen."

"I know. McKenzie and I had a big fight this afternoon. I just pray they don't elope."

"I don't think that's something you need to worry about. McKenzie isn't going to pass up the wedding of the century." She chuckled. "Besides, she is pretty mature in her decision making."

"She's going to hate me. She's as idealistic as her father when he was her age."

"I'm afraid you're right there but she'll come around. The two of you are so close."

"I don't know, Mom, I tried to discuss it with her before and there's no room in her heart for a woman who makes that choice, let alone the problem with Joel."

"When does Mitch get home?"

"He'll be home tonight."

"You need to tell him first. You'll need your husband behind you. Then you need to let those kids know they are brother and sister, before anything happens."

"It's the one good thing about them wanting to be missionaries. I believe they've waited for marriage."

"You see, there is something good in everything."

"Not much solace."

"I'm sorry honey. It's going to be a tough time for all of you. Try to see some good from this. At least you're released from thinking that your baby died. Talk to Mitch and then tell him to call me. He'll be hurting for 'Kenzie, but I'll set him straight on a few facts about life."

Brooke released the breath she didn't realize she was holding. "How can I thank you?"

"Brooke, I love you and have since the day Mitch brought you home. You get on your knees and ask God to help you tell Mitch and the kids. I'll be on my knees too. And

Brooke...Roland and I will stand behind you. Don't ever worry about that."

Chapter Forty-One

Brooke waited quietly contemplating what was about to happen. The door opened and Joel hesitated before walking over to her.

"Hello, Joel." Brooke turned to him.

"Mrs. Harris." He reached out to shake her hand. "No problems with the head... the lungs?"

"No, it seems I had an excellent doctor." The hint of a smile crossed her lips.

He sat down in the chair across from her. "So, what can I do for you?"

Her throat tightened and she looked down at her hands, now clenched in her lap. "I wasn't honest with you," she spoke barely above a whisper. "I can give you the identity of your parents."

He sat forward in his chair.

"You were right. Mark, the guy I dated in high school, is your father."

"But—"

"No wait." She forced herself to look up at him and choked out, "I'm your mother."

Their eyes locked. "I knew there was something about you. I mentioned it to McKenzie." He stopped. "That means that McKenzie and I—"

Brooke's eyes filled. "Yes…you and McKenzie are brother and sister."

He collapsed against the back of his chair and covered his eyes with his hand for a few minutes. The room was silent while Brooke waited for him to absorb the news. He got up abruptly and walked to the window. She could see his shoulders shaking.

Whether she had earned the right as his mother or not, she couldn't sit by and watch his pain. She went to him and laid a hand on his shoulder. He turned, took her in his arms and cried like a broken child.

After a time, he pulled away from her, wiped his face with his hands and led her to a couch where they sat facing each other.

"I know you were young...would you mind telling me—"

"There's no excuse for what I did." She took a deep breath. "Yes, I was young. I had a full scholarship and I was on my way to college with my best friend Lisa."

"Did Mark press you to have—?"

She reached out and clutched his arm. "No! Don't ever think that. I did it on my own and told him later. He would have married me. It was pure selfishness. I didn't want to face my parents with the truth. I didn't want to give up my plans and I've ended up hurting a lot of people. Abortion hurts more than the baby." She shook her head. "I've lived with nightmares, especially when I was pregnant with McKenzie." She hesitated before continuing. "Right after they injected the saline, you gave me a soft kick. I knew then you weren't just tissue like I'd been told. I knew you were a baby. I've lived with the shame and regret my whole life."

"We all make choices that we regret; that's why there is grace."

She reached up and brushed his face. "Oh Joel, you are so much like your grandfather...such a gentle godly man."

Joel nodded. "I remember him when he was here at the hospital."

"One thing I don't understand. I can see telling you that you were adopted but why tell you that you were aborted?"

"I have a burn scar on my knee, from the saline."

Brooke shuddered.

"They called me the miracle baby. God had his hands of protection around me. Normally aborted children have serious handicaps. Many are unable to walk, have cerebral palsy or breathing problems. All I had was a burn on my knee."

Brooke felt goose bumps all over. "Just like my painting," she breathed. "God gave me a picture of you before I even knew you were alive."

"My mom was there with you. She remembers how frightened you were."

"She was there?"

"She was the attending nurse. It was the last abortion she assisted."

"Yes..." she gazed out the window. "I remember. She had such kind eyes." She looked back at Joel.

"I'm so thankful you grew up in a Christian home. Your mom sounds like a very special lady."

"It's kind of strange isn't it? Here you are, my mother, and I'm telling you about my mom." He looked down, avoiding her eyes. "I feel kind of uncomfortable calling you Mom."

"No." She reached for his hand and gave him a tentative smile. "Call me Brooke. We have a lot of bridges to cross."

"What about McKenzie? Your argument—" Understanding registered in his eyes. "It all makes sense now."

"Mitch and I will talk to her this weekend. He'll be in Friday afternoon."

Joel leaned forward with his arms resting on his thighs. "Brooke...ah...do you think I could tell her?"

"I couldn't ask you to do that. It's my responsibility."

"I'll go along with whatever you say, but I'd rather be the one to tell her."

"Are you sure?"

He stood and shoved his hands in his pockets and stared down at the floor. "It'll be the hardest thing I've ever had to do in my life. I love her more than life, but I'd like for her to hear it from me. I'm off tonight. We'd planned to spend the evening together and this isn't something I can keep from her."

Brooke's eyes misted as she looked up at him. "I hate this, Joel. I'm so thrilled you're alive and I have another son, but I ache for you and McKenzie."

"McKenzie loves the Lord, she'll rely on God."

"I wish I shared your faith in that. Thanks to me, McKenzie has never had a difficulty in her life. I made sure she had every opportunity and I made all things better for her. She's never had to face anything of this magnitude...her faith is untested."

"Maybe God's plan is for her to grow."

Brooke shook her head and smiled at him through her tears. "How did you become so wise for your years?" She stood and gathered her purse from the chair, "Will you call me...let me know?"

"Sure," he said as he walked over to her and pulled her into a gentle hug, "I'll be in touch."

McKenzie popped her head in the door of his apartment. "Joel?"

"In the kitchen, making some of my famous spaghetti." She went up beside him and put her arm around his waist.

"You must've gotten off early. I went by after my shift and you were already gone."

"I had a conference with a patient and then I sneaked out the back door."

"You'll have to do that more often," she grinned. "What can I do to help?"

"How about slicing the bread and spread on some garlic butter. You can throw that in the oven while I finish this salad."

"I can see I'm going to have competition in the kitchen."

"I'm afraid I could never compete with the culinary training you've been getting," he teased.

"Just so you know your place." She stretched up on her toes to kiss his cheek.

They set the small table in his kitchen and visited while they ate. The food was tasteless in Joel's mouth and it hit his stomach like lead. For McKenzie's sake, he kept up the façade and had her laughing with comical descriptions of patients that day. They left the dishes and went into the living room with coffee and settled on the couch. McKenzie immediately snuggled up to him and he pulled her close, as if to protect her from the blows he was about to deliver.

"You're rather pensive tonight." McKenzie looked up at him.

Not much I can hide from her. He thought he was doing a good job covering his feelings.

"Well, let's just say that it was a day like no other."

"How's that?" She turned to face him.

"I know who my mother is…and my father."

Her eyes sparkled with excitement. "You do? How? When?"

"She came to the hospital today. That was the conference I had this afternoon."

"How did she know about you? I thought she didn't know you lived?"

"She found out while she was in the hospital. From the things I told her."

"But why would you be telling—" McKenzie searched his eyes for confirmation that she was wrong. "No—" She shook her head and her eyes filled.

His eyes misted and he could barely speak. "Yes, McKenzie, Brooke is my mother."

McKenzie's throat went dry. She tried to speak but could only shake her head. Her lower lip trembled and the tears spilled out onto her cheeks as she came to the full realization of what that meant to her and Joel. She grabbed his shirt in her fists and began pounding against his chest. "No... no..." she screamed. "I don't want you to be my brother. I want you to be my husband."

Joel sat still and let her vent against him. The blows were a relief to the blinding pain he felt in his heart. He shared her pain and anger over the loss they were facing. McKenzie fell against his chest in deep wrenching sobs that ripped through her whole being. He held her tightly until her crying softened. They remained in that position, Joel stroking her back, for an hour or more.

"I'm not going home tonight." McKenzie gritted her teeth. "I don't even want to look at her...ever again."

"Shhh," he comforted. "Don't say things you'll regret."

"I mean it. I don't want to sleep in the same house with her."

336

"You can stay here tonight, and we can talk more in the morning."

"It won't change anything."

He kissed the top of her head. "I'm going to give you something to help you sleep, okay?"

"Okay." A left-over sob shuddered through her body.

"I'll sleep out here and you can have my bed."

"No," she protested. "I can sleep out here."

"Hey." He placed two fingers against her lips. "If you're going to sleep here, you're going to follow my rules."

"All right." Her fight was gone. "I just don't want to go home." She shook her head. "Please don't make me go home."

"I won't, babe." He lifted her off the couch and carried her into his room to get her settled. With her tucked into his bed and a sedative down, he started to leave the room.

"Joel." He stopped and turned to look at her. "Please stay with me for a while." He lay down on top of the covers and held her close to him until her heard her quiet breathing and knew she was asleep. It would be their last time together he was sure.

Brooke busied herself with laundry waiting to hear from Joel. His call, the night before, had confirmed her fears that McKenzie would be bitter. Thankfully, Mitch called soon after. He'd suggested taking McKenzie to the farm for the weekend to let her get calmed down and maybe have his mother talk with her. She retrieved McKenzie's laundry. She could at least do that for her. She jumped at the sound of the phone.

"Brooke."

"How's she doing, Joel?"

"Just as I thought, she doesn't want to go home."

337

"Mitch called last night. He was going to see if she would go to the farm with him this weekend."

"Yeah, he called her this morning."

"Did she agree to go?"

"Yes." He hesitated. "Do you think you could pack up a suitcase for her? I'll come by and pick it up."

"Well, Mitch could bring it—"

"Not just for this weekend."

"Oh…"

"She's moving in with Katie and her roommate. She wanted me to get all of her things but I don't really want to go through her room. I don't have a clue what she needs."

"I'd hoped…after this weekend."

"It's not going to happen that quickly," he spoke gently. "You're going to have to give her some time."

Brooke slid onto a bar stool and held her head with her hand. "I know this was painful for you too."

"It's not just about me, Brooke. You know how she feels about abortion. She has no idea what it was like for you and she doesn't want to know right now."

"I knew she would feel this way." She hesitated before speaking again. "And how about you…how do you feel?"

"There's a big hole in my heart where McKenzie is concerned." Brooke heard the tears in his voice.

"Will you stay in touch?"

"Of course." He cleared his throat. "I'd like to know you better and Mitch, too."

"I'd like for you to spend some time with my papa. He won't be with us much longer."

"I'd like that, too."

"I'm sure we can locate Mark," she added. "I know he will be thrilled to know."

"Let's take it one step at a time. I'd like to know him, but...it's all a bit much to take in right now."

Brooke bit her bottom lip. "I was just doing some laundry for McKenzie."

"I probably won't be over before four-thirty."

"Of course, I can have it ready by then."

"I'll see you then, and Brooke," he paused, gathering his thoughts. "Let God work on McKenzie. She's a trouper like her mother."

Chapter Forty-Two

Brooke gazed out the car window at the landscape as she and Mitch sped down I-95. He reached out and placed his hand over hers rubbing the back with his thumb.

"You okay?"

She turned to smile at him. "I'm fine, just taking in the scenery."

"It's not much further. We'll be taking the next exit."

"How did you find this place?"

"It came highly recommended." He gave her a sidelong glance with a twinkle in his eye. "John comes over here to go fishing."

"We're not—"

"No." He laughed. "I've been married to you long enough to know better."

She gave him a flirty grin. "I would think we could find better things to do."

"Indeed!" He squeezed her hand and kept it safe within his.

Brooke leaned her head back and closed her eyes. Mitch had been her rock through this whole ordeal. He was shocked, of course, and quiet for a time while he absorbed her revelation. Even before taking McKenzie to the farm, he had been squarely behind her and gave her his full support.

While they were gone, Brooke had taken the opportunity to go to Clearwater. She was waist deep at this point. She may as well go ahead and take the plunge. Emma and Ben needed to know about their nephew and her papa his new grandson. What heartache she could have prevented if she had just owned up to the truth in the beginning. Even if she'd chosen to give Joel up for adoption, at least it would have been out in the open and she would have been spared these years of guilt.

With registration complete and keys in hand at the Marriott Beach Resort, Mitch drove through the manicured grounds. They passed a golf course and tennis courts, available amenities for the guests. Not so long ago, she would have been clamoring for the social interaction of those activities. Now, they represented an empty and shallow lifestyle. Brooke stepped out of the car and stretched her limbs as she gazed around. There were ten cottages, similar in style except for the varied, Key West color trim. The east coast was different, she noticed, with darker water and stronger waves churning up on the beach. She didn't care. It was the beach and a balm to her soul.

"Grab the keys, honey," Mitch said as he pulled their luggage from the trunk. "Let's take a look at our home for the next week."

She was so ready for this and hurried down the walk to unlock the door. As she pushed it open, they were met with a wall of windows looking out to an unobstructed view of the ocean.

"Heaven."

Mitch chuckled with satisfaction. "I thought you might like it."

He dropped their bags in the bedroom as Brooke stood watching the churning waters and the wide expanse of beach before her. Coming up behind her he slid his arms around her waist.

"Can we stay here forever?" she said. "We could use a new beginning."

"Wouldn't that be nice?" He kissed her neck.

"If only we could." She held his arms around her.

He squeezed her tight. "How about some beach time, and then we can get cleaned up for dinner?"

She laughed as she turned to kiss him soundly. "You're on."

They spent the afternoon soaking up the sun and walking down the beach to explore between the coral for shells and sea creatures. They laughed and talked, relishing the new companionship they were building with no secrets between them.

Brooke stretched underneath the covers and snuggled deeper into her pillow. The aroma of coffee drifted under her nose as she relished a few more minutes. Wrapped in a cozy robe she slid her feet into fuzzy slippers and went in search of her husband. Mitch sat at the table with a mug of coffee and the newspaper.

"You're up early," she said.

"Hmmm...slept like log."

"I guess we'd better go to the store and pick up a few supplies," she said as she searched through the cabinets and drawers.

"We can do that later," he said putting down his paper. "I'm taking you to breakfast. John said we've got to see this place."

"That sounds interesting." She poured herself a mug of coffee.

He got up to pour himself a second cup. "I guess it's where all the locals go."

"Sounds like an adventure."

He raised his cup to her. "I'm headed for the shower. Don't take too long." He winked at her. "I'm starved."

Brooke looked out the window at the surf, now quieter than when they'd arrived, and savored the idea of a whole week with her husband. A week to do nothing but enjoy each other's company. Something they had not done for too many years.

They sat at a heavy wooden table, thickly covered with polyurethane. There were two small mason jars filled with salt and pepper, two kinds of hot sauce and a bottle of ketchup on each table.

"Mornin' folks. Coffee?" The waitress was dressed in blue jeans and a red shirt with a monogram across the front, *Mama's Grill.*

"Yes, please," Brooke said as she looked over the menu. "And I'll just have a couple of soft-boiled eggs and an English muffin."

"I'm doing the steak, eggs and hash browns." He grinned at Brooke.

Brooke took a sip of coffee. "Do you know what this reminds me of?"

"Not a clue."

"That little restaurant you took me to, after you bought me all the paint. It was our first real date actually."

"Oh yeah." He nodded. "I'd forgotten all about that place. I wonder if they're still open."

"We'll have to check it out sometime."

Brooke glanced around the room at the salmon colored walls adorned with two gold plaster horse heads, a variety of framed, paint-by-number landscapes, and a gaudy gold framed mirror. A

343

basket of silk greenery hung in each corner. From their booth, they could see through to the counter where the cook visited with customers while he flipped eggs, bacon and pancakes.

"Hey, Joe...got any more fresh coffee?" an older gentleman called out.

"Keep your shorts on. Sally'll take care of you as soon as she can."

"Caught any fish lately?"

"Went out yesterday but didn't catch nothin', they're slowin' down right now."

"Yeah, I only caught two...was out there most of the day."

"Aw, Al, you don't catch nothin' when they're bitin," another customer said.

"You hold your tongue young fella'," the older man came back. "Thet'll be the day you can top me."

"Yeah...yeah."

"Sally, where's that coffee?"

Mitch grinned. "Looks like quaint was the word for it."

Brooke laughed. "I love it, but I can't imagine John in a place like this."

"You'd be surprised where he's comfortable"

"Meaning?"

"Meaning, all that highbrow socializing is Mallory's thing. John wasn't born into money. He's built his business from the ground up. He's just a regular guy when Mallory's not around."

"I guess I can see that. I was quite comfortable when we flew back with him from Arizona."

"Exactly."

344

Their week went far too quickly. It had been filled with hours of suntanning on the beach, reading novels in the shade of their cottage, and evening walks, hand-in-hand down the beach. Their last night, Mitch made dinner reservations at a restaurant where nothing stood between the guests and the ocean but a seamless glass wall. They indulged in green salads, grilled grouper with a fruit salsa and a sinfully chocolate dessert. The crowd was light and so they felt comfortable visiting over cappuccinos while a small band played soft jazz in the background.

Mitch reached for Brooke's hand and toyed with her fingers. "There's something I need to discuss with you, my love."

Brooke's heart took a slight lurch. "And what would that be?"

"I didn't say anything before because I wanted you to have this week free of worry.

She frowned. "You're beginning to worry me now."

He grinned. "No need to panic. It's just that…well, I'm very tired. Tired of flying out of town every week, tired of the wild Joe's I have to be around. I'm tired of the rat race."

Brooke nodded. "I can see that. I could see it in your eyes when you left each time. There was no sparkle."

"You know me well." He grinned. "I talked to Dad last weekend, when 'Kenzie and I were there. He's going to have to sell the farm."

"No."

"It's too much for him, even with the help he hired. The only way that won't happen is if I take it over."

"I think you should," she said without hesitation. "That is…if you want to."

345

"I believe I do." There was relief in his eyes at her answer. "I've been contemplating it, long before he mentioned selling." He squeezed her hand. "After everything that's happened, I believe it could be the new start you were wishing for."

A smile played about her lips. "I believe you could be right."

"You understand that it would mean selling our home in Orlando."

She looked out at the darkened sky meeting the horizon. "I know. I have no attachment to that house now. It's just a bad reminder."

"This was easier than I imagined." His eyes crinkled as he grinned at her. "Dad already has a retirement home started for them at the south end of the property. We'd probably be living with them until it's completed. You don't mind moving to the old homestead do you?"

"You're like a little boy in a candy store." Brooke laughed. "I don't mind living there at all. I love your parents and I love that house. It's home."

Mitch leaned toward her and brushed her lips with his. "I love you beautiful lady."

Brooke lay in bed listening to the rhythmic waves as they crashed against the surf. She savored the sound of her husband's breathing as he held her close even in his sleep. They had come together last night as they had in those early years, when they were young, in love and innocent of the days ahead. Yes, her husband was back and so was she. She smiled to herself in the shadowy light of early morning and snuggled her back against Mitch allowing herself to be filled with the pleasure of his closeness.

She was only slightly saddened by the thought of leaving this wonderful retreat and decided to go for one last walk down the beach. She noiselessly dressed in a pair of shorts and sweatshirt. Quietly slipping out of the bedroom door to the patio, she let her feet sink into the cool soft sand. A group of sandpipers scattered as she moved down where the waves had smoothed it hard and made it easier to walk. A deep breath filled her lungs with the salt air. How she loved the smell of the ocean.

She allowed her mind to wander back to the days when Mitch first took her to the farm and introduced her to its tranquility. What a blessing to be able to return and spend the rest of her days wandering the green hills, to ride their horses, cook in that beautiful old kitchen and yes, return to her painting. They would call Roland and Janet this morning and give them the good news. It would be the perfect place to bring Joel and Conner together. Conner would be shocked at having a brother but he wouldn't be shaken like McKenzie.

Oh my beautiful McKenzie. When will you forgive your mother? She would have to cling to Mitch's promise that time would heal the wounds. Until then, she would keep McKenzie in her prayers. That she would not be driven to any foolish decisions and would make her peace with God.

As she headed toward their cottage, she spotted a beautifully shaped shell and scooped it into her hand.

"Oh…it's broken." She was disappointed to see the piece missing from the side that was hidden.

"But still beautiful," God spoke to her heart.

"Yes Lord, I've been broken…but you can still make something beautiful. Thank you, Father, for my miracle."

Author's Notes

I began this journey in the year of 2004, pulling together information and learning about the stories of women who made the choice of abortion. The statistics used were gathered from messages of pastors and visits with women who work in the clinics providing an alternate solution to abortion.

I actively support Care Net, our local clinic for counseling and aid to women of unplanned pregnancies. The most current statistics available to me are from the Florida Office of Vital Statistics and the Florida Agency for Health Care Administration. In the year 2008, there were 87,520 reported abortions, just in the state of Florida. You will note I said *reported*. There are many that are not.

With each of these abortions comes a mother who will suffer the consequences of her actions. My purpose in writing this book was twofold. First and foremost, to enable women who might be contemplating abortion to be educated to the fact it is a baby, not tissue, and she will be left with scars of regret for her decision. Secondly, I want to encourage women who have made this choice, for whatever reason, to understand that there is forgiveness, wholeness and freedom from the nightmare they are undoubtedly living.

Lastly, I would like to say that abortion is not just about a woman and her baby. Abortion touches the lives of everyone...the father, grandparents and siblings. If you are a woman, caught in the dilemma of an unplanned pregnancy, the father in an unplanned pregnancy, or you know someone who is contemplating abortion, there is an answer. There are numerous organizations and clinics ready to help. To counsel, nurture, love and respect your particular situation. I encourage you to utilize their expert and loving care.

A place for help, whether pre-abortion or needing recovery, is available from one of the following:

National Care Net Hotline
1 800-395-HELP (4357)
www.abortionrecovery.org
www.optionline.org

Watch for McKenzie's story, *Florida House*, due out the summer
of 2014.

To connect with Linda
www.lkkennedy.com

Made in the USA
Lexington, KY
11 February 2017